Tuesday's Child

Books by Fern Michaels:

Tuesday's Child
Betrayal
Southern Comfort
To Taste the Wine
Sins of the Flesh
Sins of Omission
Return to Sender
Mr. and Miss Anonymous
Up Close and Personal
Fool Me Once
Picture Perfect
About Face
The Future Scrolls
Kentucky Sunrise
Kentucky Heat
Kentucky Rich
Plain Jane
Charming Lily
What You Wish For
The Guest List
Listen to Your Heart
Celebration
Yesterday
Finders Keepers
Annie's Rainbow
Sara's Song
Vegas Sunrise
Vegas Heat
Vegas Rich
Whitefire
Wish List
Dear Emily
Christmas at Timberwoods

The Godmothers Series:

Deadline
Late Edition
Exclusive
The Scoop

The Sisterhood Novels:

Home Free
Déjà Vu
Cross Roads
Game Over
Deadly Deals
Vanishing Act
Razor Sharp
Under the Radar
Final Justice
Collateral Damage
Fast Track
Hokus Pokus
Hide and Seek
Free Fall
Lethal Justice
Sweet Revenge
The Jury
Vendetta
Payback
Weekend Warriors

Anthologies:

Making Spirits Bright
Holiday Magic
Snow Angels
Silver Bells
Comfort and Joy
Sugar and Spice
Let it Snow
A Gift of Joy
Five Golden Rings
Deck the Halls
Jingle All the Way

FERN MICHAELS

Tuesday's Child

KENSINGTON PUBLISHING CORP.
http://www.kensingtonbooks.com

KENSINGTON BOOKS are published by

Kensington Publishing Corp.
119 West 40th Street
New York, NY 10018

ISBN-13: 978-0-7582-7838-8
ISBN-10: 0-7582-7838-1

First Trade Paperback Printing: July 2012
10 9 8 7 6 5 4 3 2 1

Printed in the United States of America

Prologue

July 2000
Dunwoody, Georgia

MIKALA AULANI, DEFENSE ATTORNEY, SITTING FIRST CHAIR IN the case of *State of Georgia* v. *Sophie Lee,* couldn't believe what she had just heard. She felt like she was carved in stone and in a time warp all rolled into one. She wanted to say something, but her tongue wouldn't work. She saw the foreman of the jury holding the paper he had just read from. She had seen the tremor in his hand and known immediately what he was going to say. And that it was not going to be good for her client. She had seen his blank expression. Now she heard the words ricocheting around inside her head, over and over and over.

Her legs were wobbly, and she was soaked with perspiration because the air-conditioning in the courthouse was broken. Overhead, a paddle fan moved sluggishly, barely stirring the stale air. A fly buzzed dangerously near her nose. She wanted to swat at it.

She risked a glance at Ryan Spenser, the prosecutor, bastard that he was, and saw the smug expression that he tried unsuccessfully to hide. Why was she even looking at the son of a bitch? She should be looking at her client, the client who had just been convicted of a heinous crime. A conviction of first-degree murder that would get her a sentence of life in prison without the possibility of parole—for a crime she didn't commit. Twenty-four-year-old dedicated nurses simply did not kill their patients, and yet that bastard Ryan had convinced a jury of seven men and five women that she had done just that. Bastard.

Mikala felt a hand on her arm and looked down, then up. Again, she heard the words but didn't comprehend them. "Is today Tuesday, Kala?" Mikala nodded. "Every single thing, bad or good, has always happened to me on a Tuesday. I guess that makes me Tuesday's Child. Thank you, Kala, for everything," Sophie Lee said quietly.

Mikala Aulani wanted to cry. She wanted to hug her client, but she was being led away. The judge was thanking the jurors for their service and discharging them. The courtroom was emptying at the speed of light. The trial of the decade had finally ended, and the reporters wanted out to report on the verdict.

Mikala—Kala to friends and peers—sat down and stared at nothing. Jay Brighton, her second chair, started to pack up their briefcases. Across the aisle, Ryan Spenser's staff was doing the same thing.

"Tough break, counselor," Spenser said. "Guess this breaks that winning streak you've been on, huh? You know what they say—the best man wins. You put on a hell of a defense, Kala, I'll give you that. I'll give you something else, too. Your client handled the verdict well. Guess you coached her for that. Just out of curiosity, what did she whisper to you before they took her away?"

Kala finally turned sideways and looked up at the spit-and-polish prosecutor, with his designer suit, power tie, pristine white shirt, and gleaming porcelain-capped teeth. He looked like an Adonis, and the media loved him. It didn't hurt that his father was the Speaker of the House in Washington, something Ryan Junior traded in on every day of his life.

Later, Kala would pat herself on her back for her comeback. The words came from God only knew where, but she said them with conviction. "She told me to put a hex on you. You know how good us Hawaiian people are at doing that. She asked me to do it tonight at midnight. You know what, Spenser? I'm going to do it, too!"

Kala loved, absolutely loved, the expression that crossed the prosecutor's face. First he turned white under his tan, then red, a feat unto itself. He made a sound that caused Kala to laugh.

The courtroom was empty except for the two of them, Spenser's people the last out the door after Jay Brighton.

All Kala had to do was sling her purse over her shoulder, and she could walk out of the room ahead of the barracuda. Defeated. She squared her shoulders and took a step across the aisle. "We both know Sophie Lee is innocent. We both know Adam Star killed his wife, Audrey, and that the two of you pinned it on my client. I'm going to appeal this verdict, and I'm going to nail your ass and Star's ass if it takes me the rest of my life. . . . But not until I get that hex going. See you around, dirtbag!"

And then, with all the aplomb she could muster, Mikala Aulani turned and walked out of the courtroom, her head held high, her shoulders squared. She didn't falter until she was outside the courthouse, where Jay Brighton waited for her.

Jay Brighton was young, young compared to her fifty-two years, young enough still to believe in the justice system. He linked his arm with Kala's, and said, "We'll get him, Kala. I'll work for free for as long as it takes. Sophie did not kill Audrey Star. She did not."

Kala's shoulders slumped even more. "We had six months to try to prove it, and we couldn't, Jay. The horse is out of the barn, and the door's locked now. Sophie will almost certainly be going to prison for the rest of her life with no possibility of parole. What makes you think we can do something now that we didn't do before?"

Jay forced a laugh that came off as more of a bark than anything else. "Well, for starters, you didn't put a hex on him. So, let's get that out of the way and get down to the business of Sophie's appeal. I want to see that winning streak of yours reinstated. And I want to see you chop off that bastard Spenser's balls. Maybe you can work that into your hex."

In spite of herself, Kala laughed, even though it was a bitter sound. "I wouldn't know a hex if it slapped me in the face."

"Then make one up. Come on, I'm buying dinner."

"It's only three o'clock," Kala said. "I don't think I can eat anything."

"Who said anything about eating? I'm thinking we need to drink our dinner, then have someone drive us home. Come on, Kala, we have a lot to talk about, and what better way than over a few drinks."

"Okay, okay. I think we should both go see Sophie tomorrow and prepare her for her sentencing next month. We need to tell her what we're planning to do. Bright and early, Jay."

"Works for me, boss."

"Yes, but will it work for Sophie Lee? That's the question, isn't it?"

Chapter 1

Dunwoody, Georgia
Ten years later

MIKALA AULANI LOOKED AROUND HER OFFICE FOR THE LAST time. Now that her thirty-five-year professional life was packed up in boxes, and the pictures, diplomas, and photographs were off the wall, her personal space looked huge. Jay would have to paint the walls to cover up the telltale signs of where all the plaques had been hung. She eyed her old leather chair, which swiveled and rocked. She really had meant to have the crack in the leather repaired; it had been on her to-do list for years and years. She wondered now why it was she'd never taken the time to do it. But, then, she found herself wondering about a lot of things lately, not that it made a difference.

Jay Brighton and Linda Carpenter, husband and wife and newly minted senior partners, carried the packed and taped boxes out to the reception area. At some point later that day, someone would come and take them to a storage unit Kala had rented a month ago. All except for the single box that sat on top of her desk. *That* box was going with her. She was personally going to carry it down to the underground garage and personally put it on the passenger seat of her car, then drive it to her home, where she would put it in a closet in her bedroom. Sophie Lee deserved a closet rather than a storage unit, where her records would never again see the light of day.

Jay Brighton stood in the doorway. "That about does it, Kala. Told you we'd have this locked down in time for you to make your retirement luncheon."

Kala looked up at her former partner and grimaced. "I decided I'm not going. Call Ben and tell him I have a bellyache."

Ben was Judge Benjamin Jefferson, Kala's significant other of twenty-five years. Ben had retired two weeks earlier, and Kala had thrown a surprise luncheon, inviting all of his peers. For no other reason except retaliation, Ben had decided to do the same for her. His theory was, if he'd had to suffer through the shitty food, the boring speeches, and the overblown testimonials, then so should she.

Newly retired judge Ben Jefferson loved Kala Aulani heart and soul. Everyone said they were a match made in heaven. Sometimes, Kala believed it, and other times, she didn't.

Stepping into the office, Jay replied, "Oh, no, I'm not calling him! You're on your own, Kala. Hey, you aren't my boss anymore, so don't you dare look at me with those puppy dog eyes. No! You sold Linda and me the firm, and I absolutely do not have to take orders anymore. Not showing up at your very own retirement luncheon would be a pretty crappy thing to do," Jay said vehemently.

Kala grinned as she stared up at her old partner. Six-foot-seven, probably the tallest lawyer ever to grace a courtroom. An imposing giant of a man, with his flaming red hair, which he hated, and his freckles, which, if anything, he hated even more. Juries loved him and his folksy manner. They likened him to themselves, just plain old ordinary people. They were wrong, of course, because there was nothing in the least ordinary about Jay Brighton, Attorney at Law. Jay had graduated at the top of his law class, had a photographic memory that did double time acting as a steel trap. He was *almost* as good a lawyer as she was, Kala thought. She'd trained him well, and he'd listened to every pearl of wisdom that came out of her mouth, soaking it all up like a sponge. Yes, one of the best things she'd ever done in her career was to hire him the minute he applied for the job. She'd never been sorry, either, and she knew he'd never regretted joining her rinky-dink law firm back in the day.

"Listen, Jay, I just want to go home and be alone. Surely you can understand that. You didn't give me a going-away present, now that I think about it. How tacky is that? So, calling Ben and canceling my luncheon will serve nicely as my going-away gift. C'mon, Jay, one last favor. I have so much to do; we leave tomorrow, and I'm not even packed. Do you have any idea how many suitcases I have to fill to go away for six whole months? Well, do you?" Kala bellowed at the top of her lungs.

Linda Carpenter, a string bean of a young woman with corkscrew curls that poked up from her head, took Jay's former position in the doorway, and bellowed in return, "I'll do it!"

Kala looked Jay in the eye, and admonished, "You do not deserve that young woman, and I'm sorry I paid for your wedding."

"Stuff it, Kala!" Jay blustered. Long years of familiarity allowed him to talk this way to his old boss. "Why do you find it so hard to accept a few well-meaning accolades? Don't give me any crap here. The reason you don't want to go to that luncheon is some asshole told you that Ryan Spenser is going to show up. With a gift. You're a bigger person than he is. Why can't you go and stare the bastard down?"

"Because I can't. This is the end of it, Jay. I'm not going. Period."

"Okay," Jay said agreeably.

Kala eyed him suspiciously, waiting for the other shoe to drop. When it didn't, Kala gathered up her laptop, her purse, her suit jacket, and dumped them on top of the Sophie Lee box. "Where's the dolly?"

"In the reception room. I'll get it."

"And I don't want or need a parade following me down to the garage," Kala shouted to Jay's retreating back.

"Like that's going to happen," Jay snorted, his eyes burning. Damn, he never thought saying good-bye was going to be so hard. He eyed his wife, who had returned to the reception area and seemed to be having the same problem he was having. The filters probably needed to be changed in the AC unit. Dust particles could really play hell with your tear ducts.

Linda grabbed her husband's arm and dragged him down the hall into the kitchen just as the door to the reception room opened. They didn't bother to look over their shoulders to see if it was a client or the mailman.

"What?" Jay blurted.

"I can't stop crying, that's what!" Linda said, burying her face in the crook of her husband's neck. "What are we going to do without her? She's the rock. She's the glue that made this law firm work. I don't think either one of us is ready to step into her shoes. What if Kala's clients don't want *us*?"

"Then it's their loss, Linda. We have our own clients. This is a thriving law firm. We have five junior partners. We have five paralegals, an office manager, and a secretary who is not only as old as God but knows how to sweet-talk people who walk in the door. We can make it work. We really can."

Linda sniffled. "Well, don't expect me to give you wake-up calls if I have to leave the house before you, and don't expect me to remind you to take your umbrella, pick up your cleaning, and get a haircut. That was Kala's job."

"Yeah, okay, I won't expect you to do that. I'll flounder around on my own," Jay said, his voice choked with emotion.

Their eyeballs popped when they heard their names being screamed at the top of Kala's lungs. They almost killed one another racing to her office. Both of them pulled up short when they saw a man with two canes lower himself to the chair opposite Kala's desk. Underneath her summer tan, Kala's face looked white. She was shaking so badly, Jay and Linda thought she was having a seizure. "What's wrong?" they both shouted in unison.

To say the man with the two canes looked like death warmed over would have been too kind a statement. He was cadaver thin, his eyes sunken, his skin sallow. It was doubtful he weighed a hundred pounds. In the thirty-odd years Jay had worked for and known Mikala Aulani, he didn't think he'd ever seen her as agitated as she was at that very moment. He didn't know what to do, so he waited, his eyes not on the man but on Kala.

"Linda, Jay, this is . . . this is Adam Star. He . . . he came here to . . . he came here to . . ."

The voice was raspy, the words almost unintelligible, but the trio understood them nonetheless.

"What Ms. Aulani is trying to say is, I came here to tell you that ten years ago, I killed my wife, Audrey. Sophie Lee is innocent. As you can see, I'm dying, and I want to make things right." One skeletal hand reached inside his jacket to withdraw a DVD. His hand shook violently when he tried to slide it across the desk toward Kala. "My lawyer has a copy of this. It shows me confessing to the murder, along with all the details. My lawyer will be turning it over to the court when I . . . am no longer here."

Three jaws dropped as three sets of eyes stared with unblinking intensity at the man.

Jay spoke first. "I guess my question would be, how much longer will it be before you are no longer here?" Jay didn't give a damn if he sounded heartless and cruel. What this man had done to Sophie Lee earned him a fat zero in consideration in Jay's opinion.

"You son of a bitch! You let that young girl go to prison for life! What kind of a monster are you?" Kala shrieked. "I knew it was you! I always knew! Now, when you're dying, you want to make it *right!* I hope you burn in hell!" Kala shrieked again.

Adam Star turned his head on its scrawny neck to Jay, and said, "I'm already on borrowed time, but I assume you want me to be more specific."

"Yeah, that would help," Jay drawled.

"Well, I'm already on borrowed time, as I just said, so I think it's safe to say I doubt I'll be here this time next week." He turned his head again to look at Kala, and replied to her question, "The kind of man who didn't have the stomach to be tied down to a paralyzed woman twenty-four/seven. I was never cut out to be the dutiful sort. The doctors said Audrey could live into her nineties with proper care. I didn't have the guts for that. Audrey demanded my constant presence, even during the night hours. I was tied to her. I couldn't breathe; she was smothering me. And yes, Ms. Aulani, I'm sure I will burn in hell." Star leaned back, the constant flow of words exhausting him.

"Why did you come here?" Kala whispered, her shrieking over.

"I owed you and your client a face-to-face. You can show her the DVD when you think it's time. She was an exceptional nurse. She actually cared about Audrey, which is more than I can say I did. Because of that, I want to give you this." The skeletal hand reached into the inside pocket of his cashmere jacket and withdrew a folded set of papers. "My last will and testament. I'm leaving everything I own, which is substantial, beyond substantial actually, to Sophie Lee. I have appointed you, Ms. Aulani, as my personal representative to see that my will is carried out the way I want it to be."

"You can't inherit if you kill someone," Jay said through clenched teeth.

"I didn't inherit a single dime when she died. Almost immediately after we were married, she put everything in my name. She said it was a wedding gift. We were very much in love. We had our whole lives ahead of us. We were 'as one,' was how she put it. She trusted me to handle her fortune for the both of us. The Star fortune already belonged to me at her death and had for some time. Therefore, I can leave it to whomever I choose, and I choose to leave it to Sophie Lee to make up for what I've done. I know Audrey would approve."

"Ryan Spenser?"

"I always suspected he knew I killed Audrey, but he was never able to prove it. On more than one occasion, he said the media would love the other-woman part of it, as they would never believe that Sophie and I were not having an affair. More meat, more fodder for the nightly news. He was right, and it was the trial of the century.

"Ryan Spenser became the golden boy. He rolled along, winning every case he tried after that one. I never saw him after the trial, but about six months ago I got a personal letter from him asking me if I would consider backing him in his run for governor next year. He, of course, didn't know I was ill, and I've been housebound since. If what you're asking me specifically is if he knew he was prosecuting an innocent woman, I would say yes. But that is just my opinion. He had the facts going for him. It was either her or me, and like I said, he couldn't prove I did it. That left only Sophie Lee, and he convinced a jury of seven men and five women that she did it."

This time the words did exhaust Adam Star. Before he closed his eyes, he pressed a button on his watch. Two male nurses barreled into the room, took one look at their patient, and scooped him up. They were out the door in thirty seconds, their patient in their arms, leaving behind three stupefied lawyers.

Kala was the first to speak, her eyes wide with wonder as she stared at the box on the top of her desk labeled SOPHIE LEE in permanent black marker. "My mind isn't working right now, so will someone please tell me what day today is?"

"Your retirement day, Kala," Linda said.

Jay knew exactly what Kala meant. His voice was pitched so low, Kala had to strain to hear the words. "It's *Tuesday,* Kala."

Kala lowered herself into the leather chair with the crack running down the middle. Gradually, she was able to focus. She reached for the stiff blue paper that covered Adam Star's last will and testament. She had to clear her throat twice before she could get the words out past her tongue. "Set up the DVD. I want to see what's on it. But first I want to read this will. If that bastard lied to us, I will kill him myself."

It took no time for Kala to read through the short, simple will. Everything appeared to be in order. She sifted through the legalese. Two persons had signed, attesting to having witnessed Adam Star's signature. It was in order and dated exactly one week prior. Everything Adam Star owned, compliments of his dead wife, Audrey Star, now belonged to Sophie Lee. Or would belong to Sophie Lee one moment after Adam Star's passing. Everything he owned amounted to hundreds of millions of dollars in stocks, bonds, real estate, and, of course, 51 percent of Star Enterprises, whatever that happened to be. Somewhere there was a yacht moored, a corporate Learjet parked somewhere else, a helicopter grounded on some helicopter pad God only knew where, two cigarette boats worth $100,000 each, berthed in Key Biscayne, Florida, and a fleet of high-end cars to the tune of $5 million. Among the listed real estate were the mansion Audrey Star had died in, a ski resort in Aspen, Colorado, and a mountaintop estate in Hawaii, overlooking the Pacific. And that was just the tip of the iceberg. The real-estate holdings ran to six pages and represented so many zeros, Kala felt light-headed.

The joke was feeble at best and didn't even draw a smile from Kala, when Jay said, "Guess Sophie can pay our bill now if this is on the up-and-up."

Kala shook her head. "We took the case pro bono, and that's the way it stays. My God, how do we tell this to Sophie?"

"Well, I don't think we should say anything at all to her until . . . until they shovel the last bit of dirt on that bastard's coffin. I'm not sure I'm buying all of this," Jay said.

"What part aren't you buying, Jay?" Kala asked.

Jay threw his hands high in the air. "The whole damn thing. Guys like Adam Star don't have a conscience. They take crap like this to their graves. The man didn't give two shits that a young girl got sent to prison for life. For *life,* Kala! Now, because he's dying, he wants to make nice. Be forgiven! Like Sophie is going to forgive him for taking ten years of her life, leaving her with no hope for a future? She has to hate his guts. How could she not hate that bastard? I don't think the word *forgiveness* is in her vocabulary these days."

Kala leaned back and steepled her fingers. "I think you're wrong. Sophie's bitch is going to be with Ryan Spenser, not with Adam Star. She knew just the way we knew that Adam was guilty. All three of us tried to convince Spenser of that, and he turned a deaf ear. Sophie will take the position that Adam tried to make it right in the end, mark my words. When Spenser finds out, if he doesn't already know, he's going to blow a gasket. And you can take that one to the bank. I think now that this has happened, it's why he was planning on attending my retirement luncheon. To see if I knew about it."

"Boy, what a shame that you're leaving for that six-month retirement vacation tomorrow," Jay said slyly as he winked at his wife. Linda did her best not to laugh out loud at Kala's expression. "Okay, let's view this cinematic masterpiece." Jay pressed a button, and Adam Star's face filled the screen.

No more than three minutes in length, the video was painful to watch. Everything Adam Star had said in the office was now verbalized, with a face to make it real. At the end, his lawyer, a man named Clayton Hughes, and two witnesses verified the date, the time, and the fact that they were in attendance when the DVD was made.

Jay turned the machine off, popped the DVD, and slipped

it into a plastic sleeve. "I think this should go in the safe. I also think we should burn maybe, let's say, three extra copies. Just for . . . whatever."

Kala nodded in agreement. "And to think today is *Tuesday*!" she said. "You're right, we'll sit on this until . . . well, until Mr. Star goes to meet his maker. In the meantime, I'm canceling my reservations for tomorrow. Linda, do me a favor and call Ben and tell him I'll meet him outside the courthouse in an hour."

"It will be my pleasure, Kala. Are you sure we can't let Sophie know?" Linda asked.

Before Kala could say anything, Jay piped up. "We're sure."

Again Kala nodded.

Chapter 2

NOW THAT SHE WAS ON THE COURTHOUSE STEPS, KALA ASKED herself why she had picked this destination to meet with her longtime significant other. "Because I'm in a state of shock and not thinking clearly, that's why," she muttered to no one in particular. She hoped Ben wouldn't keep her waiting, because it was just too damn hot to be standing out in the boiling sun.

She saw him then, and he looked just the way a judge is supposed to look. Well, a retired judge. Ben Jefferson was tall, six foot two in his bare feet. He was lean and trim, with snow white hair and a deep tan. He had a killer smile that he was fond of saying was just for Kala. Oh, he could scowl with the best of them but never at Kala, the love of his life. He was smiling now as he waved from the bottom of the tier of steps. "Missed you at your going-away party, my dear. My car is full of exquisitely wrapped presents. Just for the record, no one believed even for a minute that you had a belly ache. You don't, do you?" he asked, suddenly concerned.

Kala could never lie to this man; she loved him too much. "I didn't at the time, but I do now. Let's walk over to Snuffy's. I need a drink. A *big* drink."

Ben grabbed her arm. "What's wrong? What happened? Tell me right now! *Now,* Kala."

"Do not touch my person, Ben Jefferson! I said I need a drink, and when I have that drink in my hand, and not one second before, I will most definitely tell you exactly what is wrong." To make her point, Kala walked away in the direction of Snuffy's, the hangout of all lawyers and paralegals in the area. Many judges were known to frequent Snuffy's but usually later in the day. Ben had to jog to keep up with her. When he came abreast of her, Kala asked, "Was Ryan Spenser there?"

"He was, all decked out in summer cashmere. It looked like he'd had his teeth cleaned and polished for the occasion. His present, according to all the females there, was the most exquisitely wrapped, if that means anything."

Kala let loose with a string of profanities that forced Ben to cover his ears. "Well, if you didn't want to know, then why did you ask me?" he snapped.

"Was the package ticking?" Kala snapped back.

"I didn't check it. Will you just please tell me what the hell is wrong?"

"Not until Jim Beam and I have a long-awaited reunion. Oh, thank God it is cold in here," Kala said as she stepped through the door that Ben was holding open for her. She sailed past the bar and headed to her favorite booth, calling over her shoulder, "A double on the rocks and make it snappy!"

Not to be outdone, Ben placed the same order for himself.

The drinks appeared as if by magic. Kala reached for hers and downed it in two long, gulping swallows. Her eyes watered and her throat burned, but she held up her glass for a refill. She stared at Ben with tears running down her cheeks.

"Will you please tell me what's going on? In all the years I've known you, I've never seen you drink more than one drink, and you nurse it all night long."

"Adam Star came into the office late this morning. He's

dying, Ben. He'll be lucky if he makes it through the week. He came with two male nurses. He confessed to me, Jay, and Linda that he killed his wife and that he let Sophie go to jail for life. The son of a bitch actually made a DVD of his confession. He gave us a copy. We played it after he left. His lawyer is Clayton Hughes. And that's not all of it, either." Kala looked at her fresh drink, picked it up, and downed it. This time she squeezed her eyes shut as the liquor blazed a trail down her throat. When she could find her voice, she shouted to the barmaid to bring her a large glass of ginger ale and two cups of coffee.

Ben Jefferson stared across the table at Kala as he tried to make sense out of what she was saying. The only thing he knew for certain was that they were not going to be leaving for a six-month trip tomorrow. All he could say was, "If you drink all of that, you are going to be sick."

"Yeah, I know."

"So, what's the rest, the part that has your panties in a knot?"

"The son of a bitch gave me a copy of his will. He left his entire fortune, or I should say Audrey's fortune, to Sophie Lee. Hundreds of millions of dollars. To make up to her for what he did. You need to say something, Ben, and you need to say it *now.*"

"Does Ryan Spenser know?"

"I don't know. How was he acting at the luncheon?"

"Like a pompous ass, the way he always acts. If I had to guess, I'd say no, he doesn't know. He did get up and say something nice about you. He said you were one of his most worthy opponents and how it hurt him to the depths of his soul that he won a case against you and broke your undefeated record. He said you were one of the finest attorneys in this fair state and he was sorry you were retiring."

"And he didn't choke on the words?"

"Nope."

"I hate that bastard's fucking guts, you know that, right, Ben?" Kala singsonged.

Ben knew Kala was blitzed because she never swore. Well, hardly ever. And when she did swear, it was typically because her twenty-pound cat Shakespeare had peed on the foyer rug.

"Forget all that other stuff. You're going to get Sophie out of there, and she can get on with her life. It's wonderful, Kala. Getting her out as soon as possible should be all that you are thinking about right now. Forget the trip, forget Ryan Spenser. Let's take the will and the DVD, go to Judge Gamble for a writ of habeas corpus, and head to the prison and spring Sophie. My God, Kala, this is the best news I've ever heard."

"It is good news. It's wonderful news. It's the best news in the world, but we can't do a damn thing until that man dies."

"What? Why?"

"Because that's the way Adam Star wants it. He doesn't want to be arrested to die in prison. I guess he wants to die in what he thinks is his idea of peace. He made things right is the way I'm thinking he's thinking."

"But, Kala, if he killed his wife, he can't inherit her fortune. The will won't hold up."

"Oh, yes, it will hold up. It turns out that Audrey Star had transferred all of her holdings to her husband long before her accident and her death. Right after they were married, to be exact. It's all legal. The fortune is his to do with as he sees fit. Sophie is going to be so rich, she won't know what to do."

"It won't erase the ten years of her life she spent in prison, though," Ben said quietly.

"No, it won't. You understand I can't go away with you right now. I have to be here to help Sophie. She's going to need me like never before. I have to make a plan. I don't want her going through a media blitz. I'm going to hire a private detective to sit outside Adam Star's hospital room. I think he's in a hospital room, but I'm not sure. Those male nurses could be caring for him at his home. I know how ghoulish this sounds, and I don't care. The moment he expires, I want to be on my way to the prison to formally present that writ of habeas corpus and get Sophie released. This is where you come in, Ben. I want you to drive up to the prison, take a copy of the will and the DVD, and explain the situation to the warden and anyone else who has to be told so we can have the paperwork all ready to go and get her out of there within minutes of his receiving the writ of habeas corpus. You have to swear the warden to secrecy. Can you do that for me, sweetie?"

Sweetie. The only time Kala called him sweetie was when she wanted something she herself couldn't do or didn't want to do. He nodded agreeably. He'd lived with Sophie Lee's ghost for the past ten years just the way Kala had. He'd long ago lost count of the times Kala had dragged him with her to the prison to visit Sophie on visitors' day until Sophie herself put a stop to it by telling Kala she didn't want her to visit anymore because it was too painful. Even then, Kala had continued to make the trek to the prison, only to be turned away. The letters that she wrote faithfully were invariably returned. In the end, she had to give up. From that point on, all Kala could do was pray for the young girl she'd come to think of as a daughter.

"Okay, I think I'm going to go home now, Ben. You have things to do. Listen, you won't hurt my feelings if you want to start off the trip by yourself. I can always join you later."

"Oh, no, it doesn't work that way. I'm with you all the way on this one. I'll drive you home, and we can pick up your car later."

Outside in the sultry air, Kala looked up at Ben, and said, "This is a good thing, isn't it, Ben?"

"From Sophie's point of view, it's a home run. For Star, not so good. And I don't have an opinion as yet on Ryan Spenser. This is going to play hell with his run for governor next November. He's gearing up. He was pressing the flesh big time at your luncheon, trying to drum up support off your reputation. And just for the record, I hate his guts, too. Come along, *sweetie*, let's get you home."

Kala reared back. The only time Ben called her *sweetie* was when it was time to go to the bedroom. Ben laughed out loud at her expression.

An hour later, Kala had changed her clothes, made a pot of coffee and a sandwich, and carried it out to her shaded deck. The fat cat that she adored snuggled up against her bare ankles and purred so loud it sounded like a tune to Kala's weary ears. Then he climbed onto her lap and continued to purr. She talked to him the way she always did. He listened the way he always did, then went to sleep as Kala wound down. She still felt woozy from the two double shots of Jim Beam, but she was starting to feel better.

Sophie was going to be set free. Sophie was going to be one rich young woman. Thirty-four years of age still meant she had the best years of her life ahead of her. Yes, she'd lost most of her glorious twenties, but maybe this next decade would somehow make up for it.

Something was bothering her, something she couldn't quite put her finger on. What? In her mind, she played over every single word Adam Star had said in her office. God, why hadn't they had the good sense to record that visit? It was something he said. Something that wasn't in his confession. Dammit, what was it?

Kala reached for the cell phone she was never without and called Jay at the office. "Tell me word for word everything Adam Star said to us in the office. Something is bothering me. Something he said that wasn't on the DVD." She listened, her feet tapping the floor of the deck. Shakespeare woke and jumped off her lap, but not before he shot her a withering look.

"That's it! That's it! Okay, okay, now call around and see what hospital he's in or if he's home. He might even be admitted under another name. Oh, you did that already? He's in St. Barnabas, room 511. I'm going there right now or as soon as I can get dressed. Call Meg Stallings, the court reporter we use, and tell her to meet me there. If she's not free, get someone; I don't care who it is. I want a record of what Adam Star says when I talk to him. If I talk to him. And I want witnesses, too."

Kala finished her coffee, then poured a second cup in the kitchen as she made her way through the house. She carried the coffee with her to her bedroom, where she stripped down and changed into a pair of white linen slacks with a powder blue shell that showed off her tan. She gave her long black hair a quick brush, piled it on top of her head, finished her coffee, and headed back to the kitchen, where she called for a cab. With four shots of Jim Beam under her belt, she didn't want to take a chance of getting caught driving while under the influence.

Once Kala arrived at the hospital, it took a solid hour before she could convince the floor nurse and Adam Star's private nurses that she absolutely had to speak with him, and it was a matter of life or death. Finally, just as the court reporter appeared, the private-duty nurses relented and let them enter the room.

Kala quickly apologized for her impromptu visit and made nice while the court reporter was setting up her little machine. "I just need to ask you something, Mr. Star. You mentioned it at my office, but it wasn't on the record, and it has to be on the record, Mr. Star. For Sophie Lee's sake, it just has to be. It's about what you said concerning Mr. Spenser, the prosecutor."

Kala looked around at the machines, saw the tubes and

bags, and wanted to cry that anyone, it didn't matter who they were, had to suffer like this. She wondered if the nurses were giving their patient morphine. She asked, and one of the male nurses nodded. How good this statement was going to be would be anyone's guess if Adam Star was shot full of morphine. She waited while the nurse slipped shaved cubes of ice through the patient's dry, cracked lips.

"Mr. Star, I need to clarify something you said earlier in my office today." Quickly, Kala rattled off his admission and his opinion concerning Ryan Spenser. "So what I am asking you now is if everything I just said is a true and accurate statement of what you said in my office a short while ago?"

"Yes, it is a true and accurate statement."

"Is there anything you would like to add to that statement?"

"No."

"Then all I can do is thank you. Someone will return in short order with your statement typed out. Will you be able to sign it for a notary, who will also be here, and will your two nurses agree to being witnesses to your signing?"

"Yes."

"One last thing, is your mind clear even though you are receiving morphine?"

"My mind is as clear as yours right now. Do you want me to describe the furnishings in your office?"

In spite of herself, Kala smiled. "It couldn't hurt."

Adam Star rambled on for three minutes, then he sighed and drifted off to sleep.

Kala looked at the stenographer. "I'll have my partner take pictures of the office in short order to support what Mr. Star just described. Did you get it all?"

"I did. I can have this transcribed and be back here in ninety minutes with a notary and have it dropped off at your home by six this evening."

"That will be fine. Thanks, Meg."

Kala wanted to say something to someone but was at a loss.

Adam Star was sleeping. Both nurses were busy doing something with bags for IVs, so she patted Star's hand and left the room. She felt like crying and didn't know why. Star was paying in the most horrible way imaginable for what he'd done. She had to let it go at that. There was nothing more she could do at the moment.

Chapter 3

MIKALA AULANI LOOKED AT HERSELF IN THE MIRROR, MOVING this way, then that way. She decided she still looked as good today, at the age of sixty-two, as she had at the age of fifty. She hadn't put on any weight because she ate right, did a modicum of exercising, and had the good fortune to be born Hawaiian, one of an undeniably beautiful people. Well, almost all of them were beautiful. Some were actually ravishing.

She looked at her raven black hair and the streaks of gray running through it. Coloring those pesky gray streaks was something she debated every so often, but Ben said he liked them, insisting they made her look more like a goddess. Like a real goddess had gray hair. She snorted at the thought. One good thing about being Hawaiian was that she didn't have to worry about makeup. Hands on her hips, Kala played with her reflection in the mirror as she adjusted her minty green blouse and matching skirt. She winked at herself, kissed the air, then laughed out loud as she danced under a spray of perfume. There was just no way one could argue with 115 pounds of curves and double eyelashes at the age of sixty-two. Stupid is as stupid does. She laughed again because she knew she looked more than good for her age. Even a bit sexy. Not that she was even one little bit vain. Not her.

Time to get this show on the road. She was going into the

office. To do what, she wasn't sure. More of what she'd been doing since Tuesday, when Adam Star walked into her office and dropped his bombshell.

The death watch was on, and it was disconcerting to be so excited and at the same time sad to be waiting for someone to die. Still, donor recipients did the same thing, didn't they? In order to live, someone had to die to donate an organ for the other's survival. This wasn't all that different. Adam Star had to die so Sophie Lee could live again. Kala shook her head. She hated thoughts like this. As Jay said, no matter how you looked at it, it was one helluva mess.

Kala tried to shift her thoughts in another direction. What better than her canceled trip and Ben Jefferson? Ben had taken it well and didn't seem the least bit upset. Either that, or he was hiding his disappointment well.

She loved Ben, she really did. And the success of her thirty-five-year relationship with the retired judge, she felt sure, was because they had never married. He had his own house, and she had hers. They didn't commingle anything but their bodies, and ooooh, that was heavenly. Neither of them needed money from the other, each had robust brokerage accounts, and neither had to count their pennies or answer to each other about spending those pennies. Independence was truly a wonderful thing, Kala thought. And she planned on keeping it that way.

A time or two she and Ben had actually talked of marriage, then looked at each other and laughed, saying no, it would never work. What they had did work, and neither one of them wanted to jeopardize the relationship. Sometimes, she missed having children, and other times, she was glad she didn't have any. The world today was a crazy place; she saw it firsthand day after day in court. Ben said he felt the same way.

Number crunching of any kind was not Kala's forte as she tried to figure out how many hours it would be till Tuesday. Did she count all of today, all of Tuesday? In the end, she had to give it up because she couldn't concentrate. "Oh, God, make me stop thinking like this," she mumbled as she climbed into her racy Mercedes convertible. She could have driven to the office blindfolded, but today, she made a stop on the corner of Cedar and Central. She waited for the light to change and made a right turn into the parking lot of St. Gabriel's Catholic Church.

She was from the old school and reached into the glove box for a scarf to put on her head. She wanted to stamp her feet in fury, shake her fist at something when she found the church door locked. Her shoulders slumped until she saw a young priest headed her way. He smiled and unlocked the door, saying something about vandalism. Kala just shook her head. What kind of upbringing did kids who vandalized churches have?

The church was cool and dim, smelling faintly of incense and smoking candles. Sun streamed through the stained-glass windows, which were so vibrant in color she could only stare at them, mesmerized. She couldn't remember the last time she'd gone to church in the middle of the day. She made a mental promise to herself to come more often because it was so peaceful.

Kala bowed her head and prayed for Adam Star and his soul as he prepared for his journey to the hereafter. She prayed that Sophie Lee would be able to adjust to the outside world and that her heart and mind wouldn't be full of bitterness and hatred. Lastly, she prayed for herself, that she was doing the right thing, and asked God to take away the hate she felt for Adam Star. And Ryan Spenser. Especially Ryan Spenser.

Kala looked around, certain that something inside would have changed with her plea, but everything was the same as when the young priest had unlocked the door. She could still smell the incense and the burning candles, could still see the sun shining through the stained-glass windows, creating rainbows over the pews. Her heart felt as heavy as before, but her eyes were dry. She closed them and offered up a prayer for everyone involved in what Jay Brighton referred to as one helluva mess.

She didn't see the young priest until she was at the door. He was waiting for her so he could lock the doors again. It saddened her that such a place of comfort had to be locked down. A crazy thought swirled through her head, that maybe in the future she should call ahead, make an appointment to visit with the Lord. What was this world coming to?

Twenty-two minutes later, Kala parked her car in the underground lot and took the elevator up to her office. From the looks of things, it was business as usual except for her empty office. She hung her suit jacket and purse on an ancient bamboo coatrack and settled herself behind her shiny, empty desk. She flipped open her laptop, booted up, checked her e-mails, then her voice mail. Nothing of the slightest importance.

Even though it was late morning, and she'd had more than enough coffee, she meandered down the hall to the kitchen. She stuck her head in Jay's office and asked if there was any news.

"There's news, and then there's news plus no news. Which do you want first?" Kala shrugged. "Okay, Judge Oldstein is in the hospital having his gallbladder out. That means the two motions I had with him for today and Monday have been canceled. Jim Langley's deposition was canceled for this afternoon because he was in a fender bender, and he needs to have that checked out, plus he's a hypochondriac, as you well know. He is on his way to some bone cruncher as we speak. The closing on the Webers' new house has been put off again because the new buyers swear they saw termites even though there is a termite bond on the house. Judge Ellison's office called, and his clerk asks that you stop by sometime today for a chat. That's exactly how he put it—'a chat'—so don't grill me for more details because that's all I have."

"And . . ."

"And, Adam Star slipped into a coma during the early hours of this morning—four twenty-six to be precise. That's all I know about that, too."

"I wonder what Ruth Ellison wants to chat about," Kala mumbled to herself.

"She probably wants to rent your house in Hawaii. I seem to recall hearing something a few weeks ago at the courthouse that she cleared her docket for the entire month of August to take a much-needed vacation."

"Well, that's not going to happen. Do me a favor and call her office and point-blank tell her clerk that the house is rented through the rest of the year. It is, you know; I'm just not getting paid any rent. And if the occasion arises, and you can get it in that she has never given me a favorable ruling, go for it. I'm outta here in two weeks, so I couldn't care less what she thinks or feels."

Jay's outrage was a palpable thing. "Well, that's just great, Kala. What about me, Linda, and the rest of our associates?"

"Deal with it like I've been dealing with it for the past however many years. She's a snarky witch, and you can tell her I said that, too. You know, now that I think about it, I should call all those nasty judges who don't know their asses from their elbows and tell them a thing or two. I just might do that, too, before Ben and I leave."

Jay threw his hands in the air. "What? Did you wake up this morning and decide to take an ugly-mood pill or something? What's with you?"

Kala leaned back in her comfortable chair. She closed her eyes, and responded, "Or something, I guess. I was just venting, Jay. But do call Ruth's office and tell her the house is rented. I have no desire to go to her office today. Or any other day, so if we can nip it in the bud, that's a good thing. Besides, I am officially retired."

"What are you going to do today?" Jay asked curiously.

"I have some firming-up calls to make. And then I'm going to pay a visit to Clayton Hughes, Adam Star's attorney. We need to have a talk. I'd like to get it over with before . . . well, I'd just like to get it out of the way, and the sooner the better."

Jay was suddenly all business. "Do you want me to go with you? When you don't take notes or record the conversation, you always forget half of what went on. With me there, it won't happen."

Jay was right, and she knew it. "Do you have the time?"

"Of course. Weren't you listening when I told you about what was going on?"

"Of course I was listening. My mind wanders these days for some reason. So, if you're ready, let's head over to Mr. Hughes's office. We might as well walk—it's just a few blocks. It's hot out but not so humid, so we should be okay. Though I think it might rain later today," Kala said fretfully. "How long do people stay in a coma, do you know?"

"Sometimes years," Jay said cheerfully to get Kala's goat.

"Sometimes I really hate you, Jay Brighton."

"You could never hate me, Kala. Hatred just isn't in you. And five will get you ten, the reason you were late this morning was because you stopped at St. Gabriel's to do a little praying."

"Smart-ass," Kala shot back as she reached for her purse. "That young priest, he called you, didn't he?"

Jay laughed. He was still laughing when they walked through the revolving doors out into the bright summer sunshine. "Sun's out; don't think it's going to rain."

"It's going to rain, my knee hurts. It always rains when my knee hurts."

The partners walked along in silence until they came to a four-story brick building covered in ivy. The building housed mostly lawyers, but the fourth floor was allocated to CPAs' firms. Some of the best in the city. Kala knew that because she used Kuczkir, Bernstein, Friedman, and Schwager for all of her firm's accounting needs.

Clayton Hughes's firm was on the second floor. Kala opted for the steps, Jay following behind her. She opened the door and stepped through into another old world. Hughes, Hughes, and Dempsey was one of the oldest, most prestigious firms in the city. No new associates were ever taken on unless one of the old guard died. No one had died in years, leaving the majority of the lawyers in the seventy-plus age bracket.

Kala marched up to the receptionist and looked down at her and the desk. Both looked like they had survived the flood on the ark. Kala handed a business card to the elderly woman, smiled, and said, "I'm here about Adam Star. Would you ask Mr. Hughes if he could spare me a few minutes? I promise I'll be brief."

"No need for briefness, young lady. Clayton is just practicing his putting in his office. I think he'll welcome some company. Go right on in, third door on the right. Tell him I said it was all right."

Jay rolled his eyes as he followed Kala down the hall. Kala knocked softly and was told to enter.

Clayton looked up from his stance, his putter clutched in a death grip.

"Your receptionist said it was all right to come back here. I'm Kala Aulani, and this is my partner, Jay Brighton. We're here about Adam Star."

"Ah, yes, Adam. Sad business. Very sad business. The hospital just called a short while ago and said it was touch-and-go. I expected you sooner. Didn't you just retire, Miss Aulani? I think I heard something about that the other day."

"I did retire. I mean, I am retired, but then Mr. Star came to my office and set me back a few days. I need to talk to you. I want to understand all of this."

"Yes, I'm sure you do. Please, take a seat, and I'll tell you what I can."

Clayton Hughes was round. He was pink-cheeked. His bald head was pink, too, so it was hard to tell where his head ended and his cheeks began. He had the shrewdest blue eyes that Kala had ever seen and a nose that hooked over his upper lip. He was dressed in a bright yellow Lacoste T-shirt and wrinkled khaki pants. He wore golf shoes. He leaned forward, and said, "Ask me what you want to know, and if I can answer the question, I'll answer it, and if not, I won't. It's that simple."

Kala thought about it. His client was still alive, so attorney-client privilege prevailed unless Adam Star had given Hughes permission to discuss his affairs.

"How did Mr. Star kill his wife? He didn't discuss that part of it when he made his confession. I think my client has a right to know how it was done and why Ryan Spenser wasn't aware of it."

Chapter 4

CLAYTON HUGHES'S RUDDY ROUND FACE SEEMED TO CLOSE IN on itself. "I think I should give you both a little background as to how I came to be in the position I'm in at present. This firm represented Audrey Star's parents and, at their demise, Audrey herself as the heir to their fortune. There were no other siblings, in case you didn't know that. Actually, there were no distant cousins or aunts or uncles either.

"Abner Star, Audrey's father, made his original fortune in, of all things, storage lockers. He then deployed that fortune in many other ventures that generated staggering revenues. You'll receive all of that information when the final accounting is turned over to you.

"When Audrey came to me and said she was getting married, I wanted her to have a prenuptial agreement drawn up. She adamantly refused. She said she was in love with a fine young man, and she wasn't starting off her marriage with distrust. I argued with that young woman until I was blue in the face, but she simply would not budge.

"When she and Adam returned from their monthlong honeymoon, Audrey came back to my office and wanted all of her holdings, the whole ball of wax, transferred to her husband. She told me at the time Adam did not know what she was doing. She planned to tell him once it was a done deal. A giant surprise of sorts. 'An over-the-top wedding present,' was how she put it. Once again I argued, but when she threatened to take her business somewhere else, I had to agree to her demands. The young woman simply would not listen to anything I or our other lawyers had to say. So in the end, we did what she wanted. As far as I know, they had a wonderful marriage. They went from vacation to vacation, seeing the world, and always coming back to the Dunwoody residence to fall back and regroup until their next adventure.

"There was one other thing Audrey was adamant about, and that was not taking her husband's name. None of us here at the firm could figure that out. Everyone refers to Adam as Adam Star, but his legal name was Adam William Clements. Not that that matters, but it is something that you need to know. For some cockamamie reason, Audrey wanted Adam legally to change his last name to Star. At first he refused, and he kept refusing, but he finally gave in and had his name changed. All Audrey would say, once the name was changed, was that now they, as a couple, were Star and Star. I guess she thought it was romantic.

"As far as I or anyone else here at the firm knows, their marriage was quite blissful. From time to time I would see something in the society pages, but for the most part they were just two very private people. They donated to every charitable organization in town. They lent their names to whatever would help those less fortunate. The socialites in town referred to them as a truly golden couple. In a sense they were. Audrey was a very kind woman with a true patrician beauty. Adam was handsome, always tanned, kind, and outgoing. Audrey called him her Adonis."

Jay leaned closer to the desk. "I'm sensing we are about to hear the 'aha' moment about now."

The shrewd blue eyes focused on Jay. Hughes nodded.

"Audrey went off on safari to Africa. Alone."

"Aha!" Jay said, throwing his arms in the air.

Hughes grimaced. "It's not what you think, Mr. Brighton. Adam had a ruptured appendix and couldn't travel, so Audrey went alone. Things returned to normal or what was considered normal for the Two Stars. That's what Audrey and Adam were called around here. They continued to live in what we all assumed was marital bliss for another six, maybe it was seven years.

"And then the unbelievable happened two months after the couple returned from Africa. They went as a couple that time. Audrey loved Africa for some reason. A few days after their return, Audrey had her accident. She was on her way home from the dentist and had a head-on collision. She was not at fault; the other driver was a young boy who had just gotten his license and was speeding. Normally, she had a chauffeur drive her wherever she wanted to go, but that particular day Adam was being chauffeured somewhere and left the house not knowing—or perhaps he did know, I was never sure—that Audrey had a dentist appointment. I vaguely recall someone saying a patient had canceled, and the dentist called Audrey and asked if she wanted to take that appointment time, and she said yes. I don't know if that means anything or not. I never thought it was a 'planned' accident, if that's where your thoughts are taking you. Everything was just coincidental".

Jay rolled his eyes. Kala looked skeptical.

The elderly receptionist poked her head in the door and asked if anyone wanted coffee. "Raise your hands if you do," she said cheerfully. They all raised their hands.

"Harriet makes the best coffee in the state of Georgia," Hughes said. "And she's probably going to serve us brownies that she makes herself. She puts nuts and raisins in them. I told her she should market them, but she has no interest in doing that. We would have gladly represented her. The thing about brownies and coffee . . . I digress here."

Kala had the feeling she was Alice and had just fallen

through the rabbit hole. She tried to focus on the attorney across from her, but her thoughts were all over the map as she struggled with what she was hearing. For sure she was glad Jay was with her because she'd never be able to put it all in order the way she was hearing it. Two Stars. Now if that didn't take the cake, or in this case, the brownies, she didn't know what did.

"Harriet will be upset if we don't eat the brownies and coffee. She thrives on compliments, and the rest of the story can wait. While we partake of these goodies, tell me about yourselves."

"We're lawyers," Jay said as he stuffed a brownie in his mouth. He thought it tasted like sawdust. He managed to choke it down, then gulped the coffee. McDonald's on their worst day couldn't have made anything taste as bad.

"As Jay said, we're lawyers and represent Sophie Lee," Kala said. She *was* in the rabbit hole and trying to climb out.

"Young man," Hughes said, addressing Jay, "I know if you ask nicely, Harriet will make you a plate of brownies to take with you. She does love a compliment."

Kala looked at Jay, daring him to refuse before he joined her in the rabbit hole. She wanted to laugh. Hysterically. But somehow she managed not to. She wondered if perhaps she was destined to be an actress in her next life.

Hughes licked at one chubby finger. "Back to the accident," he said, changing course. "Audrey was hit head-on by a speeding SUV. They needed the Jaws of Life to get her out of the car. At first they didn't think she'd survive. She had the best doctors, the best surgeons in the world. As we know, she did survive but was left totally paralyzed from the waist down with intractable pain that could only be controlled through the use of an IV drip. She spent well over a year in and out of hospitals, rehab, you name it. It was hers for the asking until she put her foot down and said no more. She wanted to go home. She had the best nursing care there was out there. But she was a very demanding patient, and they weren't able to keep a nurse for more than ten days at a time. Until Miss Lee arrived. At first, Audrey took to that young lady like a duck to water. Audrey herself told me how wonderful she was when I would visit. She came to love her like a sister. I sensed . . . I sensed that Adam was jealous of that relationship. He admitted it to me later on. Audrey started making demands on Sophie, then on Adam. She was abusive, often bringing Sophie to tears. Then she'd cry and apologize to Sophie. You see, once Sophie was hired, the other two shift nurses were discharged. Sophie was on call twenty-four/seven.

"My perspective on all of that was it allowed Audrey and Sophie to bond even more. And Audrey got something else, her husband's undivided attention. She put him on call twenty-four/seven, too. If she wanted to know what the day's news headlines were at three in the morning, she would have Adam read them to her. If she wanted pickles and ice cream at five in the morning, Adam was expected to get them for her. Adam, not Sophie. She became a tyrant was how Adam put it when he came to me to make the confession.

"Audrey got perverse pleasure out of waking Adam at all hours of the night to change her diaper. She told me Adam never complained, did it all cheerfully. And he agreed with her that there was just so much Sophie could do in twenty-four hours, and the nurse did need her rest."

Clayton Hughes startled them with his next statement when he said it, and with it, they were both out of the rabbit hole and on their feet. "Did Audrey blame Adam for her accident? You bet your ass she did, although she never said the words out loud, according to Adam. If Adam hadn't had the chauffeur drive him to the shooting range where he was taking lessons, that chauffeur would have been available to take Audrey to the dentist. You'll find out sooner or later that Audrey had a deplorable driving record, so bad that her driver's license had been revoked.

"That's the background for what comes next. The way Adam explained it, it was quite simple. On Sophie's days off, Adam would hold back one or two of Audrey's medications until he had a lethal dosage available. He dissolved the pills in a bottle of water, and on the day in question, when Sophie took her bathroom break, which he had her timed at eight minutes, all he needed to do was go into Sophie's room, pour the water from the bottle into a glass, and give Audrey her next dose of medicine. Audrey could never keep up with when she was supposed to take her pills and always relied on Sophie and Adam to keep track for her. And as you know, the autopsy and tox screen determined that she died of a massive overdose."

"How soon after he poisoned her did she die? And where was he when she did? I seem to recall from the trial that he was not at home," Kala said.

"I don't know exactly. The day he said he actually did it, he left the house to go to the shooting range. For some reason he thought that was what he should do, so he did it. When he got home, Audrey was dead. You know the rest. It's all in his written statement. Harriet will give you a copy. It's all in order. I don't know why Adam didn't give it to you when he gave you his death-confession video. That's what he called the damn thing, his death-confession video.

"If there's nothing else, I have an appointment shortly I have to get ready for. I did not then nor do I now believe that that was the way it happened—despite the fact that all the evidence showed that Audrey died from an overdose of precisely what Adam said he used to kill her. I think he lied when he made that confession and was telling the truth at the time of the murder, but I don't know why. As difficult as it must have been to live with Audrey after the accident, as demanding as she was, Adam was devoted to her. I simply do not believe that he could have killed her. That is my opinion, and nothing he says now is going to change it."

Kala looked at Jay, who shrugged. Both of them got up and shook Hughes's hand.

"Thank you for taking the time to speak with us, Mr. Hughes," Kala said.

"It was a terrible thing if Adam did what he said he did, and his wife died at his hands. I hope that young woman is able to get on with her life. She'll certainly have enough money to do whatever she wants, even though it's blood money in my eyes."

There didn't seem to be anything to say to that comment, so Kala and Jay made their way out and down the hall, the receptionist hot on their heels with a tinfoil-wrapped paper plate full of brownies that she extended to Jay, who took it like it was dog poop on a silver platter. On top of the plate was a manila envelope with what they both assumed was Adam Star's written account of how he had killed his wife. Kala thanked her profusely as they scurried to the elevator and the nearest trash receptacle.

Outside, Kala looked upward, then bent to massage her knee. "Told you it was going to rain. Look at those clouds, black as the ace of spades. We should have placed a bet. So, what did you think?"

"Not much. Hughes looked like a straight shooter to me. If he says Adam lied, then I think he lied. I don't know the why of it, however. I'll let you know when I read that damn thing. Right now, I just want to get rid of these . . . these . . . this plate."

Kala laughed all the way back to the office. She was still laughing when they arrived, just before the heavens opened, and a good old-fashioned Georgia summer rainstorm commenced.

Chapter 5

KALA ADJUSTED HER SUNGLASSES, THEN REALIZED IT WAS THE sun umbrella on her terrace that needed adjusting. She loved the sun, the warmth it generated. She always felt like she could do anything, accomplish anything when the sun was out. Her Hawaiian heritage, she supposed. She craned her neck to look through the sliding doors to the giant hand-carved teak clock over her mantel, a gift from a grateful client years ago. A clock that had never lost a second of accuracy in all the time it had been hanging over her mantel. Twelve minutes past noon.

The ham-and-cheese sandwich on the plate that she'd fixed earlier didn't tempt her. She wasn't hungry, but no matter; if she suddenly got hungry, it was there for her. Maybe if Ben were there, she would have eaten it, but Ben said he was going nuts sitting around waiting for news. By news he meant Adam Star, and he also refused to refer to the waiting game as a death watch. Golf was his answer. Her answer was just to sit and wait. It was three weeks to the day that Adam Star had walked into her office and turned her world upside down.

So, there she was, alone, waiting for word. She eyed the pitcher of ice tea. The ice had almost completely melted. Well, what could you expect with the temperature in the low nineties?

Soft music wafted through the French doors, which she had left ajar. She did love the golden oldies, and so did Ben. Oftentimes they danced out here in the cool evenings after the sun went down. Ben was a romantic. So was she. At times. Soft music and balmy breezes always made her think of *back home.* Her game plan after the six-month vacation with Ben was to head that way and reclaim her roots. She wished now she had told Ben of her plans, but something inside her warned her that the timing wasn't quite right. She would, of course, extend the invitation for him to join her, but he had so many friends here, she seriously doubted he would give up his present life even for her. She *needed* to go home, that was the bottom line. Her family had made it possible for her to go to the mainland at an early age, to attend college, then law school. It was time to take her place in the family clan.

Perhaps out of guilt, perhaps not. She thought of it as guilt because while her family had been wealthy, the inheritance always went to the sons. The females were provided for, and her brothers had certainly seen to that by shipping her off to the mainland for an education. Back then, she'd thought of it as being banished from the clan, which was far from the truth.

The Aulani coffee plantation was the largest on the island and managed by her brothers and their children. It was beyond profitable. The brothers, forward thinkers, had dropped the old ways, the old customs, after a typhoon wiped out the plantation, but not before a fungus attacked the coffee-bean plants. The insurance they carried was a mere drop in the bucket for the amount of money they needed to go on. With nowhere to turn but to their sister, Kala handed over all her savings, then borrowed money to get the plantation up and running again. Today, the Aulani plantation was a major source of coffee in the US. She never regretted even for a moment the hardships she'd had to endure to make sure the plantation survived. For many, many years now, she received a full share of the profits because her brothers were fair. A house in Lahaina had been turned over to her, her grandmother's house, right on the ocean. Her brothers, their sons, the neighbors, and the workers from the plantation had refurbished the large five-bedroom house and added on to it after they bought up the two adjoining properties and made it into one. While it wasn't palatial, it was darn close to it. They said it was an act of love for her, and she believed them because, when it came right down to it, family was all that mattered in their world—her world as well. She loved going back home, loved waking up to the sound of the surf, seeing the palms swaying, hearing the rustle of the wind, staring for hours at her banyan tree, the biggest and the oldest on the island, and it was all hers. She loved the way the Hawaiian sun kissed her entire body and made her feel at peace. She hungered for that feeling.

If there was a way to get out of the six-month trip that she and Ben had planned for four years, she'd do it in a heartbeat. She knew she wouldn't really do it because she had promised Ben she would take the trip, and she never broke a promise. That wasn't exactly true, she fretted. She'd broken one promise, and that was the promise to Sophie Lee that she would successfully defend her so that she would be free. She never knew to this day if Sophie held that broken promise against her or not.

Kala didn't know how it happened or when it happened, but slowly, over the year she'd spent preparing Sophie's defense, the young woman had come to be like a daughter to her. She still, to this day, thought of her that way. Jay had told her once that Sophie, who was an orphan, said that knowing Kala was like having a mother. She'd cried when Jay told her that. She still teared up when she thought of Sophie locked up for the rest of her life.

Well, that wasn't going to happen. Soon, she'd be free. Free! God, how wonderful that was going to be for Sophie.

Kala looked down at the dried-out sandwich, at the pitcher of almost lukewarm ice tea. She sighed as she got up and carried it all into the kitchen. She might as well go to the office and pester Jay and Linda. She grimaced at the thought. Jay had threatened to kick her fanny out the door if she showed up again. Well, let him try.

Kala did a quick check of her makeup, her linen pantsuit that was so wrinkled it looked like she'd slept in it, her hair, and her sandals. She shrugged. Linen was supposed to look wrinkled. She headed out to her SUV, a Porsche Cayenne, and headed for the office. She only drove her little convertible when she wanted to show off. She much preferred the safety of the big SUV with all the crazy drivers on the road. Her cell phone rang just as she shifted gears to back out of her driveway. She had many rules when it came to driving. First and foremost, no drinking and driving. Nor would she use her cell phone or text while driving. Nothing was more important than keeping her eyes on the road, and the person could and would call back at some point. And last, never speed, always obey the law. Kala lived her life by rules, always had and always would. Besides, it was probably Ben just calling to check in. Something he did without fail when they were apart. She only wished she was half as diligent as he was.

The moment Kala opened the door to the office, she knew that *IT* had happened. That was probably what the phone call had been about when she was backing out of the driveway.

"What?" The single word exploded out of her mouth like a gunshot.

Linda took the lead, her expression one of excitement and misery all rolled into one. "Adam Star expired at precisely one thirty-six P.M. His remains are on the way to the crematorium where he will be . . . how do you say it, fried, burned, crisped up, roasted. Whatever, he is on the way. Jay has everything ready. You should go right now. Like now, Kala! Why are you still standing there? *Go!* Jay and I made all the calls.

The judge faxed the writ to the prison. The warden is waiting for you, and he promised not to bring Sophie out till you got there. For God's sake, go already!"

Jay reached for Kala's arm and literally dragged her out the door. "Before you can ask me, Kala, *yes, today is Tuesday*!"

Kala sagged against her old partner. She felt so light-headed she could barely stand. "It's finally going to happen. It is, right, Jay?"

"It damn well is, unless I have an accident on the way. The only thing I'm not sure about is if Star's death is going to leak out before we get to Sophie. Hospitals are their own gossip mills. I don't think Clayton Hughes will seek anyone out. He pretty much deferred to you, Kala. I'm not sure about the two male nurses. They don't have a clue what's been going on, at least I don't think so. They're hardened to death, but you never know. I'm driving. You just sit there, and let's go over everything one more time. Like she said, Linda and I made all of our calls, so everyone has a heads-up."

Kala's hands flapped in the air. "The private plane is gassed and sitting on the tarmac. We head straight for the airport the moment we walk out of the prison. Every detail has been taken care of. The pilot will fly Sophie straight to Hawaii, where my family will be waiting for her. They're going to take her to my house in Lahaina where, hopefully, she will agree to stay for at least six months. Time to start over with people who will care about her. My family will help her every step of the way. I have, in the back, suitcases full of things she will need until she feels confident enough to go out and about on her own. All the paperwork has been done, everything is in order. We spring her, we walk away, and that's it.

"Tomorrow morning, you will file the lawsuit against the state of Georgia and Ryan Spenser. Do not even give him a heads-up. Tomorrow you can call Clayton Hughes, and he can give a statement, but wait until late in the afternoon so it makes all the evening news shows. Do not take any calls from

Ryan Spenser. Also, tell the guard in the lobby not to let him up to our floor. I know you are getting all this because of that photographic memory of yours. I have Sophie's driver's license, which I renewed every year, her passport, which was renewed by me last year, plus an envelope full of cash until we can get her a bank account in Hawaii. I even jumped the gun and filed to have her nursing license renewed. Don't even ask me why I did all that. Maybe I had a premonition something like this was going to happen. She has a brokerage account of her own here in Georgia that we can have transferred. When we told her about the grandfather she'd never known, who only learned about her after she was in prison and left her his farm in Pennsylvania, Sophie okayed selling it, and I invested that money for her. She's not rich on her own, but we sold before the bottom fell out of the real-estate market. That four hundred thousand we got from the sale of the farm is now worth seven hundred thousand. That's Sophie's own money. The state will pony up big-time, so she will have that coming to her, too. Then, of course, there is the Star fortune. Who the hell knew storage lockers, zippers, and toothbrushes could generate the kind of money that is in that estate? I guess the elder Stars were visionaries of a sort. Can't you drive any faster, Jay? Oh, by this time tomorrow, Ben and I will be on our way to London. I do need to call him as soon as we get Sophie airborne."

"I could drive faster, but I'm not going to, so don't ask me again. I know this is a touchy subject, and I know neither one of us has mentioned it, but what do we do if Sophie doesn't want to go to Hawaii?"

Kala's lips tightened. "She's going. Sophie needs to get away from the publicity that is sure to come and get her life back. She'll see that and understand. I am prepared for a little argument, but when she realizes today is *Tuesday,* and when we tell her the story, she won't argue."

Jay's face turned stubborn. "But what if she does kick up a fuss?"

Kala's hands flapped in the air again. "Then I don't know, Jay. I guess we go to Plan B; but since we don't have a Plan B or a Plan C, we absolutely have to convince her to go with Plan A.

"I can't wait to see her. It's been seven and a half years since she cut off visitation. A day doesn't go by that I don't think about her and wonder how she's doing. The warden said she's a model prisoner, never gave them one ounce of trouble. But that's Sophie for you."

The rest of the ride to the state prison was made in silence. When they were two miles from the prison gates, Jay tossed Kala his cell phone and told her to text the warden that they were within shouting distance. "We want in, and we want out. I stressed that to him when I called earlier, but say it again."

Kala did as she was told. "The warden's return text read, 'Done. We are waiting at the door.' "

"Wow! Does that mean we don't even have to get out of the car?" Jay asked, his eyes wide.

"One of us does, to show the proper credentials. That would be me, Jay. When we return, I will sit in the back with Sophie, and you can chauffeur us to the airport. We need serious hugging time. Oh, my God! There it is!"

Inside the state prison, a tall, distinguished man with white hair and a white beard stood aside as one of the matrons brought Prisoner 9878245 to the door. He waited for the locks to open, and out walked Sophie Lee, who looked frightened to death to be where she was.

"It's okay, Miss Lee. You are being released, and you are free to leave. I wish you well."

"Free! I don't understand. What happened? What am I supposed to do, where should I go? No!" Sophie tried to pull back to return to the barred doors.

"Sophie!" Kala said, rushing forward and throwing her arms around the young woman. "Oh, Sophie, it is *sooo* good to see you!" She gathered Sophie in her arms and squeezed her so tight, Sophie could barely breathe, but she didn't tell Kala to stop.

"Am I going with you, Kala?" Sophie asked, when Kala finally released her.

"Damn straight you're going with me. You are done with this place, kiddo. Come along and don't look back. Do you hear me, don't look back! Jay is in the car."

"What happened? What about my things? They just brought me to the warden; no one said I was being released. I didn't say good-bye to anyone!"

"Is there anything you *really* want from here to take with you?"

"No, not really."

"Is there anyone you care enough about inside that you want to say good-bye to?"

"No, not really," Sophie said as she ran to Jay, who was standing by the door of his SUV. She allowed herself to be hugged, then reached up to wipe a tear trickling down Jay's cheek. "I'm really free! You got me out! I never thought it would happen. Never in a million years. Oh, you two are miracle workers! I hope you aren't upset with me, Kala, for stopping the visitation. I just couldn't keep on seeing you, then have to go back inside. I couldn't function after I would see you and Jay. It just seemed better that way."

"I understood, Sophie. Come on, get in the car. We have so much to tell you and don't have all that much time. You're going to Hawaii as soon as we drop you off at the airport."

"Hawaii! Why? Now? Why can't I stay with you till . . . till, you know, I get my bearings?"

"Yes, you're going to stay in my house in Hawaii. We need to get you as far from here as possible once the news gets out about your release and the circumstances surrounding it. My brothers are going to pick you up at the airport when you land. It's called R and R. You aren't going to give me a hard time about this, are you?"

"No, I guess not. I trust you and Jay. I guess you have your reasons. I've always dreamed of going to Hawaii. Do you think I can sleep out under the stars on the beach?"

Kala laughed. "Baby, I personally guarantee it."

"Now I am excited. Please, tell me everything."

They told her everything, ending with, "And today is *Tuesday*, Sophie!"

Chapter 6

Sophie Lee was in a daze as she stepped out of Jay's SUV. She looked to the right and saw Jay's wife, Linda, with her arms held out. She ran to her, tears trickling down her cheeks. "Jay said you two got married. I wish I could have been there," she said tearfully.

"I wish you could have been there, too. I brought my wedding album to show you," Linda said, pointing to the bag at her feet. "I'm going with you all the way to Hawaii. When Kala made the deal with the charter flight company, the pilot said he wanted three days in Hawaii before he made the return flight. Kala said okay. That means I have the same three days as he does before I have to head home. Jay and I were supposed to go to Hawaii for our honeymoon, but there was this case . . . so, we never made it."

"I'm glad for the company. I was sort of dreading it until Kala said you were going with me. I've never been outside the state of Georgia," Sophie confessed.

"Things are going to change very quickly now for you, Sophie. I want you to trust us. What we're doing for you is best."

Sophie smiled. "I trusted all of you with my life once before, so why wouldn't I trust you now? I think I'm going to be black and blue because all I've done is pinch myself since I walked out of those prison doors."

Her eyes misty with tears, Kala reached for Sophie to hug her one more time. "Time to go, kiddo. I'll see you when my trip is over. I wish I was going with you, but I made a commitment to Ben, and I have to honor it. It's best this way. When the news hits tomorrow, you, Linda, and I will all be gone. Jay can be totally invisible and completely incommunicado when he wants to be. When you get to Hawaii, I want you to keep a low profile. Linda will get you all set up, then my family will take over. Just promise me you'll do what they say."

"Of course. I don't know how to thank you, Kala, all of you. And you all worked for free all these years. Well, I can pay you back now. That's the first thing I'm going to do. Honor comes first. Most important, Kala, thank you for believing in me."

Kala didn't trust herself to speak. It looked to her like Jay was having the same problem. Another round of hugs, then Kala and Linda were tripping up the portable steps of the plane that would take Sophie to her new temporary home. Both attorneys waved so hard they thought their arms would fall off. They watched as the private jet taxied down the runway, then, like the sleek silver bird that it was, rose into the sky. When it was no more than a speck on the horizon, Kala linked her arm with Jay's. "We did good, Jay. She's going to be all right. I feel it here," Kala said, thumping her breast.

As they headed back to Jay's SUV, he said, "Call Ben now and get your plans under way for tomorrow. I don't want to see you again for six months. You hear me, Kala?"

"Of course I can hear you—the whole world can hear you. But it's six months minus three weeks," Kala shot back. "*Today is Tuesday!* It's a miracle, Jay, it really is!"

"I know. Don't go technical on me, now. Six months! I'm changing the locks on the office door, so if you come back before the six months are up, you can't get in."

Back on the road, Kala leaned back in her seat and closed her eyes. "What do you think will happen tomorrow, Jay?"

"Well, for starters, the media will have a field day. This news will be fodder for at least a week. The tabloids love this kind of stuff, so they'll put their bloodhounds on it and try to ferret out where everyone has gone. I think we did a good job of covering our butts with Sophie, but you never know. They'll be able to track you easily enough, and they will. Whatever port of call you end up in, someone will be there. Count on it."

"The Star fortune! Wall Street! That's going to be a zoo. You sure you can handle all of this? Linda won't be here for the first three days, and that is the crucial time. One other thing to bear in mind, Jay, is the five-hour time difference between here and Hawaii as well as the time difference wherever I'll be."

Jay was so outraged at Kala's words, Kala burst out laughing. "I'm not an idiot, Kala. I can handle it," he blustered. He felt sheepish because, as a matter of fact, he had forgotten the time difference. Not that he would ever admit having done so to Kala.

"Yeah, but can you handle Ryan Spenser?" Kala said as she hit the number two on her speed dial. Ben answered right away.

As Kala listened to Jay's mumbling that he could handle Spenser with both hands tied behind his back, she tried to talk over him to Ben. "Get the earliest flight you can get in the morning, and we're outta here. Uh-huh. Of course I'm serious, and no, six o'clock is not too early for me. Sophie is airborne, and Jay and I are on the way home. I never unpacked my bags, so just load them into the car. Why don't you cook dinner tonight; we'll eat out on the terrace, and we'll be having a guest. Jay doesn't know how to cook. Okay, I'll see you at my place around six."

They rode for a while in silence, each busy with his or her own thoughts. Back in town on their way to the office, Jay finally broke the silence. "Kala, *exactly* how do you want me to handle Ryan Spenser? By the way, you never said what he gave you for a going-away present. Someone said it was gorgeously wrapped."

Kala burst out laughing. "It was a picture of the both of us taken at some symposium where we were both guest speakers. I think the man has extra teeth in his mouth. Anyway, I threw it in the trash. I was going to keep the frame, but then I changed my mind. Handle him however you want, Jay, but don't let him walk roughshod over you. He'll try. He's going to go nuclear when he hears the news. I'm glad I won't be here to see it. I detest that man. I just wonder how many of the other people he prosecuted are innocent like Sophie. In short, he scares me, Jay. And don't for one minute underestimate him. He's a slimy devil."

"Thanks for the warning," Jay said as he waited for the gate at the underground parking garage to swing open. "You coming up?"

"No. I want some time for myself, and I have to stop at the store to buy dinner so Ben can cook it for us. I'll see you at home later. Don't be late. Ben likes to eat on time."

Outside the car, Jay walked Kala to her own vehicle and waited till she was inside and the motor was running. He gave off a sloppy salute and waited for her to drive down the ramp before he headed for the elevator to take him up to the office. He felt emotionally exhausted and physically drained, and he already missed his wife.

The single hostess aboard the private jet gently touched Sophie's shoulder. Sophie opened her eyes and stared up at the smiling woman. "The captain asks that you buckle up as we're preparing our descent to Kahului Airport." Expecting to see a smile from the nameless passenger, the hostess was stunned to see a panicked expression just as Linda came instantly awake.

"How much time before we land? What time is it?" Sophie

demanded. The hostess blinked at the panic that had invaded the young woman's voice.

Linda worked at her lips, which felt dry and cracked for some reason. She looked down at her watch. She'd forgotten to turn her watch backward to allow for the time change. Her mind raced. She knew exactly why Sophie was panicking. She mentally calculated the time change, the flight time. They were down to the wire. In thirty-seven minutes, it would be *Wednesday* morning.

The hostess smiled again. "We had excellent tailwinds. Actually, we're early. That's the good news."

"What's the bad news?" Linda barked. Out of the corner of her eye, she could see Sophie kneading her hands. "We need a definite time for wheels on the ground. If you don't know, ask the pilot. Tell him we have to be on the ground before midnight. I don't care what he has to do, but we have to be on the ground before midnight. Nothing else is acceptable. Go, now!"

Sophie's knuckles were white as she rubbed and twisted her hands. "You don't think I'm crazy, do you, Linda?"

"Not one little bit. This just might be one of those things that are beyond the pilot's control, Sophie. I'm so sorry, wheels on the ground before midnight was something none of us thought about. There shouldn't be much air traffic at this hour, so the pilot should get clearance to land with no problem. I don't know, Sophie, let's just hope for the best."

The hostess was back, the smile still on her face. Linda took the smile as a good sign. "Captain Ortega said we'll be wheels on the ground at eleven fifty-one. If not, you get your money back." At the stricken look on both women's faces, she quickly added, "That was a joke. If Captain Ortega said wheels on the ground at eleven fifty-one, then it's wheels on the ground at eleven fifty-one."

Linda reached for Sophie's hand and squeezed it. "We'll make it," she whispered.

Sophie nodded.

The private Learjet's wheels kissed the ground at exactly 11:50 local time. It took another three minutes to taxi to the slot assigned to private planes, another two minutes to come to a complete stop, then a minute for the hostess to open the hatch and drop the portable set of steps. The moment the hostess motioned for the two women to come forward and disembark, Sophie barreled up the aisle, was out the door and galloping down the steps to the tarmac, Linda right on her heels.

"What time is it, Linda?" Sophie shouted.

"Two minutes to midnight! We made it, Sophie! We made it!" She reached for Sophie's arms and hugged her as they danced around in a circle like two lunatics.

The pilot and hostess stood in the open doorway staring at their two passengers. "Hey, we just fly and deliver them. We got them here on time, so maybe we'll each get a bonus, and if that doesn't happen, we made two people really happy tonight. Wanna go for a drink somewhere? First, we have to lock this baby down, then we can take in some nightlife." But neither moved as they watched the two women make their way to where a crowd of locals waited for them behind the gates, leis in hand.

"You think those women are VIPs or something?" the hostess asked the captain.

"Or something. Not our business. All we need to think about for the next few days is warm sand, gentle breezes, and golden sun. We are in Hawaii! What's not to love?"

"You're right, it's none of our business," the hostess said, flashing a winning smile that Captain Ortega thought was beautiful.

Across the tarmac under the lights, the entire Aulani family waited for one of the maintenance crews to unlock the gate that would allow Sophie and Linda to walk through, where they were immediately showered with deliciously scented leis, one after the other. And then everyone started to jabber at once. A baby in a front papoose sling started to cry while other children held out additional leis that Sophie and Linda accepted with smiling faces.

An older man, deeply tanned, with snow white hair, came forward. He held out a beautiful white orchid lei. "It means welcome and the love of our family. I am Sam, Kala's oldest brother. She has entrusted you to my care. These people gathered here are our family. We came here to make you welcome. The hour is late; tomorrow, today actually, we will gather at the house and make a luau for you and your friend. Welcome to Hawaii, Miss Sophie, and welcome to you, too, Miss Linda. We have a car waiting to take you to the house. My grandson Kiki will drive you."

The baby started to cry again as the group urged Sophie and Linda forward.

The two-hour trip was made in silence for no good reason. Later, Linda said it was the jet lag that had tired them out even though they'd slept for most of the trip.

When the car came to a stop in the driveway of crushed shells, Sophie got out and looked up at the stars. "This is real, isn't it, Linda? I'm not dreaming, am I? Tell me I am not going to wake up back in prison. I want to hear the words, Linda, so please humor me, and say them, okay?"

"This is so real, it's scary. You are not dreaming. You are not going to wake up back in prison. This is the beginning of your new life, Sophie, so start enjoying it right now!"

"In that case, I'm walking down to that beach right now, and I'm going to sleep under the stars. Kala said I could do that. I'm going to keep all these sweet-smelling leis and use them as a pillow. Want to join me?"

"Try keeping me away. Just you try," Linda said, sprinting through the yard and down to the sandy beach, Sophie right behind her.

Linda stopped right at the water's edge. "Tell me something, *Tuesday's Child*—that's what Kala always called you, by the way. Tell me exactly what you feel right this moment in time."

"I feel like . . . I feel like I could fly if I flapped my arms. I feel safe, happy, and blessed that I'm here. I want to shout it to the world and to thank . . . everyone, even Adam Star."

"Then do it!" Linda challenged her.

Sophie screamed until she was hoarse, her screams muffled by the roar of the ocean. The only one who could hear her was Linda.

Chapter 7

Sophie Lee woke slowly. She was full of sand from head to toe, even had sand in her mouth. She tried to spit it out. Looking around, she was stunned to realize that everything had not been a bad dream after all. She really was in Hawaii, and she really had slept on the beach under the stars.

It was still dark out, with a few stars twinkling overhead, but the new day was going to chase the darkness away within minutes. She could see a faint glow of light on the horizon. A new day. Wednesday, to be precise. Wednesday was good; not as good as Tuesday, but still good. Sophie sat up and hugged her knees as she waited for the sun to creep over the horizon. Her first sunrise in Hawaii. How good was that? Pretty darn good, she thought. She stared, transfixed, at the huge orange ball and the dark, velvety shadows, which were fast disappearing.

The first day of her new life. And it was a new life. She needed to think about that. Really think about it. Yesterday was still a blur in her mind. Events had moved at the speed of light, with no time really to sort through it all. Adam Star was dead. Adam Star had gone to Kala and confessed that he had killed his wife. Even though Kala and her legal team had suspected that all along, they had been unable to prove it. Given their absolute certainty that Sophie hadn't killed Audrey Star, the only other person who could have done it was Audrey's husband. Adam Star had left her his fortune. The Star fortune, whatever that might be. She, personally, had over $700,000 in a brokerage account. That meant she could buy whatever she wanted. Within reason. She had an active driver's license, a current passport, and her nursing license was going to be given back to her. All thanks to Kala, Jay, and Linda. In a million years, she would never be able to thank the three of them for believing in her, standing by her, fighting for her. How could she ever repay them? Not that they wanted to be repaid. So many times during the trial they had all said they were doing the job they were trained to do. That turned her thoughts to Ryan Spenser, the man who had sent her to prison for life even though he did not have a shred of evidence that she, and not Adam, had killed Audrey Star.

During her ten years in prison she had tried not to think about Spenser, but she'd been unsuccessful. Plotting his death day after day was the only way she could fall asleep at night. She made promises to herself during those ten years that if she ever got out of prison, she would go after him and make him wish he were dead. In the darkness of her cell she tortured him, flayed his muscular body, tossed him to the coyotes in the desert, drowned him at sea. She particularly liked the scenario where she carved her initials over every inch of his body. The scenario where she managed to hog-tie him, then kicked and stomped him to within an inch of his life wasn't bad either. She grimaced at her ugly, evil thoughts.

Those thoughts had carried her to the faster-than-lightning extraction from the state of Georgia. What were the lawyers so concerned about? She didn't fully understand Linda's explanation of what they were anticipating happening once the news broke about Star's death, his confession, and her release from prison.

Sophie continued to hug her knees, her thoughts on her current situation. It must be noon by now back on the East Coast. Was news of her release public knowledge yet? Had

Adam Star's death made it to the obituary page? She wished she knew. But what she wanted to know more than anything was Ryan Spenser's reaction to the news of Adam Star's confession, his death, and his cremation. She wondered what Spenser looked like now, ten years later. Was he still so arrogant, so cocky, so mean-spirited? Leopards didn't change their spots, Kala had said.

Sophie had never hated anyone in her whole life, not even the bullies back in the orphanage. She understood they were just venting at their circumstances, trying to get through the days. They wanted to belong to someone just the way she did, but she had accepted early on that there was no one out there who would magically appear and whisk her away to a wonderful life. The nuns had explained that part of life to her and she had listened and accepted it. The bullies had not. She'd had friends back then, during those days, girls as well as boys. Life at St. Gabriel's had not been bad. She survived by being obedient. Sister Julie had said life was all about being a good person and going by the rules. You had to obey them. When you weren't obedient, that was when trouble happened.

Sophie had tried to be a good person and live her life by the rules, and for her effort, she'd gotten a sentence of life in prison. She was going to write a letter to Sister Julie and tell her about that. What would be her response? Probably something along the lines of: God never gives you more than you can handle. Well, right now that wasn't working for her. So what if she handled it. So what!

She shouldn't have had to handle it. She'd been a good person. But . . . she could hear sweet Sister Julie say, "Now, now, Sophie, take a look at where you are! Look at where God has placed you. He's given you your freedom and a fortune to go along with that freedom. He was testing you. You must forgive."

"Yeah, right. Forgive who? That skunk Adam Star? Ryan Spenser, who pinned the killing on me and sent me to prison?

The people who kept me locked up for ten long years? I'm supposed to forgive those people? Well, Sister Julie, that is not going to happen, and the word *forgiveness* is no longer in my vocabulary."

A wave washed up and over her legs. The water was deliciously warm.

Farther down the beach, Linda yelped and jerked upright, her expression so comical, Sophie burst out laughing. Good Lord, when was the last time she had laughed out loud? So long ago she couldn't remember.

"I think it's time to go inside, don't you? Since we're covered with sand, maybe we should dunk ourselves first, what do you think?" This was another first; she had an idea, and she voiced it. Almost as good as making a decision.

Linda tried to spit the sand out of her mouth. Her corkscrew curls stood out at crazy angles all over her head. "I cannot believe I actually slept on the beach under the stars. I can't wait to tell Jay; he's going to be so jealous."

Sophie was already on her feet. She reached for Linda's hand to pull her up. "The ocean is as warm as bathwater. Look how blue the water is, Linda. Isn't it beautiful?"

Together, they walked down to the water's edge, the water lapping around their ankles. "It was hard to tell last night, but this looks like a private beach. I guess it belongs to Kala. I read something on the plane yesterday that said the population here is only around nine thousand during the off-season and around forty thousand during the season, which I assume is the winter. Amazing. Can you swim, Sophie?"

"Yes, but not well. Patty and I took lessons at the YWCA. I'll just wade out and wash the sand off."

"That's another thing for you to do while you're here. Learn to swim like a pro, learn how to make those gorgeous leis, and learn the hula. Boy, you sure are going to be busy, and you know what, Sophie? You earned every minute of your time here. We really slept on the beach, and no one came near us. Un-be-liev-able!"

Ten minutes later both women walked back toward the sprawling house set amid lush foliage. "I can't wait to see the inside. I guess that young boy took our bags inside. Kala said there is a housekeeper, a cousin, I think she said. She's going to be cooking and cleaning for you, and I'm not sure about this, but probably waiting on you hand and foot."

"I don't want anyone waiting on me hand and foot, Linda. I'm not feeble. I want to do all that myself. Well, okay, I don't want to do the cleaning, but I know how to do it. We had chores at the orphanage."

"Well, rules are rules. These are Kala's rules. I don't think it would behoove either of us to break those rules."

"I know a thing or two about rules, and you're right," Sophie said as she stepped onto the lanai. She gasped. She'd never seen such a wild profusion of colorful flowers in her life. At first she thought they were growing wild, but then realized all the plants were perfectly manicured. There were orchids, beautiful, gorgeous orchids of all sizes, plumeria, white and pink, that smelled heavenly, hibiscus so brilliant in color they almost burned Sophie's eyeballs. In the middle of the lanai, a table was set for breakfast, with pristine white dishes. The chairs were teak and their cushions covered in brilliant colors to match the rainbow of flowers. A glider that swung back and forth was nestled next to a small fountain, whose trickling water was guaranteed to induce sleep. Sophie thought it one of the prettiest sights she'd ever seen. She said so. "They must have a wonderful gardener. When I had kitchen duty in prison, I tried to grow basil and parsley, but the plants died on me."

"I'm going to take pictures and send them to Jay. I want him to eat his heart out. In a nice way of course." Linda giggled. "Are you going to fight me for that glider?"

"Yes. I think I'll sleep out here tonight. How wonderful it will be to be surrounded by flowers and the stars overhead as I fall off to sleep. I almost can't wait."

"Well, in that case, I guess I'll have to opt for a nice soft bed with gentle breezes wafting through the open windows. I'm sure the scent of the flowers will drift upward. I am so hungry, are you?"

"I could eat something, but I'm not starving if that's what you mean. I think I'm too excited to eat. Can that magic phone you have check on what's going on back in Georgia?"

"It can, and I will do that as soon as we take a shower and have some breakfast. Come along, Sophie. I think it's time we met your housekeeper."

Her name was Mally, and it was hard to tell her age. She could have been forty or she could have been sixty, not that it mattered. She was small-boned like Kala, and it was easy to see the family resemblance. She'd coiled her thick, silky hair in a braid around her head like a crown. Her eyes were bright and inquisitive. Her smile was shy and welcoming as she hugged Sophie, then Linda. She stepped back and picked up the two leis that were on the kitchen counter. She draped them around the women's necks, first Sophie's, then Linda's. "You wear all the time. Make you smile. You go now and take shower. I cook for you when you come downstairs."

"I could get real used to this in a hurry," Linda said, as they made their way through the house. It was breathtakingly gorgeous, and everywhere they looked, they could see Kala's fine touches. Everything gleamed and sparkled, and the heady scent of the plumeria was everywhere.

"I like it that everything is so open, all those French doors and the sheer curtains billowing about, the paddle fans stirring the scented air, all this beautiful teakwood, the floors, the furniture. . . . It's like something out of a movie. I am so jealous of you, Sophie, that you are going to be living here while I'm back in good old Dunwoody, Georgia." It was all said in fun, and Sophie knew it. She laughed as they mounted the stairs to the second floor.

"Look at this balcony; you can see the entire downstairs from here," Sophie said in awe. "Why is Kala living stateside when she could be here?"

"She's needed stateside for people like you. People here don't *need* her the way she's needed back home. That's the best answer I can give you, Sophie."

"I understand. Now which room is mine and which one is yours?"

"I guess whichever one has our stuff. I'm thinking someone probably unpacked our things, and we're good to go. Yep, this one is mine," Linda said as she opened a bedroom door. "Oh, my God! Is this beautiful or what? Look at that pineapple bed! You need steps to get in it. I've only ever seen pictures of rooms like this."

Linda was talking to dead air; Sophie was down the hall opening the door to her room. She stood in the doorway and simply stared as she tried to drink in the room that was to be hers for as long as she stayed there. It was beyond anything she could ever have imagined. There was no ceiling, just the roofline of teakwood. A long pole from the peak held a paddle fan that whirred soundlessly. Everywhere she looked, there were vases of fresh-cut flowers, the scent intoxicating. She could see her reflection in the shiny floors. Sheer organza rippled from the open French doors outside her own private balcony, with two chairs like the ones on the lanai. Her bed was the same as Linda's except for the coverlet, which was pale yellow with appliqués of tiny green leaves. She had the same set of three steps to get into it.

Sophie made a promise to herself to jump on the bed later. She looked in the closet to see a wide array of clothes, evidently the things Kala had bought for her that were in the huge suitcase that had been carried onto the plane. Sundresses, slacks, blouses, shorts, and dressy dresses. All cotton, linen, or silk. In the whole of her life, she had never had anything as fine as what she was seeing.

In a far corner tucked into a small alcove was a desk of sorts, which held a computer, a phone, and, mounted above it, a television set. All the comforts anyone could ever want.

Sophie made her way into the bathroom and stopped short.

She reached for the doorframe to steady herself. It wasn't just a bathroom. It was a grotto, with brick walls that held moss and water trickling down. Within it was a huge Jacuzzi with twelve jets. All tiled to match the grotto walls and floor. The shower was clear glass and spouted twenty-seven jets. Sophie counted them. The vanity was white and gold, with three sinks. In the middle were bottles and jars and jugs and pots of lotions, shampoos, and perfumes. The towels on the racks were thick and thirsty and bigger than twin sheets. They were mint green with the initials KA on them. She laughed when she saw the bidet. Oh, if the prisoners back in Georgia could only see this. She was glad they couldn't. What they didn't see couldn't make them hunger for it.

Sophie stripped down and piled her wet clothes in one of the three sinks because she didn't know what else to do with them. She turned on the twenty-seven jets in the shower and danced under all of the gushing water. She soaped up and rinsed three times, each time using a different bath gel. She also washed her hair three times, using different shampoos and conditioners. When she saw that her skin was starting to pucker, she got out of the shower and wrapped herself in one of the green towels.

Sophie took her time poking through the clothing in the walk-in closet. She finally chose a yellow sundress splashed with white daisies and spaghetti straps. On the floor she found a pair of thong sandals with matching daisies on the bands. She brushed out her hair and hoped that at some point she could get a fashionable haircut in town. She wondered if she smelled as good as she felt.

Sophie looked at the little clock on the night table: 7:45. Lunch hour back in Georgia. She shrugged; there was nothing she could do about the time. And right now it was time to eat because her stomach was growling. She walked down the hall and saw Linda sitting on the pineapple bed.

"I want to live here." Linda laughed.

"With or without Jay?" Sophie said.

"Only with Jay." Linda jumped off the bed and linked her arm with Sophie's. Together, they made their way downstairs and back out to the lanai, where Mally served them macadamia-banana pancakes with banana syrup, fresh mangoes, and crispy fried bacon strips. Fresh flowers and a silver urn of Aulani coffee sat in the middle of the table. Mally served them gracefully. Both women ate like it was their last meal.

Mally cleared the table, leaving them with their coffee. She returned a few minutes later with the dinner menu, which read simply, "LUAU." Linda squealed with pleasure, and Sophie drooled.

"Find out what is going on back in Georgia. I can't wait any longer, Linda."

"You're the boss. This, by the way, is something called a Droid. You can do everything but wash your car and paint your house on this gizmo. Be patient now, and before you know it, I'll have everything at my fingertips."

"Why don't you just call the office and *ask* what's going on?" Sophie said. "You can put it on speakerphone, and I can hear both ends of the conversation. It will save you from repeating everything to me."

"I guess that makes sense. Okay, here we go."

Chapter 8

Sophie leaned back on the glider, her feet swinging slightly to make it move back and forth as she listened to Linda talk to her husband. A smile tugged at the corners of her lips as she listened to what she called *kitchey koo* talk between husband and wife before they got down to serious business. Her mind wandered a little as she considered how she was going to spend the day. The beach, of course, a swim in the sapphire water, another walk down the shore, possibly a nap here on the lanai. Or perhaps no nap. She got down to the business of mapping out her life and what she was going to be doing once Linda left and she was on her own.

She thought then about her old friends from the orphanage and wondered what they were doing. She wished now that she hadn't cut them off when she went to prison the way she'd cut off Kala, Jay, and Linda. How wonderful it would be to call them up and say hello. Dominic Mancuso, otherwise known as Nick; Patricia Molnar, Patty to her friends; and Jonathan Dempsey, also called Jon. Best friends. Today the term was *best buds.* That was the four of them back at St. Gabriel's. Ten years was a long time to lose track of three of the people you loved most in life.

They had been there for her during the trial, steadfast, testifying on her behalf. Even Sisters Julie and Helen had testified for her. Not that it did any good. And she had kicked them out of her life. She told herself she was doing them a favor because they didn't need a jailbird for a friend. They had lives, good lives, and she didn't want to burden them with her miserable existence. Their memories would have to suffice.

What would they think when the news came out about her release and that she was out of prison? They would have no way to find her. If she wanted to reconnect with her old friends, it would be up to her to initiate contact. Did she have the guts to do that? At the moment, she just didn't know.

There had never been the slightest doubt in her mind that Nick would be successful. And she had been right. The number two golfer in the country. She hadn't been at all surprised to hear that. Patty, too. Jon, now that was a different story. Jon was the weak one of the four, the gentlest, the kindest, and not the least bit motivated. Jon was frail, too, something about his immune system. She hoped he was all right.

Sophie wondered where her *things* were. No one had said, and she hadn't asked once she was convicted. Who packed up the little efficiency apartment she had shared with Patty? Did they toss her belongings, or did they store them? She wondered if Linda knew. There wasn't anything she really cared about except her books, her address book, and some costume jewelry she'd saved up to buy. A strand of pretty pearls and a gold bracelet. A gold chain with a locket that Nick had given her the first year they were all out on their own. Surely whoever packed up her things wouldn't have thrown those away. When it came right down to it, she didn't care about the forty-dollar string of pearls or the sixty-dollar bracelet, but she did care about the locket Nick had given her. She cared about it because of the minuscule picture of the four of them that Sister Helen had taken for just that purpose.

Sophie almost laughed out loud when she noticed Linda wiggling her fingers in her direction. Obviously, the kitchey koo part of the conversation was over, and they were finally down to business. She shook her head that she understood and leaned forward to hear better. Jay was talking.

"I really have no news other than that Kala called for a status report. She said they were on their way to see Big Ben. One of the investigators called in and said that at six-oh-five last night, Adam Star, as we knew him, had been cremated and his ashes were placed in a burnished bronze urn. The nameplate on the urn reads ADAM WILLIAM CLEMENTS. Not Star. And the director of the crematorium told the investigator that Adam's wife's nameplate had been changed a month ago. Her urn now reads AUDREY STAR CLEMENTS. Both urns are in a crypt of sorts since there was no one to claim them. Bought and paid for by Adam.

"I filed the suit Kala drew up against the state of Georgia before five o'clock yesterday. Today, there were four calls I didn't take from the state's attorneys. Guess they want to try for some kind of settlement for Sophie's wrongful imprisonment. I'm going to let them sweat so the media can have their field day. I can tell you what their offer will be first crack out of the barrel—ten years salary and a little extra thrown in for taking ten years of her life. Kala said to start at two point five million a year and come down to only two million for every year of prison. She said twenty million dollars was fair."

Sophie fell back against the cushions on the glider. *Twenty million dollars!* That had to be just about all the money in the world. "Is it tax free?" she managed to squeak.

Linda started to laugh and couldn't stop. She had no idea if the settlement was tax free or not. She asked Jay.

"Yep!"

Sophie grew so light-headed she had to drop her head between her knees. She made a mental note to add to her to-do list: how to spend $20 million. How many pieces of paper would she need for *that*?

Sophie didn't realize Linda had ended the call until she sat down next to her on the glider. She hugged Sophie so tight she grunted.

"Is that possible? That they would pay me that much money?"

"Kala seems to think so. She convinced Jay, and he just convinced me. The firm will take a third of that. You do realize that, right, Sophie?"

"Of course. Is that enough?"

"It's enough, trust me. Do you want to make a little bet here as to how soon you get the money?"

"Don't these things take *years*?"

"Not when you have someone like Jay being a PITA. I'd say three weeks, tops."

Sophie frowned. "What's a PITA?"

Linda laughed. "A pain in the ass."

"Oh. Then I guess that's a KISS."

"Yeah, keep it simple, stupid. Now you're getting it. Okay, listen. I need you to sign this bank card. I'm going to town. Kiki is picking me up. I'm going to get the lay of the land of this town and open your account at the Hawaiian Bank branch where one of Kala's cousins works. She did it all—I just have to show up. This way when you need money, you can hit an ATM or go through the drive-through. Kala really means it when she says you need to keep a low profile and not be out and about for a while. Spenser and his camp are going to try to locate you. We do not want that. You okay with all of this? It pretty much means you are confined to this house, the beach, and surroundings."

"I'm fine with it, Linda. I have no desire to go anywhere right now. I'll follow all instructions to the letter. I don't want you to worry about me."

"Then I won't worry, but Jay will. We have Plan B in effect, and what that is this. If one of the cousins comes for you and tells you it's time to relocate, you go. That means Spenser or someone in his camp or maybe the tabloids has put two and two together and figured out Kala sent you here, then went off somewhere so they couldn't bug her. I'm no seer, but I think you're only good here for about a week once the news gets out. Spenser is looking at his career going up in smoke, so he's going to leave no stone unturned. You okay with that, too?"

"I am. I'm going to take a walk on the beach and get some sun and maybe take a swim."

"Before you go, Sophie, you asked about something earlier that leads me to believe that you were so excited when Kala and Jay explained everything to you that you did not take in something very important."

"What did I ask about, Linda? Did I do something wrong?"

"No, honey, nothing is wrong. What you asked about was whether the twenty million was tax free. Which told me that since you saw that question as significant, you did not understand just how wealthy you are. Or will be once Adam Star's estate is settled."

"Linda, I remember their telling me that I had inherited some money from Mr. Star. But—"

"Sophie, you did not just inherit 'some money.' You inherited an estate worth hundreds of millions of dollars. When that estate is settled, you will be one of the richest women in America. And the difference between a tax-free twenty million and a taxable twenty million is, in your circumstances, almost negligible. Chump change."

Sophie sat there, stunned. Seemingly incapable of speech, she got up and started into the house, shaking her head as if to clear it of cobwebs.

"Use sunblock, this sun is wicked," Linda called after her.

"Yes, Mother." Recovering from her daze, Sophie laughed as she headed into the house to change into a bathing suit. "See you when I see you," she called airily.

Friday's weather was a repeat of Wednesday's and Thursday's. In other words a perfect day, in Sophie's opinion.

It was the end of the workday in Georgia and lunchtime for Sophie and Linda. And when lunch was over, Linda would head to the airport for the long flight back to Georgia and her husband.

Both women had just been served what looked like a wonderful shrimp scampi and a mango-pineapple-banana salad when Linda's cell rang. Both their eyes popped wide, knowing it had to be Jay on the other end of the line. In other words, news. The succulent-looking lunch was forgotten.

Sophie mouthed the word *speakerphone.* Linda obliged.

Jay Brighton's words were crystal clear. "Here we go, ladies . . . and let me be the first to say I have never felt this popular in my entire life. Everyone in this state wants a part of me. The media is giving this a full-court press. Sophie, you are big news. It's all they are talking about. The warden at the women's prison gave a brief interview, said how Sophie was a model prisoner. Said how the paperwork was in order. Said how Adam Star called the shots and wouldn't accept anything except the deal his lawyer brokered, which translates to no one could do anything or say anything until he was dead. Told about the meetings he had with Adam's lawyer, Clayton Hughes.

"Adam's video has been on the news every hour on the hour. The judge who signed off on Sophie's release has so far refused to be interviewed.

"Ryan Spenser has called here every ten minutes. Mavis is threatening to quit if we don't get someone to help her field the calls. We have to keep the office doors locked, and I canceled all appointments till Monday. Reporters are camped outside. I might have to sleep here.

"In addition to all of that, the state's attorneys called again this morning. I chopped them off at the knees and told them straight out what our deal was. Told them not to bother me again unless we had an agreement.

"They are now showing the urns at the mortuary. Guess the

director thought it might be good for business. The media is giving them so much press, so why not."

"That's it! That's all you have?" Linda shrieked.

"What? That's not enough! What more do you want?" Jay started to grumble and mutter under his breath about not being able to satisfy women.

"Oh, honey, you *more* than satisfy me. We just want to know more about Spenser and what his mood is, you know, so we can bask in his misery."

"Well, he ain't happy, that's for sure. He's pissed to the teeth that he didn't know a thing and heard it when the rest of the world heard it. That's what he said when he left a message on our voice mail. So far he has not given an interview, and the media are saying he's involved in something and can't do interviews right now. The translation to that is, he's in deep shit with a twenty-million-dollar-payout that is going to haunt his ass for many days and months to come. This is when it's going to get interesting, so stay tuned."

When the conversation turned personal, Sophie moved away to sift through what she had just heard. She rolled her eyes and shrugged her shoulders at Linda's gleeful look.

"At last we got one up on that SOB," Linda said when the call ended. "I'm glad he's scrambling; he deserves to grovel. And truth be told, I'd pay through the nose to see Ryan Spenser grovel. You know that old saying, *what goes around comes around?* His business just came around. Jay said, depending on how he feels, he might pick a reporter and give a sort of/kind of/make of it what you will interview. Meaning, of course, your old friend who works for the *Atlanta Journal-Constitution.* He said he's going to throw something out there that will make Spenser pee green. Don't even ask because he wouldn't tell me. He'll call if he does it.

"As much as I hate to eat and run, that's what I have to do, Sophie. Everything is all set for you. Remember to keep your stuff ready and handy, so if they come for you, you can leave in a heartbeat. It's wheels up at three for me, so I have just enough time to eat and get to the airport. I really hate to leave, but I'm needed back at the office," Linda said as she shoveled the delectable scampi into her mouth.

Sophie picked at her food; it was delicious, but her thoughts weren't on food, Ryan Spenser, or things back in Georgia. Her mind was preoccupied with her old friends. She finally asked Linda to find out where her personal things were, and if she found them, to send them on to her by overnight mail. Linda promised.

Twenty minutes later, Sophie was waving good-bye to Linda from the driveway. Tears were rolling down her cheeks.

She was alone again. "Do not feel sorry for yourself," she muttered over and over as she made her way into the house and up the stairs to her room, where she changed into her bathing suit, which Mally had washed and dried. She pulled on a yellow wrap, made her way back outside, and ran down to the beach. She waded into the water and swam until she got tired. She didn't see a soul anywhere nearby the entire time.

Back in her room, Sophie shed her wet clothes, took a shower, dressed again, then turned on the television. She blinked, then blinked again as she adjusted the volume on the set. Jay Brighton was talking outside the office to a gaggle of reporters.

"I'm only going to make one comment, so listen up and don't pester me afterward, because this is all you're going to get. My client, Sophie Lee, has authorized this firm to hire four additional associates to go back through all the court trials that Ryan Spenser has prosecuted from the day of her conviction. In addition to those four associates, she has authorized the firm to hire an additional four associates to go back and review all of Ryan Spenser's cases for ten years prior to her conviction.

"As you all know, those cases are a matter of public record.

We have also been authorized to hire as many private investigators as we need to do whatever needs to be done. In short, our client feels money is no object when it comes to vindication. That's all, ladies and gentlemen. I meant it—no more questions, no more comments," Jay said as he made his way to the parking garage and his car. The gaggle trailed behind him, shooting out questions he refused to answer. Jay Brighton was a man of his word. He did, however, wink at Patty Molnar.

Chapter 9

THE REASON FOR THE SEVEN FORTY-FIVE EARLY-MORNING MEETing of attorneys was the media. The powers that be in the state of Georgia were patiently waiting for their star, Ryan Spenser, to make his appearance. Coffee had already been poured, sweet rolls depleted from the silver tray in the middle of the conference table.

The men and two women looked at one another. One of the men, a white-haired older gentleman who could have passed for Santa, spoke. "We did tell him eight o'clock so that we could talk. He is not late. So far I haven't heard a word from anyone at this table."

They all started to talk at once, the voice of one of the women a shade more shrill than the others. The gist of the comments was that they didn't have $20 million in their coffers to hand over to Sophie Lee, courtesy of the Aulani, Brighton, Brighton, and Darrow law firm.

"Furthermore, if what the media said last night about the firm's hiring all those extra attorneys to go after Spenser's old cases is correct, we're looking at megamillion-dollar payouts down the road. Everyone Spenser ever prosecuted will head to their neighborhood lawyer to file suits. They'll win, too. The public doesn't like to hear that innocent people were sent to prison. The trust will be gone. Every Tom, Dick, and

Harry in the state of Georgia will go after us even if it's for jaywalking," the guy with the white hair and beard sputtered.

The woman with the shrill voice chirped up. "You're all convicting Ryan before you know if he's guilty or not. He goes with the facts he has, the proof, when he goes to court. You're all ready to do the very thing you're accusing him of doing. Stop being so disgusting."

A slick-looking young guy with a tint to his styled locks smirked, and said, "And you came to this conclusion because of . . . pillow talk. Everyone knows about your affair with Ryan Spenser, so maybe you need to cool your jets here and let more impartial minds prevail."

The stunning blonde turned crimson as she started to sputter and mutter. "I had dinner with the man, that was it."

"Not according to Spenser's next-door neighbor, who, by the way, hates Spenser's guts," the slick, good-looking young guy said.

"Enough!" the Santa figure shouted just as the door to the elegant conference room opened, and Ryan Spenser stepped in. He did not look like a man going to meet his executioner. Everyone at the table, especially the stunning blonde, recognized his cockiness, his arrogance, and saw no trace of a defeated attitude. And all were well aware of Spenser's political ambitions and the powerful people he and his daddy knew.

No one offered to pour Spenser coffee, so he served it himself with a steady hand. He took a long sip before he spoke. "I resent this meeting. This whole circus is ludicrous, but as you all know, with the media, it has to run its course."

"It will grow legs, Spenser," a man in a subdued charcoal gray suit said ominously. "If you think this is going to go away anytime soon, think again. So don't try blowing smoke in our direction."

A short distinguished man, the lead attorney for the state in matters of this kind, leaned forward. His bright blue eyes were icy when he shoved the morning edition of the *Atlanta Journal-Constitution* toward Spenser. "Take a look at this, Spenser! A good look!"

Ryan Spenser looked down to see a huge picture of Sophie Lee, in color, above the fold. His stomach knotted up. "It's Sophie Lee," was all he said.

The same short man said, "You're damn right it's Sophie Lee. She's everyone's daughter, sister, cousin, the girl next door. She's wholesome. She's a goddamn nurse who put herself through nursing school working two jobs so she could take care of sick people. She's apple pie and ice cream. And let's not forget she's an *orphan!*

"You sent an orphan to prison for life for a crime she did not commit. It's a damn miracle that that orphan, that girl next door, is now out of prison. You took away her youth, her hopes, her dreams. The media are going to play that up for all it's worth. Imagine the anguish she's been through for ten long years! Just try to imagine it because the people in this state have already imagined it, and they have weighed in, and they want blood. *Yours!*"

Spenser felt the knot in his stomach move up to his chest. This was not supposed to be happening. On the way over he had rehearsed his speech, which, unfortunately, was now no longer in his memory bank. All he could say was, "I went to court with facts, with only what I could prove at the time. Are you all forgetting that a jury of that woman's peers found her guilty?"

The Santa figure spoke. "That jury is being interviewed by the press today, every last one of them. By next week, they'll all have contracts to write books. I heard on the car radio on the way here this morning that a publisher in New York said he'd pay ten million dollars to Sophie Lee to write a book. The only problem is, the publisher can't find Sophie Lee to make the offer. It appears she's gone to ground somewhere. Probably to plot your demise, and this state's as well. In case you aren't getting the picture here, Spenser, this state is going to go bankrupt. Goddamn it, Spenser, say something."

"What do you want me to say? I said I prosecuted Sophie Lee to the best of my ability. I went where the proof and facts led me. I find it appalling that you and the media are blaming me. All I did was present the case; the jury is who you should be going after, not me. I can assure you that my other cases are bulletproof. But to be sure and to leave no stone unturned, I am going to put together a team of investigators to go over everything with a microscope. What else do you want me to say?"

The short man snorted. "Twenty years of cases, ten before Lee and ten after, and you sit here and tell me all of them are bulletproof. Aulani, Brighton, Brighton, and Darrow are on this like fleas on a dog. You better start praying, Spenser. All it's going to take is one irregularity. Another thing. From where I'm standing, it looks to me like you can kiss your political aspirations good-bye. No one is going to vote for someone like you, a prosecutor who sent that poor innocent girl to prison for life."

Ryan Spenser felt sick to his stomach. Everything he'd heard in this room only spelled doom and gloom. If they were right, he might end up being a Walmart greeter before this was all over.

Since arrogance was Spenser's middle name, he calmly finished his coffee, stood up, and said, "I have an office to run and things to do. If you like, I can give you a report daily, biweekly, or weekly on my progress. I want to assure you that I am on top of this."

The room was silent. It remained silent until the door closed behind Ryan Spenser.

And then all hell broke loose. The contingent of state functionaries banged their fists on the shiny conference table so hard, the coffee urn toppled over, spilling coffee all over the folders and pads lined up like soldiers, at which point the blame game began in earnest. Name-calling followed. Only the cocky young man remained silent, taking it all in.

The Santa figure, the designated chairman for the meeting, whistled so shrilly the room went silent. "Enough already. We are going to appoint our own task force and go in behind those schmucks from the Aulani firm to make sure we're on top of this. In the meantime, someone go to that firm and try to talk sense into those people. Flat out tell them we don't have twenty million to dish out to that young woman. Explain what's going to happen when they open that Pandora's box of old cases."

The stunning blonde eyed the Santa. She squared her shoulders and asked what they were going to do to Ryan Spenser.

"Nail his ass to the wall," the blonde's female counterpart called over her shoulder as she exited into the hallway.

"And you think he won't retaliate? As you pointed out earlier, remember who his daddy is and remember all those important people he dines with, plays golf with, and vacations with. Chew on that, gentlemen," the stunning blonde with the shrill voice said. She said *gentlemen* because there were only four men left in the room. "And before any of you can get up the guts to ask me, no, I don't kiss and tell."

"Son of a bitch!" the tall, distinguished man swore. "Talk about being between a rock and a hard place. There's no way out of this; we're going to have to pay up. The media will hound us, and this is never going to go away."

The Santa figured rubbed at his chin. "Maybe if we could locate Sophie Lee, we could cut a deal with her."

The other three men snorted at once. "Are you out of your mind? You couldn't go near that young woman even if she were standing outside this door. She lawyered up. You can only deal with her attorneys," the lead attorney for the state shot back.

"I have a meeting with the attorney general this morning

about this mess, so I have to leave now. I'll copy all of you on the results. In the meantime, no interviews, and someone, for God's sake, find that young woman. I don't care what it takes."

The three remaining men watched the lead attorney walk out of the room, their eyes full of misery, except for the slick young guy, who started to laugh. "This is exactly what I love about politics: you never know what's going to go down. It's the challenge, gentlemen, the chase, the adrenaline rush. Well, good luck," he said, waving airily as he left.

"Who the hell hired that guy, and who is he?" the Santa asked the only remaining person in the room.

The two men looked at one another.

"I never saw him before."

"I thought he came with you."

"I think he said he was with . . . crap, I can't remember."

The stunning blonde's counterpart walked back into the room, accompanied by the lead attorney. "He's with the Aulani law firm, gentlemen," she said. "He just walked in here and took a seat, and no one questioned him. Out in the hall, I just asked him who he was since this was a closed meeting. He was laughing his head off when he handed me his business card." The woman tossed the card on the table as the lead attorney took his seat again. "That, gentlemen, is what you are up against. And may the best man win."

The men looked down at the pristine white card with the engraved name on it like it was a coiled rattlesnake. Three heads craned to read the name.

"Jonas Emanuel Darrow."

"Nah, he can't be . . ."

"Clarence Darrow's great-grandson? Why the hell can't he be his grandson?" the Santa shot back.

"Google the bastard," the lead attorney for the state said.

"I thought you had a meeting with the attorney general."

"I do, but I want to know if this guy is who he says he is, so I can report it. Will you just do what I tell you?

Ten minutes later, after the report on Mr. Darrow came back, the lead attorney said, "Yep, the son of a bitch is who he says he is. I take that to mean we're screwed blue."

No one said a word as they packed up their briefcases. "Well, I was right about one thing. This case has already grown a leg. Wait ten minutes, and six more will sprout," the man in the charcoal gray suit said.

Chapter 10

Ryan Spenser's staff of three women and three men were on tenterhooks as they waited for their boss to return from his early command-performance meeting. All of them looked wary and uneasy as they tried to imagine what had taken place and what their roles would be when their boss returned to the office. The woman who was senior to the others whispered, "We'll know by the expression on his face when he walks through the door. Let's go over the checklist one more time."

"Coffee's fresh, pastries are under the dome so they don't dry out."

"E-mails are taken care of."

"The Lee transcript has been opened, and everything is on Mr. Spenser's desk. Even Kala Aulani's appeals. Files are stacked next to the desk."

"The plants have been watered."

"All his appointments were canceled for the day."

The senior member of the staff nodded as she brushed at an imaginary speck of lint from her jacket sleeve. "Then we just wait."

"Maybe we should go back to our respective offices so he doesn't think—"

"Good idea," the senior member said as she walked away in

relief. The others scattered like mice who had just smelled a cat coming in their direction.

The clock in the foyer read 8:50 when Ryan Spenser stormed through the door. He took a moment to glare at the receptionist, then slammed through the double doors that led to a hallway and his office at the end of it. "Everyone! My office!" he roared like a lion as he rushed to his suite.

When they heard the roar, the staff scurried again like the mice they were. They stood at attention, waiting for the shouts, the demands, the threats that Ryan Spenser was famous for.

"Coffee?"

"Here, sir," a mousy looking young man who had graduated summa cum laude from Yale University said, his hands shaking as he set a cup of coffee on his boss's desk. He almost fainted with relief when he realized he hadn't spilled a drop.

The mousy young man stepped back into the precise line, his hands folded in front of him like the others, as if they were soldiers at a drill parade waiting for orders. No one blinked, no one twitched, and no one coughed.

Spenser looked down at his desk. His three daily newspapers were neatly lined up. The *Atlanta Journal-Constitution*, the *Wall Street Journal*, and the *New York Times*. He almost spewed the coffee he had in his mouth when he stared down at the color photo of Sophie Lee. His insides started to churn at how innocent she looked, how normal. They were right—she was the girl next door. A crazy thought invaded his mind. How could she be the girl next door when she was an orphan? *Orphan* was the magic word.

Spenser fixed his gaze on his senior staff member. "I want a full background on Sophie Lee from the moment she came out of some woman's womb. I want twelve of the best investigators we have going at this full bore. Yes, I know a lot of that is in the transcript and in our files, but we are going to start from scratch as if this were day one in preparing for trial. Forget what's in those files," he said, pointing to the boxes neatly lined up at the side of his desk. "We need information yesterday. We work around the clock until we get this resolved. Screw up, and you're on the unemployment line. From this moment on, your lives are mine. If I sink, you all go with me. No interviews. Is that understood?" Six heads bobbed as one. "Now listen up, and listen good."

They listened, making mental notes as to their various assignments, then nodded again, until their boss was satisfied that they understood what their jobs were to be.

"Here's a tip. Shake the tabloid trees. Those sleazy reporters know ways to get information we can only dream about utilizing. Promise them whatever the hell you have to promise. Pay them, do whatever it takes. In the end, they'll probably get the information we need before our investigators can. And you also need to know this. At the meeting this morning there was a stranger there. His name was Jonas Emanuel Darrow. He's the great-grandson of Clarence Darrow. He works for the Aulani firm, and he just marched into that private meeting like he belonged and sat his ass down and listened to everything that was said. He was a goddamn spy, and no one knew it. I didn't know it either until one of the conferees called me on my cell after I left the meeting. The son of a bitch now has the inside track. We're all going to look like fools on the next newscast. Did you all hear what I said? He just marched in there like he belonged, and no one knew who the hell he was. We all look like idiots. You're all still standing here. What part of what I just said didn't you understand?"

The mad rush for the doorway would have been comical any other time. Not so that day.

Spenser drained his coffee and fervently wished he'd dosed it with something a little stronger. He buzzed his secretary and held up his cup for her. Just now, that very second, Ryan Spenser couldn't help wishing that he were dead.

When his secretary returned, Spenser could not avoid

frowning at the few drops of coffee that had spilled over into the saucer. Looking up, he asked, "Where are the messages, the e-mails? How many calls did we get from the media?"

"It's all there on your desk, sir. Your father has called five times this morning and said to tell you he wants you to call him the moment you get into the office. I explained about the early-morning meeting. He said he didn't care about early-morning meetings and to remind you he is your father, and if you don't call him, he's coming here. That was verbatim, sir. Do you want me to ring him for you?"

"No! Absolutely not! I'll deal with my father. Do not let anyone near this office."

"Of course, sir." The secretary backed out of the room and quietly closed the door behind her. She felt so dizzy that she had to sit down. Every light on the telephone console was a glowing red button. She hated that console.

She also hated the pompous ass sitting behind the closed door. It was like this anytime he heard from his father, another real piece of work, whatever his position. I should have quit years ago, she thought. But at sixty years of age, who would hire me?

She had two more years until that glorious day; then she could thumb her nose at this place. On the other hand, given what was going on these days, she might not get the chance to thumb her nose at the jackass she worked for. She crossed her fingers that Ryan Spenser would go down for the count on the very same day she was scheduled to retire. She shot a hate-filled glance at the closed door as she jabbed at one of the glowing red buttons.

Inside the suite of offices where everyone feared to tread, Ryan Spenser sat in his custom-made chair and rubbed his temples. He had a killer headache, one that six Advil had not alleviated. He also felt sick to his stomach. Just the thought of calling his domineering father made him want to puke. He took great gulps of air, hoping to relax himself. Someone had told him once it was a marvelous way to shift into the neutral zone when under pressure. Obviously, that person had lied, because it wasn't working.

Spenser looked around at his office, his home away from home. He loved it there. He *belonged* there. At least until he moved into the governor's mansion, where he would truly belong. The suite had been decorated by some long-ago paramour whose name he no longer remembered. Cherrywood, one-of-a-kind window treatments, splendid comfortable furniture you could get lost in. Ankle-deep carpeting, the best that money could buy, luscious green plants. His own private lavatory complete with shower. He even had a closet, where he kept several changes of clothes. Built-ins galore and a private bar that didn't emerge from its hidden recess until he pressed a button. Another button revealed a concealed safe deep enough to hold his life's most memorable moments. And enough cash to see him through any kind of trouble that found its way to his doorstep. All paid for from his robust trust fund, at no expense to the taxpayers.

These two rooms were his lair, his sanctuary. Today, though, they felt more like a prison, however luxurious. He removed his designer jacket and tossed it across the room, where it landed on one of the deep, comfortable chairs. He jerked at his tie. It landed on top of the jacket. He rolled up the sleeves of his pristine white shirt. He didn't feel one bit better, and his head continued to thump and pound inside his skull. He continued to massage his temples as he tried to contemplate his next move. A skilled politician, he knew this was do-or-die stuff, and he had to come off just right. If his father was running true to form, he probably already had Spenser's speech drafted for him.

Spenser wanted to cry as he looked back at the turns in the road he'd taken. What if he had missed, say, just one of those turns, and today he was a plumber or a mailman? Would he be happy? Hell no! He didn't know the first thing about plumbing other than you turned on water and turned it off. A mailman was out of the question. They kept getting bitten by dogs and delivered mail bombs and anthrax to unsuspecting recipients. Who the hell wanted to be a mailman? No, he was right where he was supposed to be at that point in his life.

Spenser picked up the paper and stared at the picture of a smiling Sophie Lee. God, how he hated that young woman. And for sitting her ass in prison, she was going to get $20 million from the state of Georgia. That was practically a given. She was also, or at least would be shortly, one of the richest people in the country thanks to Adam Star's having left her the Star fortune. That kind of money could and would bury him. Where the hell had Kala Aulani sent her? For all he knew, she could be with Sophie right that minute, but Kala was too smart for that. She'd spirited her away, far away, that was for sure.

It all came back to the tabloids' investigative reporters. The first picture of Sophie Lee, wherever she was, would pay enough money to put three kids through college. He reminded himself that he hated Kala Aulani.

Maybe Kala sent her to Mumbai. That sure as hell was far enough away. Or the Hindu Kush. Even farther. Or was it? He'd have to look that up. Kala was crafty, though; she could have stashed Sophie Lee someplace in Georgia, right under their noses.

Spenser's mind traveled back in time to the day Sophie Lee's verdict was read and the courtroom was empty except for him and Kala. He'd asked her what the girl had whispered to her, and she said . . . she said . . . Kala had said, "She told me to put a hex on you." Had she?

He thought about karma then. What goes around comes around threefold, or was it tenfold? He couldn't remember. Well, that was why they had Google, wasn't it? He'd dated some woman who was into the stars and all that psychobabble, and she was big on karma.

Spenser's arm snaked out. He buzzed his secretary. "Did the Aulani firm send over Adam Star's video?" he barked.

"No, sir, they did not."

"Well, call them and tell them if I don't have it in an hour, I'm going to file a motion with the court saying they are withholding evidence. Never mind, just call Jay Brighton for me."

"I can do that, sir, but the last time I called, the person answering the phone said their office is not taking any calls from you. Do you want me to try again?"

"Son of a bitch! Who the hell do they think they are?" he roared into the intercom.

"They say they are the Aulani, Brighton, Brighton, and Darrow law firm when they answer the phone," the secretary responded smartly. Spenser missed the sarcasm. He broke the connection and decided to e-mail Jay Brighton.

Hawaii? Maybe Kala sent the girl to Hawaii. No, that was too obvious. Or was it? He thought about that old saying, "Keep your friends close, your enemies closer." Kala had a huge family still in Hawaii. He'd read an article about her right after she announced her retirement, and she had talked about the Aulanis' coffee business, the huge family, and how she couldn't wait to go back to her roots. That huge family would take care of Sophie Lee. Probably guard her with their lives. Strangers poking around would get nowhere with a family like that. Then he thought about another old saying, "Money talks and bullshit walks." Yeah, yeah, Kala probably sent her to Hawaii. Well, he'd just throw that out to the media and let them take it from there. He made a mental wager with himself that Kala Aulani would cut her six-month vacation short and suddenly return to Hawaii if he did that. Oh, yeah.

Spenser pulled out his cell phone, took a deep breath, and hit number four on his speed dial—his father's number. Much as he hated to do it, he really had to return his father's call.

Chapter 11

It was hard to tell who was more nervous, Ryan Spenser or his staff. They watched him roll his shoulders, shoot his cuffs, and square his shoulders again before he took one last look at the short speech he was about to give at his first press conference since Sophie Lee had been released from prison. He was clearly very nervous, but his arrogance was still there, written all over him.

Half the members of his staff hoped he would pull it off because they knew he meant it when he said they could all find themselves on the unemployment line. The other half, the half who hated his guts, hoped he would fall flat on his face.

None of the staff had seen his prepared remarks, which he'd memorized earlier, but two of them had seen it roll out of the fax machine, which meant his daddy, who was the Speaker of the House in Washington, DC, or someone on the staff of his uncle the governor, had actually written the speech. The only thing those who had seen it communicated to the others was that it was short, just two paragraphs.

"Time to go, sir," one of the staff members said as she looked down at the incoming text on her cell phone. "The reporters are waiting."

"They can wait. Who's front and center?"

The same staff member, anticipating the question, had already asked the question to the person who had sent her the original text. She looked down at the incoming text. She cringed. "Patty Molnar, the *Atlantic Journal-Constitution*'s star reporter." Or, as they called the paper around the courthouse, the *AJC*.

Ryan Spenser felt a slight tremor in his knees. He tried to ignore it as he stood as tall as he could. He hated Patty Molnar almost as much as he hated Sophie Lee because of the position he was in. He didn't just hate the reporter, he *really hated* her. The reason he hated her was because Patty Molnar was Sophie Lee's best friend, along with that star golfer, Dominic Mancuso. Every goddamn day of Sophie Lee's trial, Molnar had attacked him in the *AJC*. Mancuso, Atlanta's golfing star, had added his comments to Molnar's vitriolic writings, and the news carried them twenty-four/seven. Until . . . his father stepped in and had a Come to Jesus meeting with the powers that be at the *AJC*. Successfully muzzled, Molnar, according to his sources, had a vendetta against him, and there she was with the opportunity to claim her fifteen minutes in the spotlight. After that day's press conference and interview session with the members of the jury that had convicted Sophie Lee, she'd be the most-sought-after reporter in the country, probably more famous than Woodward and Bernstein. God help him.

"I don't need a goddamn parade, people. I can do this on my own." Spenser glared at his staff as he headed out of his office to beard, in this case, the lioness by the name of Patty Molnar. He had one bad moment as he stared at himself in the shiny brass of the elevator. He'd forgotten to floss that morning. "Shit!" he muttered.

He strode from the elevator like a man with a purpose—and he indeed had a purpose, a very important one—to save his own skin and his reputation, not to mention his political aspirations.

He made his way to a room at the far end of the hall that

had been set up for the press conference, and, afterward, the interviews with the members of the jury in Sophie Lee's trial. Interviews by the same group of reporters to whom he would be addressing his remarks, led by Patty Molnar. He did not envy any of those jurors. Not one little bit.

Spenser eyed the podium at the front of the room and walked toward it with long strides. He knew all eyes were on him, and he was glad that he was wearing his Hugo Boss suit and the pricey new linen shirt he'd purchased just for this occasion. The power tie he'd chosen was just the right touch. He looked out at the small sea of reporters and locked eyes with Patty Molnar. In his life he had never seen a more evil, vindictive smile. His stomach muscles tightened into one gigantic knot.

"Good afternoon, ladies and gentlemen. I have a prepared statement, which I will read. I will not be taking any questions afterward as I have a meeting scheduled directly after this press conference. So, let me get started.

"No one is more saddened than I am that Sophie Lee was imprisoned for a crime she apparently did not commit. When the case was brought to trial, I argued it on the basis of the evidence that was presented to me. I gave the case one hundred and ten percent. I left no stone unturned. I presented my case, and the jury of Miss Lee's peers found her guilty. A judge sentenced her to life in prison. I sincerely regret that Miss Lee spent ten years in prison for a crime she didn't commit. I cannot turn the clock back, and if I could, I would still present the same case I presented ten years ago. The only positive aspect of all of this is that Adam Star made things right at the end before his death, and Miss Lee was released to go on with her life.

"I would like to say at this time that I am not at all certain in my own mind that Adam Star's deathbed confession is truthful. My staff and I are working on that as we speak. As we have updates, you will all be notified via a press release. Now, if you'll excuse me, I have an office to run and an old case to look into."

Spenser didn't want to look at Patty Molnar, had no intention of looking at Patty Molnar, but he couldn't help himself. He saw the same evil, vindictive smile he'd seen when he walked into the room. The knot in his stomach tightened till he thought he wouldn't be able to take another breath. When he reached the hallway, he walked faster than he had ever walked in his entire life to the men's room, and, once inside, he leaned against the door and took great gulping breaths of air. And then he started to shake and couldn't stop. He ran to one of the stalls and closed the door until he could get himself under control.

Spenser took deep breaths, pep-talked himself, then slapped at his own face to try to calm down. He couldn't stay there. He needed to get back to his office, so he could watch the reporters grill Sophie Lee's jury.

On the way back to his office, he couldn't erase Patty Molnar's smile from his mind. She was out to get him. Maybe no one else had seen it, but he'd seen her flip him the bird ever so subtly.

Inside his headquarters, Spenser ripped at his Hugo Boss jacket and the power tie as he stomped his way into his office and slammed the door. He knew, without even asking, that his staff thought he had come off in the interview as a real shithead. He knew because there had been no one in the outer offices, and he *felt* like a shithead. He should have written his own goddamn speech. And he never should have said that Star's deathbed confession was suspect. Or that it merely appeared that Sophie Lee had not committed the crime for which she had spent ten years in jail. Never never never!

Spenser clicked on the television set. He pressed a button on the console and demanded coffee he didn't want. It appeared within seconds. Cup poised, he watched the screen as the jurors, all but juror number seven, who had died three years into Sophie Lee's incarceration, filed into the room. There were also five alternate jurors who followed the other eleven jurors and took their seats on one of the long sides of a large conference table.

It was a full-court press, with all the wires and cables and cameras. The press—print as well as cable and the major news channels—were seated in four rows of seats that had been set up earlier. Patty Molnar had the best seat in the house, front row center. She was seated directly in front of the jurors.

Spenser's eyes caught movement in the rear of the room. He felt his heart take on an extra beat when he realized who he was seeing in the back of the room. The golf pro Dominic Mancuso. Another best friend of Sophie Lee and Patty Molnar. Where was the other best friend, Jonathan something or other? Dempsey, that was his name. And then another person entered the room and took a seat next to Mancuso. Jonas Emanuel Darrow! Spenser knew without a shadow of a doubt that he was carrying sixteen subpoenas somewhere on his person. The minute this slaughter was over, Jed, as Darrow was called by his peers, would swoop in and serve all those lovely blue subpoenas. Spenser continued to watch, a sick expression on his face as Jed shook hands with Mancuso. Allies? But of course. And after the subpoenas were served, Patty Molnar, Dominic Mancuso, and Jed would all belly up to the bar and hoist a drink to his fall from grace.

Ryan Spenser wanted to cry.

Spenser's mood lightened just a little as he listened to the softball questions being asked of the jurors. None of the media or the reporters got up, instead shouting out their questions from their seats. The answers were terse, yeses and nos, with no elaboration. Clearly, the eleven jurors did not like being in the limelight like this. All of them looked wary and uncomfortable.

And then it was Patty Molnar's turn. She got up, microphone in hand, and approached the table. Under her arm she had a stack of files. From a paper in her hand she went down the list, saying each and every juror's name. Even the alternates. Each juror nodded as his or her name was mentioned.

"I have here a profile of each of you. I know everything about each of you from the day you were born. The *Atlanta Journal-Constitution* will be publishing these profiles in tomorrow's paper. I'm going to ask you some questions now, and I want to warn you ahead of time that most reporters don't ask questions they don't already know the answers to. We're kind of like lawyers in that respect. Well, some of us, anyway."

Spenser glared at the television set. The jurors looked uneasy, he could see that. After all, he'd had a full month of staring at them ten years ago as he tried to figure out how they were going to vote. Especially the foreman. He'd aged, that was for sure.

"First question. Is it true that you all rushed your verdict because juror number four's wife was going into labor, and he wanted to get to the hospital even though five other jurors were voting for acquittal?"

Juror number four bristled, his face turning as red as a candy apple. "That's not true!"

"Actually, it is true. I have here in your file the time you left the courthouse after the jury rendered their verdict and the time your six-pound-three-ounce baby boy was born. Whose name, by the way, is Daniel Robert Rumsen Junior. The time difference between the reading of the verdict and the birth of your son is exactly ninety-four minutes. I don't think you're going to get a book deal, juror number four."

"It was all his idea," juror number three, a sixty-year-old woman with white hair, said, pointing to the foreman. "There were four other holdouts, and I was one of them. He hammered at us and hammered at us. He kept saying that the facts were as plain as the noses on our faces even if we couldn't see them. He called the five of us stupid. He said we were uneducated." Three other jurors nodded in agreement. "Oh, and one other thing—he said the prosecutor had an almost perfect record on convictions and wouldn't have brought the case to trial if he didn't think he could win it."

Juror number eight, a young woman around thirty-five or so, raised her hand. "The foreman told us that you can't trust a foreigner, meaning Miss Aulani. Like Hawaii is foreign." She sniffed. "Of course, ten years ago we didn't have a president who was born in Hawaii. He browbeat us and kept calling us stupid, especially the women. He reminded us every day that because he was a school principal, he was smarter than all of us put together."

"Guess none of you are going to get that extra fifteen minutes of fame," the reporter from the *Atlanta Journal-Constitution* observed, "and no book deals, either. *None of you are credible.* You getting what I'm saying?"

No one said a word.

"So then, Mr. Foreman, what do you have to say to these comments?" Patty asked, shoving the microphone as close to his face as she could.

"I am not going to lower myself by responding. We voted our consciences. We did exactly what the judge told us to do. And just for the record, I am not looking for a book deal. And before you can ask how I now sleep at night, my answer is the same: I did my duty and went with the facts. And I sleep very well, thank you very much, Miss Big Shot Reporter. Molar, is it?

"I am sorry that young woman had to spend ten years in jail. I truly am sorry. I am sure that we all are, but none of us can unring that particular bell."

Patty Molnar smiled, knowing that what she was going to say was utter nonsense, but she said it anyway. "Well, there is sorry, and then there is sorry. How sorry will you be when that young woman, whose name, in case you have forgotten, is Sophie Lee, files a lawsuit against all of you? You do know she has already filed a suit against the state of Georgia for twenty million. It's my understanding another suit is going to be filed against Ryan Spenser. Lawyers are expensive in this state. Some of them actually charge four hundred dollars an hour." Patty thought she heard several gasps of shock as she wondered again if what she had just said was true or not, not that she cared even one little bit at that point.

Juror number ten, a middle-aged housewife, started to cry. "Well, I for one can't sleep, and I don't mind telling you that either. I regret my vote. I regretted it the moment I voted. I even had to go to a therapist to try to get past that. It still haunts me. I want to cry for Miss Lee and what we did to her. And the worst part was she was an orphan with no family to help see her through that awful ordeal. I hope she gets the twenty million dollars, and that's not nearly enough to make up for ten years behind bars. Speaking strictly for myself, I wouldn't take a book deal if they paid me my weight in gold."

Nine of the jurors and the alternates nodded. Not so the foreman and juror number four.

Chairs were pushed back as the jurors signaled that, as far as they were concerned, the interview was over. Patty turned and nodded to Nick Mancuso to stand by the door until Jed could serve his subpoenas. She wanted to laugh at the startled expressions on the faces of the foreman and juror number four when Jed read off their names and handed them the subpoenas.

"Lawyer up, ladies and gentlemen," Patty shouted as a cameraman for CNN shoved a microphone in her face. She swatted it away.

As Patty headed to the back of the room, she heard the television reporter from CNN say, "That was Patty Molnar from *AJC,* who just tried to knock the mike out of my hand. She has a big dog in this fight since she's a personal friend of Sophie Lee."

Nick Mancuso was grinning from ear to ear. "Duffy's Pub, and I'm buying."

"What about your golf tournament?" Patty asked as she linked her arm with that of her best friend. "I wish Jon was here to see this," she whispered.

"Yeah, me, too, but I think he's watching us from above. By the way, I had to book a later flight to Hawaii."

Jed clapped Nick on the back, then hugged Patty. After all, she was his significant other.

Upstairs, in his plush office, Ryan Spenser turned off the television set. Just as he did, his cell phone started to ring. He had no doubt whatsoever that it was his father, so he didn't even bother to take the phone out of his pocket. For all he cared, his old man could call from then till the cows came home or hell froze over, and he still wouldn't answer it.

Chapter 12

PATTY MOLNAR WAS BREATHLESS FOR SOME REASON AS SHE TOOK her seat in a booth in back of the pub. Her adrenaline was at an all-time high. Home run for Sophie. She inched closer to Jed, liking the feel of him next to her. She watched as Nick yanked at his tie and shrugged out of his lightweight summer jacket. Jed did the same thing. Even though it was cool in the pub, they'd sweated a gallon of perspiration on their walk from the courthouse.

Duffy's Pub was just like any other pub, now minus the stale odor of cigarette smoke. It was all mahogany and brass, comfortable wide booths, and superefficient waiters and waitresses. The food was excellent because all Duffy's served were half-pound Kobe beef burgers on homemade, from-scratch buns and onion rings made on the premises with their own batter. From opening to closing, the beer flowed freely from a large keg that was the centerpiece of the pub. Every seat at the bar was full, even at that time of day, because lawyers and reporters weren't held to hard-and-fast schedules. Duffy's was the epitome of the perfect watering hole. A place to meet and greet. A place to snag a pickup. A place to bitch and moan and plot someone's downfall, usually some ornery judge, after a harrowing day in court.

The little group made small talk when the waiter took their

orders, which really wasn't necessary, more a formality because everyone got the same thing, a burger to die for, out-of-this-world onion rings, and beer so cold it froze your nostrils when you brought the glass to your lips.

The moment the waitress was out of sight, the threesome started to jabber at once. The gist of the yammering was, How do you think it went?

Jed looked thoughtful. "I'm not sure I can call it. Those women were pretty damn feisty. They let themselves be bamboozled by that *educated* foreman. Ten years ago, they could live with it, but now, ten years later, with all that's happened, they're no longer comfortable. They're either going to go to ground, give out no interviews at all, or their consciences are going to make them feel so guilty that they want vengeance. And who better to throw to the wolves than the foreman and juror number four. Toss in Ryan Spenser, and you have a very explosive mixture. I'm going with the latter, but that's just my opinion." He turned to Patty, and said, "You were great, honey."

Patty beamed.

"Do you two have any idea how sappy you look?" Nick growled, as their cold beer arrived. They picked up their glasses. Nick made the toast. "To Sophie Lee!"

"You still have a thing for Sophie, huh?" Jed said quietly. He wasn't being snide or brash, and Nick responded in kind, his eyes on Patty.

"Always did, but she could never get past that big-brother thing. I got past it. I was hoping, and we were actually making progress, when the dark stuff hit the fan. Where is she, Jed?"

Jed sighed as he flopped back against the booth. "You know I can't tell you that. I would if I could. Don't badger me, please."

"Yeah, Nick, don't badger him. If he tells anyone, it will be me, right, sweetie?"

"Wrong!" Jed held up his glass for a refill. He had it in seconds.

"I thought it went well back there," Nick said.

"It did. It went so well, Spenser is in hiding. No one is going to see him for a while, trust me on that. He really stuck his foot in it when he said he wasn't sure if Star's deathbed confession was legit."

Patty's cell phone chirped just as their food arrived. She pulled it out of her pocket and looked at the incoming text, her jaw dropping. Her face turned as white as the blouse she was wearing. Tears puddled in her eyes. "I don't believe this," she whispered.

Nick immediately leaned over as Jed crowded next to Patty to read the text.

"This is from my boss. He just . . . he just fired me. For unprofessional behavior."

Nick and Jed both exploded with the two most famous words in the English language at the same time. "Oh, shit!"

"*Oh, shit* is right," Patty said, chomping down on her burger, tears dripping down her cheeks. Patty Molnar never had a problem with her appetite when she was upset.

"Let's consider this a blessing in disguise. I'll call a press conference as soon as I get back to the office. The fix is in, and we can play this for all it's worth. The daddy, Mr. Speaker, or the uncle governator must have gotten to the paper. Maybe both. Your boss is an idiot. This is not going to play well for Daddy's little boy. Don't cry, honey, you can come work for us. Same salary as you were getting at the paper. Sophie will be delighted you are on our payroll. You're an investigative reporter; only difference is, you'll be investigating for us. Win-win!" Jed said, holding up his glass. "Three refills!"

"That's so sweet of you," Patty hiccuped. "You always come to my rescue, but are you sure Jay and Linda will be okay with your hiring me?"

"As you know, they officially made me a partner when this whole thing started. The actual vote was yesterday even though all the letterheads, business cards, and the like were changed the day after Star died. It was Kala's idea, just before she retired, and Jay and Linda agreed. So, yes, I can offer you a job. Kala even had my name put on the door a couple of months ago. Everyone in town knows it, I just haven't talked about it. Didn't want to jinx anything."

Nick sighed. "Well, that's a relief. I won't be going off to Hawaii with that worry on my mind. Can't throw my game off like that.

"I'd sue those bastards, Patty. Can you do that, Jed?"

"Damn straight we can do that, and I'll take it on myself. I'll make you rich, honey, then we can retire in style. The firm gets a third, just so you know that right up front." Jed chuckled at his own wit.

"I never liked my boss. He doesn't like women reporters." Patty snuggled next to her savior and smiled at Nick.

"Hey, big guy, how long you gonna be in Hawaii?" Jed asked.

"Five days. Maybe six. One day traveling, two for the tournament. It's one of those two-day match-play deals—one day to take in the islands, as I've never been there, and one day traveling back home. I picked up a new endorsement last week, so I have to be back to shoot the first commercial."

"I think we should order another beer and toast Nick as the next Tiger Woods," Jed said playfully as he hugged Patty closer. "Or maybe not, considering the way the former number one has been playing the past two years."

As happy as he was for his best friend, Patty, Nick still felt jealous that she had the love of her life—and she certainly deserved it—while he had no romantic attachments. The prospects of finding his one true love seemed pretty remote at the moment. "Listen, Jed, will you tell Sophie—wherever she is, and I know you know where she is—to get in touch with me and Patty the first chance she gets? Don't tell her about Jon, though. I think Patty and I should do that. We were such a team back then," he said with a catch in his voice. Patty blinked, but she didn't say anything. She bit down on her lower lip so she wouldn't cry at the mention of their old friend Jon.

"I think we should go now. I want to stop by the *AJC* to pick up my belongings and flip my boss the bird while I'm doing it."

"We'll go with you," Jed said as he reached for the check.

"Yeah, we'll all flip him the bird," Nick said, struggling into his jacket. "If the time is right, and I get a chance, I'll tell him that I'm going to tell my sponsors not to advertise in his paper. Like Kala and Jay always say, money talks and bullshit walks."

"You'd do that for me, honest, Nick?" Patty said, throwing her arms around him.

"Why wouldn't I do that? You're my best friend, the sister I never had. Of course I'd do it for you." And he meant every word of what he'd just said.

The threesome left Duffy's and headed back toward the courthouse and the parking garage, where they picked up their respective cars and headed toward the offices of the *Atlanta Journal-Constitution.*

Patty was the lead car in the parade. Traffic was heavy, so she had time to think and rehearse what she was going to say to J. T. Fry, her boss. But she knew in the end she probably wouldn't say half the things she was rehearsing because she was a serene kind of gal. She liked her job, really liked it, and she was good at it. What she didn't like was her boss and his cavalier attitude where women were concerned. All it had taken was one confrontation with him in which she had threatened a lawsuit for discrimination. From that moment on, she knew she was on J.T.'s kick list. Everyone else at the paper knew it, too.

Twenty minutes later, Patty pulled into the parking garage and parked in the spot she'd earned month after month as reporter of the month. She waited for Nick and Jed to find parking spots. The three of them took the elevator to her floor, where she proceeded to clean out her cubicle. Her colleagues waved halfheartedly. Obviously, the news had already spread. One of her fellow reporters jerked his head toward the kitchen, which meant J. T. was getting coffee or having lunch. Patty nodded as she loaded Nick and Jed with her personal belongings, which weren't all that much. She motioned for them to follow her to the kitchen.

The newsroom went silent, the reporters' fingers poised over their keyboards, but no keys were struck. If possible, they wanted to hear what was going down in the kitchen.

"Yo, J. T. Just picked up my things and wanted to say good-bye. And to tell you how much I really hate your guts. And to tell you what I think of your journalistic politics. Any newspaperman who lets someone dictate to him about free press stinks in my opinion. I also want to tell you if you need to get in touch with me, you can reach me at the Aulani law firm. Ooops, it's now called Aulani, Brighton, Brighton, and Darrow. I accepted a position there thirty minutes ago.

"Where are my manners? This is Dominic Mancuso and Jonas Emanuel Darrow. Jonas is my new boss. Boys, this is my old boss, J. T. Fry, a man who can be bought."

Nick stepped forward, shifted the load in his arms, and said, "I'm notifying all my sponsors that if they advertise with this paper, I'll cancel my contracts with them."

Jed stepped next to Nick, and said, "And I'm the guy who is going to file a discrimination suit against you personally and this paper as soon as I get back to the office."

"See ya around, fatso," Patty said, referring to J. T.'s exceptional girth.

Back in the newsroom on their way out, Patty's colleagues high-fived her, grinning from ear to ear. She grinned back. Damn, she felt good. So good, in fact, she wanted to go somewhere to celebrate. Well, first things first; maybe later.

Back in the parking garage, Patty's belongings were dumped in the trunk of her car. Then it was time to say good-bye to Nick. God, how she hated good-byes. She hugged her best friend, told him to fly with the angels the way Sister Julie had always sent them off. "Be sure to bring me a present when you come back and not a shitty souvenir you found at some beach market. I want a quality present." Tears trickled down her cheek for the second time that day. Nick's hug was fierce. She backed away as Jed stepped forward and gave his friend a manly hug. Nick clapped him on the back.

"Ya know, you really should stay a little longer than what you planned. You know, enjoy yourself a little. Live it up. I know you're going to win that tournament, so you should celebrate." Jed winked, hoping Nick would pick up on what he was trying to tell him.

"Can't. I have that commercial to shoot."

Jed snorted. "I can get you a postponement on that with no sweat." He winked again. Nick's eyes almost popped out of his head.

"Yeah, yeah, I just . . . yeah, sounds good. See if you can get me a week, and I'll be ready to shoot when I get back. You guys take care now, you hear?"

Patty and Jed stood with their arms around each other as Nick peeled away.

"Sophie's in Hawaii, isn't she?"

"Now, what makes you say that?" Jed said, heading for his car.

"Because I'm an investigative reporter, and I saw that wink you think I didn't see. So there!"

Jed laughed as he settled himself into his snappy money green Porsche Boxter.

"Damn," was all Patty could think of to say as she climbed behind the wheel.

Chapter 13

NICK MANCUSO WALKED OFF THE GOLF COURSE AND HEADED TO the clubhouse. He knew from past tournaments it was going to take him a full hour, possibly two, before he could take a shower and change his clothes. He'd played the match and won, and now he had another game to play, the social game that helped get him to where he was.

Dripping with sweat, he swiped at his forehead with the sleeve of his endorsed shirt, jammed his endorsed ball cap back on his head, and smiled, his eyes searching for the good-looking young guy whose last name was Aulani. But he couldn't see him among the throngs of well-wishers who were waiting to shake his hand and congratulate him.

It had been hot out there on the course even with the ocean breezes. A kind of heat he wasn't used to. His hip was aching, too, so that hadn't helped. Bone on bone was what the orthopedic doctor had said. Thirty-four and in need of a hip transplant. Ridiculous! But it wasn't ridiculous; he'd consulted three top-notch orthopedic surgeons, viewed his X-rays. He hungered for some Advil and the hot tub at his hotel the way a man who was stranded in the desert hungered for a drink. Soon.

Nick wanted to check to see if he had any texts from the mainland, but he couldn't do that either, not till he had some privacy. Now, though, he had to prepare for the photo op, accept his trophy, and bank the very large check that would be handed to him.

Nick sucked in his breath as he stared out the wraparound windows of the elite clubhouse. He loved Hawaii, what he'd seen of it so far. He gazed at the lush green lawn, the swaying palms, the verdant vegetation, and the colorful flowers that Hawaii was known for. He sniffed the half dozen or so leis that had been draped around his neck the moment he'd beaten his final opponent, three and two. He wasn't sure, but he rather thought that a person could get drunk on the scent if they inhaled it long enough.

Nick gulped at a glass of ginger ale and finished it in two swallows. He reached for a second glass and finished it, too. He eyed the tempting buffet and decided to pass on food. He could always eat later.

Exactly three hours and twenty-three minutes later, Nick let himself into his hotel suite. He literally ran to the bedroom for his cell phone. Six text messages, five from Patty. One from a friend back home congratulating him. He read them hungrily even though there was nothing there to tell him where Sophie Lee was, if she was indeed on the island. He read them twice so he could think about them when he hit the shower and the hot tub.

Nick almost passed out with the relief he felt when he lowered himself into the swirling hot water. Someone, the maid he assumed, had placed several leis in the hot tub, and the scent was so pleasing Nick closed his eyes and gave himself up to the moment and let his mind drift. He thought about Patty, Sophie, and Jon, and how close the four of them had been, how much they'd shared, all their hopes and dreams for the future. Jon was gone now, succumbing to some virus that attacked his delicate immune system while he'd worked as a missionary in the jungles of Peru. He, Sophie, and Patty had always looked out for Jon, as he was frail and far from healthy. Jon was the one who was always the voice of reason. He'd been so devastated at Sophie's conviction, he'd had a nervous breakdown. The moment the verdict was read, he'd headed for the airport and Peru. Nick had gotten daily reports on Jon's condition from the head missionary, for all the good he or Patty could do. He remembered how Jon had stood for one minute in the courtroom, eyed Patty and Nick, tears streaming down his face, then he was gone. His ashes had been sent to St. Gabriel's, and the nuns had given those ashes to Nick. He still had them in his bedroom back in Dunwoody. He knew he would keep them forever. Sometimes, Patty asked to keep them for a week or so, and he always allowed it. She would return them, her eyes moist, and give him that little smile that was just for him.

Patty, with the sparkling green eyes, feisty to the core, all 105 pounds of her, had taken Jon's death so hard, she had cried for weeks. All she kept saying over and over was how could God do this to them, rob her and Nick of their sister and brother? The answer she always came up with was maybe because they weren't blood brothers and sisters. She'd demanded answers from the nuns back then. She'd gone there like the spitfire she was and refused to accept their explanations. As far as he knew, she'd never gone to church again. Surprise! Surprise! He hadn't gone, either. They, whoever they were, said that God worked in mysterious ways. He guessed now that it was true because Sophie was back among the living. All he had to do was find her.

As he luxuriated in the steaming water, Nick replayed Patty's other texts. She liked working at the firm. What was not to like, working alongside her fiancé? The hiring of the new associates had gone at the speed of light. Investigators had been hired, and she was in charge of all of them. She said she loved issuing orders to big burly guys and blond bombshells. Blond bombshells, she said, were ideal investigators.

Another text said that the new hires were busy with the

court transcripts. She herself was going over them with a fine-tooth comb. So far nothing concrete was jumping out, though there was something niggling at her that she felt was important but couldn't put her finger on.

The last text congratulated Nick on his win and contained a reminder to bring Patty a present. Nick smiled at the last comment. Earlier in the morning, he'd made arrangements to send two dozen plumeria leis to Kala's office. Of course he would buy his best friend a trinket of some kind. Patty did love presents, that was for sure. He knew it wasn't the actual gift she wanted but him taking the time to pick out something just for her. And as she pointed out numerous times, she wasn't the least bit ashamed of reminding him. She'd always brought him something back, too, when she went on the road covering a story.

Nick leaned back on the leather headrest and closed his eyes. Either the Advil was working or the Jacuzzi was doing its job. Probably both. He felt so good, he actually catnapped for the next twenty minutes. He used up another forty minutes showering, shaving, and dressing.

Now what was he supposed to do at eight-thirty in the evening, Hawaiian time? He'd sent the entourage he traveled with home. Actually, they should be boarding their flight that very minute. He was alone, and he savored the peace and quiet.

Dressed in creased khakis and a white golf shirt that showed off his tan, he headed out of his suite to the elevator and the bar in the lobby. What better place to find out information than from a bartender. He hated doing it, but he was going to trade on his celebrity to gain information.

Heads turned when Nick walked into the bar. The patrons started to whisper among themselves, but no one approached him. For as long as he could remember, people just never came up to him unless it was after a tournament. Patty said he gave off an aura of some kind that said *stay away*, and people recognized it and gave him the space he needed.

Nick took a seat at the far end of the bar. He nodded to a few people and turned away. *Stay away,* the nod said. The bartender, a handsome young guy with dark eyes, grinned and said, "Congratulations, Mr. Mancuso! What can I get you?"

"A cold beer would be great."

"Coming up. Glass?"

"Nah." The bartender grinned as he placed the uncapped beer on a round cardboard disk. He reached under the bar and brought up a bowl of peanuts and some other kind of mix that looked crunchy and salty. He waited just a few moments to see if Nick would initiate conversation. His face lit up like a Christmas tree when Nick asked him if he knew Kala Aulani.

"You know it! She's a second cousin of mine. Great lady. She lives here on the island, you know. Well, when she's here she lives here. Guess that doesn't make sense. She lives stateside in Georgia and comes back once a year or so. Usually for the family reunion. Really nice lady. Do you know her?"

"Actually, I do. One of my friends works for her firm. She's on a six-month vacation because she retired." He hated to lie, but he lied anyway. "Kala does legal work for me from time to time. I'm going to miss her because now someone else has to do my work."

The bartender relaxed. The guy knew stuff about his cousin that no one else knew, so he had to be legit, and besides, he was the number two golfer in the country. "One of her partners was here a few days ago. Didn't stay long."

"That so? Must have been Linda."

Convinced that it was okay to keep talking to this guy, seeing as how he knew the partner's name and all, the bartender said, "Yeah. Yeah, that was her name. Guess she was doing some business for Kala since she's away."

Nick swigged at the beer and picked at the nuts in the bowl. Macadamia nuts. His favorite. Now all he had to do was find out where Kala's house was. He struggled for nonchalance when he swiveled around on the bar stool and looked around the room. "I think her house is somewhere around here," he said vaguely. "Hey, can I buy you a beer?"

"Can't drink on duty. Yeah, she lives on Liliuokalani Street, the biggest house on the street."

"I knew it was something like that. I wouldn't even try to spell it. Well, if you see her before I do, give her my regards. Tell her had she been here, I would have taken her out to dinner. It's been a tough day, so I think I'm going to retire. Thanks for the conversation. Nice meeting you." Nick stuck out his hand and so did the bartender.

Suddenly shy, the bartender asked for his autograph. It wasn't just one autograph, though. It was several dozen for his assorted cousins and nephews. "And a few nieces." He grinned.

Nick laughed and signed his name on cocktail napkins till his hand went numb. He waved and left the bar and took the elevator to his room. He popped another beer from the small fridge and carried it out to his balcony. He sat down and propped his feet up on the table and tried to relax. It was still light out. He could have taken a taxi to Kala's house. He told himself it was better to wait till morning. He'd have all night to dream about Sophie Lee. If he was right, he might even *see* Sophie Lee.

Downstairs in the bar, the happy-go-lucky bartender made sure all his customers were served and needing nothing before he made a call on his cell phone. "Kiki, listen up." The bartender rattled off what had happened with the golfer Nick Mancuso. "You told me to report anything with all the statesiders here, so I'm reporting. I think the guy is who he said he is, and he knew Kala, and she did legal work for him. No, he said he was sorry she wasn't here because he would have taken her to dinner. He didn't say how much longer he would be here, but his people left the hotel earlier and are probably on the eight o'clock flight to California. I checked with the front desk, and Mr. Mancuso is the only one who remained behind. He signed a bunch of autographs. Nice guy, but he did want to know where Kala lived, and I told him. I have one of the bellboys watching to see if he leaves his suite. Yeah, Kiki, you do owe me."

The bartender stared out across the room. He felt like a snitch, and he didn't like the feeling.

But family came first. That was all there was to it.

Chapter 14

Sophie Lee was watching a recap of the golf tournament with tears in her eyes. In a million years she never thought Nick would be the second leading golfer in the country. She knew that he would be a success in whatever he did, but golf had never entered her mind. She remembered how he caddied on the weekends, thanks to Father Davidson, who had gotten him the job. The best perk, though, was that the part-time job came with free golf lessons.

When Nick lined up his winding forty-foot birdie putt on the fifteenth hole and it undulated into the cup, Sophie held her breath before letting out a whoop of joy as both clenched fists shot in the air. "Way to go, Nick!"

And Nick was right here, so close she could walk to his hotel. She could even call the hotel and leave a message. Did she dare? She wanted to call him so bad she could taste the feeling, but she knew she wouldn't. She had promised to follow the rules, and she would keep that promise. Sister Julie had taught them early on that if you didn't live by the rules, then you courted disaster. And this time, she would follow the rules to the letter.

Sophie Lee loved Nick Mancuso. She had loved him from the age of seven but had never let on, not for a minute. One day, when she was sixteen, Sister Julie had taken her aside and had a long talk about what the nun called the birds and the bees. Sister Julie had also said that Father Davidson was having the same talk with Nick. From that day on, many eyes were on them, and that was okay; neither one of them minded. They were friends. Just friends. No one could get inside her mind, or know what she dreamed about at night. Well, that was then, and this was now.

Sophie continued to watch the recap of the tournament, riveted. When the cameras were still on her old friend in the clubhouse, she could restrain herself no longer. The tears came gushing and flowing down her cheeks. So close and yet so far away.

Just as the sportscaster was asking Nick how long he was staying in the islands, Sophie heard voices in the downstairs foyer. Kiki. What was he doing there at that time of the evening? She half heard Nick say he was going to stay on a few more days to do some island hopping because he wanted to see and possibly play on Hawaii's other famous golf courses. She was more intent on listening to what Kiki was saying, but she couldn't understand a word because he and Mally were talking in their own language. While Mally understood English, speaking it was another matter. Pidgin English was how Kiki had explained it to her. Mally was shy and worried that her English wouldn't be understood, so she kept all conversations short and relied on her smiles to get her points across.

Sophie knew there was a problem by the tone of Kiki's voice, and she also knew in her gut that the problem was Dominic Mancuso. She waited a few more minutes before she made her way into the huge walk-in closet to pick up the packed bag that was ready for her. She was holding it when Kiki knocked on her door. Without saying a word, she followed him out to the hall and down the long staircase. Mally hugged her, then placed a lei around her neck.

Settled in the car, Sophie was struck again by how handsome the young man was. He looked like he belonged on a surfboard in a television commercial advertising the islands.

"We're not going far. A cousin who is on the mainland on sabbatical has offered his house for emergencies. We take care of it for him. There is only one hitch." He grinned. "You have to take care of his dog. She's a female, and her name is Ursula. We call her Sula. She guards the house, and we take turns taking her for walks and feeding her, but she can do all of that herself. It is our obligation to do this. With a family as large as ours, there is always someone willing to do what is needed. Sula will also take care of you. By the way, no cook or housekeeper this time around. But someone will do your shopping, and there's plenty of food in the fridge. You still stay to ground until they say otherwise. You can still walk the beach, swim, whatever you want, but do not go to town. You call us at the numbers we gave you if something comes up. Like I said, Sula will take care of you. You okay with this, Sophie?"

She was okay with it. And she liked the idea of no one else being in the house with her. She knew how to cook and clean. What she liked best about the move was the dog. She loved animals. "Is this move because of Nick?"

"Yes," Kiki said curtly. "And another reason. Two reservations were made from the district attorney's office in Georgia for an early-morning flight tomorrow. A cousin works for Hawaiian Airlines."

"Oh," was all Sophie could think to say.

"My cousin has already called Kala's office to tell them, so you see the importance of the move. Your golfing friend just wants to renew your friendship; the others want something else."

Sophie nodded. "I wonder if they *know* I'm here or just suspect that I'm here."

"Your friend might have something to do with it. He's here,

and they know you know each other and have a history. They probably have someone watching him. Who that would be, I don't know. We have cousins in Hawaii Five-0, and they would tell us. They have a duty, I'm told, to help out fellow law-enforcement agencies. Having said that, they will let us know first, and we are not a chatty people. We will smother them in leis and go about our business."

In spite of herself, Sophie laughed.

"Okay, we're here. Let me introduce you to Ursula. I think I should tell you, she does not like that name. If you call her Ursula, she will ignore you. She responds only to Sula."

"I'll remember that."

Kiki got out and reached for Sophie's bag. "Just so you know, your neighbors are watching us, so don't get spooked. It's a good thing." Kiki whistled sharply and a dog almost as big as a small pony galloped across the lawn, skidded to a stop, then held up his paw for Kiki to shake, which he promptly did. "Sula is very formal. It's your turn." Sophie held out her hand to shake the dog's paw. Sula let loose with a soft woof of welcome. "Sula loves company. She also loves it when you make her a lei. A small one. I don't know why that is.

"Okay, Sula, Sophie is your new best friend. Give her the tour while I . . . go along, I'll be in in a few minutes."

Sophie followed the huge dog from room to room. When Sula wanted her to see something of particular interest, she nudged her thigh. "I see it, the old treat jar. Okay, here we go." Sophie opened a bright yellow jar that said TREATS on the front and handed over a chew bone.

Spinning in a circle to take it all in, Sophie said, "Oh, wow, I love this house! I love all this teak, the marble floors, the French doors, and that lanai is to die for. I think you and I are going to spend a lot of time out there. I know how to cook. Or do you just eat dog food?" Sula stopped chewing and looked up at her as if to say, What do you think? Sophie laughed.

By the time Sula finished her chew bone, Kiki was back in the house. "All set?"

"Yep." She grinned from ear to ear as Sula nudged Kiki toward the front door.

"See? That's what I meant. She's telling me it's time to go, and she'll take over now. I'll see you when I see you." Sula gave Kiki one last nudge. When the door closed behind him, she reared up and shoved the dead bolt into place with a paw that was as big as Sophie's open palm. She looked over at Sophie for approval.

"That's great, you even know how to lock up. Good girl! Okay, that's your job from now on. Well, it's still early, so let's go outside on the lanai and drink some pineapple juice. I'll give you another treat, and we can cuddle on that big lounge chair out there and look at the stars."

Sula cocked her head to better observe her new temporary mistress before she headed back to the treat bowl. Sophie laughed out loud when the dog barked twice—surely it meant *two* treats.

Comfortably settled into a lounge with a frosty glass of fresh pineapple juice, her arm around the huge dog, Sophie started to talk and couldn't stop. Finally, someone to listen to her who would not judge, talk back, disapprove. When she cried, Sula licked her tears. When she said with all the vehemence she could muster, "I hate that man. I really hate him, Sula. He took away ten years of my life; that's why I'm here now with you. I need him to pay for what he did to me. He didn't have a shred of evidence that I was the one who killed her and not Adam Star. But he was so sure, and he convinced that jury. I know God is going to punish me for my evil thoughts, but right now I don't care. If it weren't for him, I might . . . Nick would . . ." She never finished what she was going to say because she was so tired and filled with anxiety that she fell asleep in midsentence.

Sula wiggled free of Sophie's embrace when she was satisfied her new mistress's breathing was even and steady. She inched to the corner of the lounge chair and dropped her big head onto her paws. She did not go to sleep. She sat on guard all through the night and into the early hours of the morning until Sophie woke. Only then did she trot off to the dense undergrowth surrounding the small compact house to do what she had to do.

Meanwhile, while Sophie was taking an early-morning swim with Sula, just minutes away from Sophie's new residence, Nick Mancuso was knocking on the front door of Kala Aulani's house.

Mally, already alerted to the news that someone was going to come looking for Sophie, opened the door, a huge smile on her face. She continued to smile as Nick presented his case. She started to jabber in her own language, to Nick's dismay. He reached for his wallet and pulled out a picture of himself and Sophie taken when she'd graduated nursing school. Mally smiled and nodded and then shrugged. Nick pointed to the house and Mally again shook her head as though perplexed at where he was pointing. Kiki had told her to invite him into the house, wave her arms about to indicate he could look around, then offer him a glass of pineapple juice, so she did just that. Unsure what the little woman was telling him, Nick stepped over the threshold. Mally waved her arms about again, so he started to walk around and marvel at the house that belonged to Kala. He even walked upstairs and poked his head into the different rooms.

Downstairs, he accepted the glass of pineapple juice, drained it, and nodded to Mally, but not before she draped a fragrant lei around his neck.

"You come back Miss Kala here."

There was nothing for Nick to do but leave. He'd been so sure, so very sure that Sophie was here. What the hell did that wink Jed gave him mean? Maybe he was just jerking his chain. Nah, Jed wouldn't do that. He knew that Nick had feelings, strong feelings for Sophie. Maybe she wasn't there in *that* house, but she was in Hawaii somewhere. He felt it in his bones.

Nick walked back to his five-star hotel and made arrangements to do some island hopping. If nothing else, and he didn't actually play a round of golf, he at least had to be able to say he'd *visited* all the golf courses Hawaii had to offer. Besides, his hip needed a break. Unable to sleep last night, he had pored over all the colorful magazines and brochures the hotel had provided. He had an itinerary for the day, then he'd head home in the morning. He knew he'd never be able to find Sophie if Kala had hidden her, so there was no point in staying. So much for hope springing eternal and all that jazz.

As he walked along, following the shortcut the hotel concierge had provided, he noticed the biggest dog he'd ever seen in his life frolicking at the edge of the water alongside a slim young girl. It had been years since he had anything remotely like fun. Ah, well, one of these days, he decided, he'd take some time off and do just that. Maybe once he made his mind up to have the hip-replacement surgery, he'd come back there to recuperate. Maybe. That was like saying someday I'm going to do all these things when I get around to it. The sad part was, someday rarely arrived.

Where are you, Sophie? I know you're here somewhere. I just know it. I feel like you're just a heartbeat away.

With the five-hour time difference between Hawaii and Georgia, Ryan Spenser's two ADAs stepped off the plane and looked around. Ginger Albright and Don Clark looked at each other as much as to say, I think I'm going to like this four-day minivacation. They'd flown coach, and each knew that their hotel accommodations would be less than desirable. Their food stipend was small. Ginger called it miserly. It didn't really matter to either one of them because they were in *Hawaii.* The only request they made was for their rental vehicle to be an open jeep.

The jeep came with a road map and a GPS.

In less than an hour, they were on their way to a place called Monarch Suites. One suite for the two of them, one regular bed and a couch that opened to a bed. One bathroom. Ginger rolled her eyes, and said, "You get the couch, and I get first dibs on the bathroom." Don agreed because he had no other choice—Ginger was senior to him.

An hour after checking in to the fleabag, as Don called it, they were wearing shorts and Hawaiian shirts they had picked up at the airport so they could blend in with the locals. The only problem was, they looked like tourists. Pale tourists.

"Okay, kid, let's go find Sophie Lee," Don said as he straightened his cap a little more firmly on his head. He slipped on his shades. Definitely incognito.

Ginger giggled. "You have to be kidding me, Don. There's no way we're going to find that young woman. Even if she's here, Kala Aulani has her so well stashed, even a drug-sniffing dog couldn't find her. Assuming, of course, she had drugs on her person."

"I don't even know why the hell we're here, Ginger. What does Spenser think this is going to get him? Sophie Lee is free. There's nothing he can do about it. It's all legal, and it's all been squared away. What? He thinks he can send in some goons and take her out? That's pretty damn stupid if you ask me. I don't know what his game plan is. When A can't get me to B, I start to worry." His voice was fretful as he ranted on. "I'm just not getting it. Sophie's free. Why did Aulani stash her somewhere? Why is Spenser looking for her? What could she possibly say or do now that would make a difference?"

"Yeah, me, too. Do you think maybe it might have something to do with Aulani filing a lawsuit against the state? Maybe he wants to chop her off at the knees. Hell, Don, I don't have the faintest idea, and if you want the honest truth,

I hope we *don't* find her. Sure, we'll do some looking in the obvious places, but not all that hard. We're lawyers, not private detectives. I suppose he sent us because it would cost too much to send real investigators, who would not put up with the crap we're putting up with."

Chapter 15

THE AULANI LAW FIRM, NOW KNOWN OFFICIALLY AS AULANI, Brighton, Brighton, and Darrow, resembled a Chinese fire drill gone awry. The four fax machines spit out paper at the speed of light, the three copy machines were hot to the touch, with all the copies being run through the automatic feed, computers clicked and hummed as documents were hammered out almost as fast as the fingers typing them could hit the keys. Cell phones pinged and buzzed, some to snappy tunes that set everyone's teeth on edge. The firm's main number was backlogged, with some thirty-seven callers waiting to be heard. Associates, the partners, and the paralegals were shouting to one another as though they were on the floor of the Chicago Board of Trade with its open outcry trading system.

Patty Molnar brought her fingers to her lips and whistled the way Jon had taught her years and years ago back at the orphanage. The sound was so shrill that people clapped their hands over their ears. All sound ceased except that of the machines, which continued to work at warp speed. They all stared at Patty to see what this break in work meant. She waved her index finger in a half circle to indicate she wanted the attention of the new investigators she'd hired. "All of you, follow me."

Inside the conference room, which could comfortably seat twelve, Patty took her seat at the head of the table. She looked around at the people she'd just hired; the three blond bombshells looked just the way she wanted them to look. Blond wigs, false eyelashes, plenty of makeup, glossy lips, sparkling white teeth, curvy where they were supposed to be curvy. The curves were encased in eye-opening spandex. The stiletto heels glistened with rhinestones and shiny sequins. The bombshells stopped just short of looking like ladies of the evening. Patty didn't think the man who could resist their charms had yet been born. She grinned, and said, "I do like your style, ladies."

Patty turned her focus to the three male investigators. Studs—although she wouldn't know a stud if she tripped over him. All were Adonis good-looking. Or as Linda said when her husband was not in earshot, "Those guys are ripped." All three were tanned and buff, with killer smiles to match their killer bodies. There was nothing shabby about their killer résumés either. All six investigators were on summer vacation from their last year at various law schools. A good crew.

"Okay, guys, here's the deal, so listen up. I'm going to separate you into three teams, boy-girl, boy-girl, boy-girl. I want you to go back to the day Adam William Clements was born and get me everything until the day he died. When I say everything, I mean everything, no matter how insignificant you might think it is. The same thing goes for Audrey Star, Adam's wife, who inherited the Star fortune. Last but not least, I want the same thing for Ryan Spenser. Work together on his father—the Speaker of the House—the uncle, who is governor of Georgia, and the governor's wife. And don't forget Spenser's mother. Do a good job, and your last year's tuition will be paid in full by this firm, and you'll all get nice going-back-to-school bonuses as well. Any questions?"

Adonis number one looked at Patty and smiled. She felt herself melt for a second. "Yes?"

"What if we have to pay sources before they agree to talk?"

"You go with your gut. Don't be overly generous, but don't be stingy either. You know what they say, money talks and bullshit walks. They say that a lot around this office. We'll pay whatever it takes if it's legit. One last thing, and I'm glad you brought it up." The last and only question, which told her she had made the right selection.

"Try and rip us off, and we'll go after you. You won't be able to hide, so let's keep this on the up-and-up with meticulous records, names, dates, places, and most important, phone numbers that actually work if we need to make contact again. I want a report on my desk at the end of each business day. Signed by both members of each team. Two sets of eyes see things differently, two minds interpret things differently, so make sure you include everything in your reports. I'm going to leave you all now so you can divide up your work, decide who is qualified to work with which person."

"Wait, one more question," Adonis number one said. "Do we have a time frame here?"

"You do. It was up yesterday," Patty said, closing the door behind her. Damn, those guys were good-looking. And on her very, very, very best day, she couldn't even come close to looking like the bombshells. On the other hand, she seriously doubted any one of the six had two best friends like Nick and Sophie or a fiancé like Jed. Well, no one gets it all, she told herself happily as she made her way back to where the Chinese fire drill was still going on like . . . a Chinese fire drill.

Patty looked down at the strap watch on her wrist. It was an old-fashioned Timex, the kind they advertised with "They take a lickin' but keep on tickin'." Sophie and Nick had watches just like hers. Nick was even wearing his when he played in the tournament. She frowned; whatever it was she'd been trying to remember was still niggling at her. Thinking about the watches brought the elusive thought front and center. What the heck was it? Whatever it was, it still wasn't ready to pop into her conscious mind.

Patty made her way through the chaos and found a secluded cubicle at the very back of the suite that was next to Kala's old office. She sat down, took a deep breath, and sent off a text to Nick.

Three hours later, Nick read the message as he waited to get off the plane. He smiled. Patty was so on top of things. Welcome home, indeed. He grinned. It was Patty's not-so-subtle way of reminding him of the present he was supposed to bring her. It wasn't the money at all. Patty would be satisfied with a bottle of sand from one of the famous black beaches, which was exactly what he was bringing her.

Nick wished now he had opted to fly home on the private jet that had been offered, but accepting gifts like that didn't sit well with him. He'd opted for commercial and first-class. His hip ached unbearably from the long flight even though he'd gotten up numerous times to walk up and down the aisle. He didn't want to take any more Advil—he'd gone through more than enough for one day. According to the pilot, it was raining, and damp weather always added to his discomfort. Then he looked out the window and saw that the jet was parked on the tarmac, not at a gate, which meant they would have to go down the portable stairs and walk across the tarmac in the rain. In an hour, he'd be home and in his hot tub. He held on to that thought as he picked up his gear from the overhead bin and got in line behind two other people. Damn, make that two hours, possibly three.

How could he have forgotten the welcoming committee that would be waiting for him indoors? He made a mental note to call his orthopedic surgeon as soon as he got home to ask him if he could get another shot of that jelly they pumped into his hip joint. He wasn't hopeful the doctor would agree. It was time for the surgery he'd put off long enough. The main reason he'd put off the surgery was because the doctors—and he had the best of the best—couldn't guarantee he would be able to play golf the way he had been playing. The most they would say was, he would be able to play golf after a reasonable length of time with therapy, but they didn't know about the grueling tournament schedule that had gotten him to where he was in the golf world.

A minute later, it was all moot. Nick's hip locked into place, and he slipped on the slick third step of the portable stairway. He tumbled to the bottom. Never in his life had he felt such incredible pain. It was so bad, he blacked out. When he came to, he was on a gurney and being loaded into an ambulance.

Kala's entire office saw the accident. Patty was out the door within seconds and got to the hospital just as they were wheeling Nick through the wide double doors of the emergency room. Tears were running down her face as she raced to catch up with the running EMTs. "Nick!"

"Don't worry, I didn't forget your present," he shouted feebly. Then he was gone through another set of double doors.

"Jerk!" Nick was okay; he wasn't going to die if he could yell at her like that. "Thank you, God, thank you, God!"

Patty sat down on a bench near the door. She'd catch the EMT guys on their way out. She started to cry again. She knew it was Nick's hip. People didn't die with broken hips or when they got hip replacements, something Nick had been trying to avoid. Nick was her rock. Actually, he was everyone's rock. He'd confided in her two years ago when he'd been diagnosed with rheumatoid arthritis. He'd sworn her to secrecy. Like she would ever breathe a word of Nick's business to anyone. Not even to Jed.

The tears continued to flow. What would Nick do if he couldn't play golf? She couldn't even begin to imagine what he would do. Maybe write a book. Nick's writing a book was the silliest idea she'd ever had. Maybe not a book per se but more like a golfing manual. He'd do better writing a book about what it meant to be a friend and benefactor to St.

Gabriel's. Who would buy something like that? Other golfers? Even that was doubtful. Teach kids to play golf the way someone had taught him? Good possibility. Sell his own brand of golf clubs?

How could life be so unfair? The four of them had started off their lives with no parents, been put in an orphanage, and never knew what it was like to have a real family. That part was even okay because the four of them had found each other. They were their own little family. Then Sophie was arrested for murder and sent to prison for life for a crime another person had just confessed to committing and lost ten years of her life. Then Jon, who only wanted to do good in the world, had died from some crazy-ass jungle virus. Now Nick with his bone-on-bone hip. She couldn't help but wonder what was in store for her. She felt a shiver of apprehension ripple up her spine.

Patty swiped at her eyes with the sleeve of her shirt as she got up to talk to the EMTs. In the end, they really couldn't tell her anything that she hadn't seen on television other than to say that Nick's doctors were on the way.

Outside, in the now-pouring rain, Patty could see the media vans rolling up. She saw her replacement from *AJC*, who groaned when she saw Patty. Patty flipped her the bird and hustled over to the Fox reporter and asked him up front if he wanted to interview her since she was first on the scene and had actually spoken to her friend Nick. The reporter snapped her up like she was the last donut on the plate. When no one except her replacement was looking, Patty offered up a single-digit salute for the second time.

Ten thousand miles away across the Pacific, Sophie Lee watched a recap of the day's news before retiring for the night. Her eyes almost popped out of her head as her jaw dropped when she saw her best friend in the whole world tumble down the portable set of steps that had been wheeled up to the plane. She clutched at her chest at the pandemonium she was witnessing. She hardly dared to breathe as she watched an ambulance careening across the tarmac minutes later, and her best friend in the whole world was loaded onto a stretcher and into the wailing ambulance. She listened to the words, heard them, digested them, then started to really cry.

Sophie continued to listen as reporter after reporter vaguely implied that there were rumors about Nick's hips and what it would mean to his golf game and to the sport in general. Then they went on to Nick's endorsements and what it would mean to all the companies who sponsored him. It always came down to money with these guys, Sophie thought. She hugged Sula, who was busy trying to lick at Sophie's tears.

"Money really is the root of all evil, you know that, Sula?" She gasped when she saw Patty and the Fox reporter. Good, good, really good. Patty was there for Nick. Good old Patty. God, how she missed her. Sophie listened to what she was saying as she hugged Sula close. How great she looked. She couldn't believe it when she heard the reporter say Patty had been fired from the *AJC* and was now working as an investigator for the Aulani law firm.

An hour passed as Sophie flipped from one station to the next. She couldn't get enough of the rehashing. She had the reporters' verbiage memorized as the hour moved on. She needed to go back to Georgia. She really did. Another hour passed, then, gloriously, there was Patty standing outside the hospital talking to a Fox reporter. Again. Sophie's tears welled once more at the sight of her friend. How good she looked. How *pissed* she looked. Sophie saw how upbeat she was trying to be, but she was hurting big-time. Hurting for Nick. Patty tried to make light of what he'd said to her as he was being rushed into the operating room, and she ended with, "And I still don't know what he brought me back from Hawaii." In spite of herself, Sophie laughed. That was Patty.

Then the reporter overstepped his bounds by asking Patty her personal opinion on what she thought Nick would do if the rumors were true about his physical condition. Patty backed away, her eyes narrowed into slits. She waved airily and headed for her car, the *AJC* reporter hot on her heels.

"Hey, Patty, don't blame me for getting fired."

"What?" Patty retaliated. "Do you have a guilty conscience or something?"

"No, I don't. They handed me your job. You know how it works. Either I took it, or I was on the unemployment line. You would have done the same thing."

She was right. It was an ugly business. "If I had a secret and wanted to share it with a newspaper, and your paper offered me ten times what another paper offered me, I'd turn it down and go with the other guy. You guys got bought off, you blinked. That's not the kind of journalism I subscribe to. Good luck," Patty said as she stomped away through the rain.

Patty got in, slammed the car door, and started up the engine. She was going home to cry some more in the little house Nick held the mortgage on. The day after Sophie had been taken off to prison, Nick came by the apartment she had shared with Sophie and helped her move, along with three of his friends. It wasn't like she had a choice. Nick and his friends had just showed up, packed up hers and Sophie's stuff, and moved her into an investment house he had only recently bought with the proceeds from his first tournament win. He said she had enough going on in her mind and didn't need the memories of her life with Sophie in the ratty little apartment they lived in. And, of course, he was exactly right. Nick was always right. Well, almost all of the time.

And it was a nice little house, three bedrooms, three baths, a nice family room, wraparound deck, wonderful shrubbery, and flowers galore in the spring and summer. Nick even cut the lawn for her from time to time. Big brother Nick.

Patty started wailing so loud, she turned on the radio to drown out her misery.

Big brother Nick. God, how she loved him. Even if she had a flesh-and-blood brother, she couldn't have loved him any more than she loved Nick. How blessed she was that Jed understood her feelings for Nick and wasn't the least bit jealous. Jed truly understood that Sophie and Nick would always come first in her life no matter how much she loved him.

Chapter 16

Retired judge Ben Jefferson stood on the balcony of the hotel he and Kala were staying in. It offered a perfect view of Paris in all its romantic glory. Not that he was actually seeing or appreciating it; his mind was a thousand miles away. He never should have insisted on this trip, but he and Kala had been planning it for over a year. She'd been as gung ho as he was in the planning stages and had done most of the work on it herself. All was well until the day Adam Clements, a.k.a. Adam Star, walked into Kala's office and turned her world upside down. And his world as well.

The trip simply wasn't working, that was the bottom line. Kala was forcing herself to enjoy herself, but the effort it took was beyond painful to watch. She barely picked at the delectable food, she hurried from one sightseeing adventure to the next like she had a time frame where she couldn't waste even a minute. He knew if he quizzed her at the end of the day, she would have struggled to remember what it was they had seen or where they had gone.

Ben looked down at his watch just as the phone in the elegant suite rang. He walked back inside and picked it up. He thanked the concierge as he jotted down what he was being told on a notepad alongside the phone. He looked around the room, then across the hall to the door, where their packed bags waited for a bellhop to take them to the lobby. On his own, he'd made the decision to leave, to go back to Georgia. He knew in his heart, in his gut, Kala would not protest. If she had to, she would run all the way to the airport and leave the bags behind if she knew that was the only way to return to Georgia.

Ben looked at his watch again. Kala should be returning any minute now from her spa appointment. There would be just enough time for her to shower and dress in the clothes he'd laid out on the bed for her before he finished packing their bags. He no sooner finished his thought than Kala breezed through the suite.

"What's up with the bags?" she asked as she headed for the bathroom.

"I packed for us. I had the concierge change our tickets. We're going home, so shake it, or we'll miss the flight."

Kala stopped in her tracks. "Don't you think you should have consulted with me first, Ben? What if I'm not ready to go home?"

"Oh, you're ready, my dear. You've been ready since the day we left. I've known you most of your adult life, and I can truthfully say I have never seen you more miserable than you've been since we left Georgia. We have not had one moment of fun, and I say that lightly since we are of an age where fun is whatever we want to make it. You don't eat, you aren't the least bit interested in sightseeing. We don't even have conversations about our day at the end of the day. This vacation is a chore. You're working at it harder than you would work at preparing for a six-month murder trial. Now, go take your shower, get dressed, and we're outta here."

In a flash, Kala was in the huge marble bathroom, stripping off her clothes. She turned on the shower, talking past the door she'd left slightly ajar. "Have I really been that bad?"

"Yes."

Inside the shower, Kala grinned as she lathered up her

thick dark hair. She was going home. Yessss. "You could have sweet-talked that just a little, doncha think? What was the final decision breaker for you?" she called out.

"A week ago when you saw Nick Mancuso take that tumble at the airport. And all those transatlantic calls to Sophie and your people in Hawaii."

"You noticed that, huh?"

"Yeah," Ben drawled. "You know, this might be a good time to talk about that plan you have to retire back in Hawaii. When were you going to tell me about it?"

Kala's heart fluttered in her chest. There it was, the thing she couldn't bring herself to talk about to Ben. Now or never. She'd thought when it was time, they'd be sitting on her nubby wheat-colored sofa with wineglasses in their hands. She never thought she'd be naked in a shower in Paris, when she had to confess to her plans. She felt like crying for some reason.

"I was trying to find just the right moment. Originally, I thought when the trip was over, and we were back home. I never in a million years thought life would turn upside down the way it is now. I love you, Ben. You know that. I know your life is back in Georgia, your friends are there. I realize you have no real family to speak of, but your friends are your family, as you've pointed out to me time and again. You like going to the courthouse, you love talking to your fellow judges. You enjoy playing golf with them, and you live for the days those very same judges call or want to meet with you to ask your opinion on cases. I didn't want . . . I didn't think I should . . . what I'm trying to say here is, if you knew what I was planning, why didn't you say something? We've been together over thirty-five years; that gives you the right to ask, to demand answers. Besides, I didn't want to be rebuffed."

"And you figured this out all on your own, is that it?" Ben held up a huge white towel for Kala to wrap herself in the moment she stepped out of the shower. Ben wasn't sure if what he was seeing were tears on Kala's cheeks or just water droplets from the shower. He thought they were tears.

"Well, yeah, I did. You're telling me I was wrong to do that? Okay, do you want to retire with me to Hawaii once this Sophie mess is all settled?"

"Hell, yes, I do."

"Really, Ben? Truly you do?" They were definitely tears, he decided, as he took her in his arms.

"Wouldn't have it any other way. Haven't you noticed how my friends have all migrated to other climates? You went with me to four funerals this year. The younger judges aren't the least bit interested in this old fart's opinions. I can play golf anywhere. What I can't do without is you. For a top-notch lawyer, you can be pretty dense sometimes, my love. Maybe I can teach some law classes at the University of Hawaii. If they'll have me. How many cousins do you have at the university?"

Kala laughed. It was a joke about her family and all the cousins, nieces, and nephews. "Quite a few, actually. I'm sure we can get you a gig there."

"What will you be doing?" Ben asked curiously.

Kala whirled around and stared up at Ben. "I thought I'd plan my wedding. No way in hell can I move back home and live in sin. The elders would never permit it. So I'm thinking a real island wedding with a luau. I'm going to wear the traditional garb, do the hula for my new husband in my grass skirt, which I will make myself, and I will wear the traditional crown of flowers. That's *my* game plan."

"Are you asking me to marry you, Kala Aulani? Because if you are, I accept. What I won't do is wear a loincloth to your grass skirt." Well damn, he was excited.

"Sure you will," Kala said, tweaking his cheek. "Well, now that that's all settled, how do I look for our trip back home?"

"Marvelous. No loincloth."

"Then I can't marry you," Kala said, sashaying to the foyer, where all the bags waited. She opened the door and crooked her finger in his direction. "I promise to make it worth your while."

"Well, in that case . . ."

Twelve hours later, thanks to a four-hour layover, Kala and Ben were pushing a dolly with all their luggage toward the EXIT sign at Hartsdale-Jackson International Airport.

Outside, in the cool evening air, Kala looked around as she sniffed a familiar scent. Plumeria. Plumeria there in Georgia? Impossible! It must be perfume. Walking toward her, decked out in flowered Hawaiian shirts, was a couple she vaguely recognized. They both wore leis. Just another vacationing couple returning from Hawaii. My ass, she thought. She wouldn't bet the rent on it, but she thought the couple were assistant DAs who worked for Ryan Spenser. She gave Ben a slight nudge to the side so that he could see what she was seeing. She watched the frown build on Ben's face as he tried to figure out if he knew the colorful couple or not.

A van slid gracefully to the curb, and Jay and Jed hopped out. Within seconds, the mountain of luggage was stashed in the back, and Kala and Ben were inside, buckled up and ready to go.

"Take a good look and tell me if you recognize those two decked out in Hawaiian garb," Kala hissed.

Jed craned his neck. "Oh, yeah, that's Ginger Albright and Don Clark, Spenser's ADAs. Looks like maybe they're just coming back from a vacation in Hawaii." He laughed. Jay joined in.

"They fit the description your people called in to us daily, Kala. They had pictures of Sophie they showed to practically everyone on the island. With no results, of course. They gave it their best shot. They were everywhere, didn't miss a beat. Grocery stores, beauty shops, nail salons, various spas, all the hotels, the banks, the post office. They hired some kids to patrol the beaches. They handed out copies of Sophie's picture like she was a wanted criminal with a bounty on her head. But, I am happy to report, they came up dry, and as you can see, they returned home with their tails between their legs." Jay laughed again, the sound so contagious the others laughed with him.

"Damn, it's good to be home," Kala said. Ben reached for her hand and squeezed it hard. She squeezed back.

Ryan Spenser looked at the mountain of paper on his desk. Then he looked down at the entire transcript of the Sophie Lee trial. He'd been lugging it back and forth from home to the office for days. Then he looked at the newspapers his secretary had placed on his already cluttered desk alongside a deep pile of phone messages, most of them from reporters and, of course, the Speaker and his uncle the governor. As much as he didn't want to, Spenser picked up the *AJC* and snapped it open. Nothing above the fold. That was good. Nothing below the fold, either. That was good, too. The Speaker and the governor should be happy about that.

Spenser spit on his finger and turned the page. Top left-hand corner in bold print, the words glared at him. "Seven new cases added to Spenser's backlog. Lawyers furious at the prospect of their clients wrongfully imprisoned. All vowing to overturn past convictions."

Spenser felt sick to his stomach. This would go on for years, destroying all his dreams of stepping into the governor's mansion. He'd be damn lucky if they didn't cart his ass off to some federal prison. He goddamn well did not deserve this.

Rage filled Spenser at the situation he was in. Blind rage. All-encompassing rage. *Eye of the tiger.*

Spenser felt like he was in a trance. It was almost impossible to pull his eyes away from the Sophie Lee transcript when he heard the knock on his door. He bent over and banged his head so hard on the desk he literally saw stars. The pain brought him back to reality. He barked an order to come in. He glared with narrowed eyes at his two ADAs.

Ginger took the lead. "We came up dry. Not one person—and we spoke to thousands of people—would admit to seeing Sophie Lee. We covered the island from one end to the other. We didn't leave one stone unturned."

"And yet you both somehow managed to get a nice suntan," Spenser snarled.

"We were on foot most of the time and in the sun, *sir,*" Don Clark said, his attitude toward his boss apparent in his tone of voice. "It's hot in Hawaii."

Ginger picked up the ball, and said, "Is there anything else you want us to do, sir?"

Spenser looked at the mess on his desk, wishing he knew what the hell it all was. "I want you to go to the evidence locker and bring me everything in it. If they give you a problem, have them call me. And Sophie Lee's personal possessions, if there are any."

"Yes, sir," the ADAs said as they turned and left the room.

Outside in the hallway, Ginger grimaced. "Ten years later he wants the evidence that he used to convict Sophie Lee? My bet is Sophie Lee's personal possessions were picked up by her lawyer or her friend the reporter. What do you think, Don?"

Don shrugged. "Who the hell knows? I wasn't even in Georgia when that case went down. It's customary for the next of kin to take possession of the defendant's property once the police release it. Since Sophie Lee was an orphan with no next of kin, then either the reporter friend or her lawyer probably has it, and lots of luck trying to retrieve it. That son of a bitch is just grasping at straws now. He's going down, and he knows it, and even his Speaker of the House daddy isn't going to be able to help him. In case you haven't figured it out, Ginger, I got a hard-on hate for Spenser."

Ginger laughed. "Join the club. Listen, just because no one likes that cocky bastard doesn't mean he did something wrong. He went to court with what he had, and a jury agreed with him. He could still come out of this okay, and everyone out there might be spinning their wheels for nothing. Come on, let's get on this so we can go home and get some sleep. I do like your tan, though, ADA Clark," she added with a smirk.

Twenty minutes later, covered with grime and dust, the two attorneys looked at the empty box labeled SOPHIE LEE and the date, which was ten years earlier. They smiled in the dim light.

"No way in hell is Spenser going to believe this! Someone's head is going to roll." Ginger shoved the empty box back into its niche. "Let's see where Lee's personal possessions are and who signed for the evidence to be taken out."

Another thirty minutes went by before the two detectives had a name; Kala Aulani had signed out Sophie Lee's personal possessions. Don read from the list. Watch, purse, keys, billfold, assorted purse junk, laptop, clothing, and shoes. There were no signatures for the contents of the evidence locker.

"Looks like Aulani didn't even ask to see what was in the evidence locker. The cops are pretty uptight about that end of it. They keep pretty meticulous records from what I've seen over the years. We can't hang that on her, but Spenser sure as hell will try," Ginger said.

Ginger flipped through the pages of the logbook, but there was nothing to find other than Kala Aulani's signature for the release of Sophie Lee's personal possessions.

"Well, someone took it all out," Ginger said. "Spenser is never going to believe this. Who was on duty when Kala signed out Lee's personal effects?"

"Donna Holmes. Never heard of her," Don said. He looked over at the grizzled older officer who was reading the sports page under a dim yellow reading lamp. "Hey, Drucker, do you know who Donna Holmes is?" The officer shook his head.

Back upstairs, Ginger logged on to the first computer she came to and ran a check on Donna Holmes. Fifteen minutes later Ginger said, "She's a detective at this precinct. According to this," she added, pointing to the computer screen, "she was a rookie, fresh out of the academy and assigned to the evidence locker because that guy we just saw back there was in the hospital with a ruptured appendix. It was her first assignment on the force. Guess we have to talk to her."

"Can't we just call her? I need some sleep. This jet lag is killing me. Weren't we supposed to eat almonds or something?"

"Huh?" Ginger said, a stupid look on her face.

"I think I heard somewhere that if you eat almonds, you won't have jet lag," Don said lamely.

Ginger rolled her eyes. She'd never heard such a thing. Cell phone in hand, she was already dialing Donna Holmes's work cell. The voice that came through was brisk and cool. "Holmes, what can I do for you, Ms. Albright?"

"A lot. Can you meet us somewhere in the next ten minutes? We need to talk with you about something important."

"How about right out front? I'm parking in the lot as we speak."

"Ten minutes tops, and you can head for home, Don. Try to look alert. You look like you're in a trance of some kind," Ginger said.

Donna Holmes looked like the girl next door who had grown up into an adult and hadn't changed a bit. She was neat and tidy, just a touch of makeup. Her eyes were clear and steady, her handshake firm.

Ginger took the lead and explained what they wanted to know. Donna responded:

"That was ten years ago. My first assignment when I got to the force. I hated every minute of being stuck down there. I did read a lot of books and magazines, I can tell you that. I couldn't wait for Drucker to get out of the hospital. I just don't remember anything about what you're asking. If Miss Aulani signed out her client's stuff, what's the problem? Shouldn't you be talking to her?"

"She signed out Sophie Lee's personal stuff, you know, watch, purse, clothes, that kind of thing. The evidence box was *empty.* What we want to know is where that evidence is. No one signed it out, but the box is empty. Is it even remotely possible that being new on the job, you gave her the evidence contents *and* the personal stuff?" Ginger asked.

Any other time and under other circumstances, the look of blind panic on Donna Holmes's face might have been funny. Right then, that minute, it was not funny.

"This is about Ryan Spenser, right?" Holmes didn't wait for a response. "I don't remember doing that, but I'm not saying I didn't. I was overwhelmed, and I hated being cooped up in that dungeon. I don't know how Drucker does it. I felt like a vampire down there. I don't know what to say other than I might have given her everything. What's going to happen now?"

Ginger and Don both shrugged.

"Do you remember what was in the evidence bin?"

Holmes's face puckered up. "I want to help, and if I screwed up, I'll take responsibility. I can't be sure, and I'm guessing. Laptops, I think, and I don't even know why I'm saying that as in plural. I don't have any recollection of even looking in that box, but if I'm saying laptops, where did I get that from?" The detective shrugged her slim shoulders and frowned. "How much trouble is this going to cause?"

Ginger's eyes sparked. "Could be a lot, could be none, depends on Spenser and how mad he is. Is it possible you're thinking of the laptop in Sophie Lee's personal effects."

Holmes shook her head. "No. I seem to remember multiple laptops and thinking who needs all these laptops? It's vague in my mind. Like I said, I'm guessing here. Did you talk to the person who signed out the stuff?"

"Not yet. Okay, listen, keep thinking about this and call me if you remember anything, anything at all." Ginger scribbled both hers and Don's work cell numbers along with their personal numbers on a sheet of paper she ripped out of a notebook she always carried with her. She handed it over.

Both lawyers watched Donna Holmes walk away. "I think she gave Aulani the whole ball of wax. Think about it. Why would Aulani even mention it to anyone? None of it would ever have come to light if Spenser hadn't asked for it. She probably used all that stuff from evidence when she filed all of her appeals. I'm not sure what that makes her guilty of, if anything. Sophie Lee was found guilty by a jury of her peers. The appeals didn't work. Why open up that can of worms?"

Ginger Albright looked uneasy as she stared at her fellow ADA. "We're not going to get to first base with Kala Aulani."

"Well, I'm not going to worry about it. I'm going home to eat some almonds. And then I'm hitting the sack. Don't call me unless they find Spenser's dead body somewhere."

"What? You're leaving me to go back and . . . and . . ."

"Yeah. Maybe you can sweet-talk him," Don said, trotting around the building to where his car was parked.

"Why do I always get the shit detail?" Ginger groaned as she retraced her steps and took the elevator to Ryan Spenser's office. When Spenser's secretary told her Spenser had left to attend a meeting, Ginger almost fainted in relief. The secretary took notes as Ginger rattled off what had happened at the evidence locker and at her and Don's meeting with Donna Holmes.

"Oh, this is not good."

"No, it isn't, and I, for one, don't give a good rat's ass, either. I'm just the messenger," Ginger said cheerfully. "And I heard somewhere that shooting the messenger has gone out of style. See you when I see you."

Chapter 17

KALA AULANI AND JAY BRIGHTON STEPPED OUT OF THE ELEVAtor onto the floor of the attorney general's suite of offices. "I appreciate your coming along, Kala, but I could have handled this myself. You did tell me when you left that you were not going to stick your nose into the firm's business and that you *really* were retired. And yet, here we are! You just got back from Paris a few hours ago. Why don't you have jet lag like everyone else?" Jay groused under his breath.

Kala smoothed down the wrinkles of her white linen jacket and skirt, which now looked like she had slept in them. Underneath the jacket she wore a scarlet silk blouse that matched the flower she'd pinned above her ear. She was in battle-dress mode. "That's all partially true, Jay. But you left off the part where I said I was going to see Sophie's case through to the end. I don't have jet lag because I ate almonds. I never get jet lag. Besides, I couldn't pass up a chance to see Ryan Spenser again. You think he'll offer to kiss my feet to make this all go away? A small wager, Jay. Mr. Spenser is going to be downright testy today. I read the headlines this morning," Kala said, as she stepped through the doors to the reception area.

"Nice digs. Our taxpayer dollars at work," she murmured, as Jay gave their names to the gorgeous receptionist with the two-inch-long fingernails that were painted bloodred. Kala looked down at her own French manicure, which she'd gotten at the spa before they left to return home. A lovely manicure it was and truly French.

"How do you suppose that chick wipes her rear end with those nails?" Jay hissed in Kala's ear as they took seats in the reception area.

"And how do you think I would know the answer to that?"

Jay shrugged. Kala had to fight to keep from laughing.

"Did you rehearse a speech or anything, or are you going in cold turkey?" Jay asked in a jittery voice.

Kala fixed a steely gaze on Jay and grinned. "Here's the deal. I'll say, 'Pay my client what I asked, or we're outta here, and I'll hold a press conference within an hour of my leaving.' Do you think that will work?"

"Well, gee whiz, I don't see why not. You're the eight-hundred-pound gorilla in the room. Hell, they might even give you a check *before* you walk out of here. You do know you're all wrinkled, right?"

"Linen is supposed to wrinkle. Don't you know anything about women's fashions?"

"No," Jay snapped as he whipped to his feet the moment the door off the reception area opened. He turned to look at Kala, and as always in tense moments, he thought her one of the most beautiful women he'd ever had the pleasure of meeting. She was still as beautiful as she had been the day she'd hired him light-years ago. At that moment, she not only looked beautiful, she looked intimidating as hell. No one was going to push this lady around. No one.

All the men seated at the conference table, and there were a lot of them, rose when Kala and Jay entered the room. The lone woman remained seated. No one missed the red hibiscus flower in Kala's ear. Early on in her career, Kala had given numerous interviews and said that wearing the flower meant she was a female warrior and ready to go into battle. Red was for going into battle, and white was for victory. Of course, she had made that up out of whole cloth, but no one but she and

Jay knew it was make-believe Hawaiian folklore, fully on a par with the bit about putting a hex on Ryan Spenser. She had a standing order at a local flower shop to supply her with the gorgeous flowers whenever she demanded them. One time she had refused to enter the courtroom until one was delivered to her out in the court hallway. The flower shop's delivery truck had not been on time that particular day. She'd made headlines that day and switched to a white hibiscus when the jury came back with their verdict.

The amenities over, coffee poured, pens in hand, mostly Montblanc, the informal meeting was ready to get under way. Nothing chintzy about this group, Kala thought. When no one made an effort to be first to speak, Kala decided to take the bull by the horns. First, though, she fiddled with the flower in her ear for just a few moments. When she was satisfied the flower was secure, Kala leaned forward, arms crossed on the table. Just another folksy meeting. Not.

"This is the second meeting you've called with my firm, and yes, I am once again a member of the firm before you can ask. Let's get right to it. You have our numbers. You all know what has been going on. My client is demanding restitution, and she will not budge on the numbers. So that leaves us where we were at your last meeting with my associate, Mr. Brighton, who is sitting beside me right now. I'm not here to dicker, to negotiate, or to play games, and I have absolutely no desire to play nice. Time is money, people. Maybe all of you on the taxpayer dole can waste your time, but I go by billable hours as do all lawyers."

Kala held up her hand. "One person here at this table speak to me. Give me your position right now and don't tell me you don't have a position. Don't go the route the state has no money. If you don't have it, *find it.* I'm not interested in hearing any of that. The clock is ticking, people." Kala leaned back in her chair. Her slender fingers caressed the flower in her hair.

Someone cleared his throat. Feet shuffled under the polished conference table. Eyes flinty and steely glared at Kala and her partner from around the table.

A lone voice that sounded like it was a mixture of molasses and grit finally spoke. "We have no other choice but to agree to your terms. We want a protective order on this. We're giving in to your demands with four payments over two years. It's the best we can do. The first payment of five million by ten o'clock tomorrow morning followed by the second payment on December thirty-first. The same payment schedule for next year."

Kala fiddled with the scarlet flower in her hair before she slid her chair back and rose to her feet. "Nice try! Two payments, the first payable now, the second payment due December thirty-first. Of this year. Divide ten and one-half years into the total payment, then tell me if any one of you sitting at this table would spend those years in prison for any amount of money. Just one of you." Kala looked at first one face, then another, finally coming to rest on Ryan Spenser. "What, all of a sudden you're clams? Tomorrow morning, my office, check in hand. And have Mr. Spenser deliver it. There is nothing else to negotiate, so my partner and I will see ourselves out."

Kala reached up and plucked the brilliant-colored hibiscus from her hair. She walked around the table and dropped it in front of Ryan Spenser. She leaned over and whispered loud enough for the others at the table to hear her. "And I haven't even started with you yet."

Outside in the reception area, Jay clapped Kala on the back. "Nice going in there. Do you really think Spenser will show tomorrow with check in hand?"

"Oh yeahhhh," Kala drawled. "He might even have a bell around his neck to announce his arrival." They both laughed all the way down in the elevator. They were still chuckling when they walked into the office at ten-thirty.

At eleven-thirty, retired Judge Ben Jefferson called Kala on the phone to tell her that Ryan Spenser had filed a suit against her, accusing her of stealing evidence from the evidence locker in the Sophie Lee trial.

"He had also conned some judge into signing a search warrant to search your house and your offices, one of those young squirts I was telling you about back in Paris. Not to worry, my dear, I still have a few loyal friends at the courthouse. And remember, I'm still a lawyer; I filed a motion to quash it on your behalf. You can take it from there."

"Oh, Ben, thank you. Don't you want to know how it went at the meeting?"

"Only if you tell me you lost, which I assume you didn't; otherwise, Spenser wouldn't have asked for a search warrant and filed the suit. Are you going to call a press conference? Congratulations!"

"Nah. I don't want to come across as cocky just yet. You wanna take me to dinner to celebrate? Oh, one other thing, Ben. If you have time today, stop by the post office to pick up my mail. Drop it off at my house, and I'll go through it tonight. There's probably going to be a lot since I stopped the mail the day of my retirement party. Take a big box with you."

"No problem. I have to pick up my own. Anything else you need me to do?"

"I think that'll do it. Thanks, Ben."

"For you, Kala, anything." Kala knew he meant it. She smiled at how easy their relationship was, had always been.

"Remember now, you promised to wear a white hibiscus in your hair."

"You got it." Kala giggled like a schoolgirl.

Kala returned to the business at hand after ending the phone call. "Does anyone know where Patty is?"

Linda poked her head out of her doorway, and said, "She told me she was going to check on Nick and would be back in an hour. You can reach her on her cell if you need her right away."

"No, that's okay. I can wait till she gets back."

Kala walked back to the kitchen and poured herself an ice-cold glass of pineapple juice. She sat down at the old table and ran the morning's activities over in her mind. She wanted to call Sophie to tell her they were almost to the home stretch and that, as of tomorrow, she would be $10 million richer, but thought better of the idea. Better to call Sophie when she had the check in hand. She finished her juice and returned to her office, calling out to Linda to send Patty to her office when she got back.

In her office, Kala flopped down and started to drum her fingers on the desk. She needed a game plan. She'd run with the moment. Ben said that was one of her major faults. Not that he was criticizing her, because when she did that, the outcome was usually positive. There was a lot to be said for confidence, and she certainly had plenty of that. Her heart kicked up a beat when she closed her eyes, envisioning Ryan Spenser handing her a check for $10 million.

Kala's thoughts turned black when she contemplated the warrant and the suit Ben had told her about. Her mind raced back in time to the day she'd gone with Patty to the precinct to retrieve Sophie's personal possessions. If she remembered correctly, it was three days after the sentencing that sent Sophie to prison for life without the possibility of parole. She and Patty had had a good cry before they entered the precinct's doors. She'd signed her name on the log sheet and left Patty to wait for Sophie's things because she had to be in court to file a motion for something or other. She'd talked to Patty later in the day to ask how it went. If memory served her right, Patty said she'd taken the box home and hadn't even opened it. She said she just couldn't look at Sophie's things, and that was the same day Nick and his friends had moved her out of the apartment she and Sophie had shared.

Kala wondered if Patty had ever looked at Sophie's belongings. More to the point, where were they? Was it possible the officer on duty had given Patty the things that were in the evidence locker along with Sophie's personal belongings by mistake? Anything was possible, she decided. She squeezed her eyes shut, trying to remember if she'd seen the list of items that had been tagged. She simply couldn't remember, but more than likely no, she had not seen the list, she decided. To the best of her recollection, there had not been much in the way of personal possessions left behind at the Star mansion when Sophie was arrested. A few clothes, her cell phone, her purse and whatever she carried in it, lipstick, tissues, keys, her ancient laptop, toiletries, that sort of thing. She had a vague memory of Patty saying at some point, though, that Sophie's laptop was at the apartment. If that was the case, then the detectives had probably taken it from the apartment. Was it in the personal possession box or the evidence box? She simply could not remember.

Patty had said that on her days off, Sophie always returned to the apartment she shared with Patty. She did her laundry and would return to the mansion with a small duffel to last her until her next day off. Spenser had not made an issue at trial over any of those things; nor had she when she filed her various appeals after sentencing. So what was the big deal?

Kala knew what the big deal was. Spenser was saying—no, *accusing* her of taking stuff out of the evidence locker, things he *had* used at trial. If somehow the officer on duty had mistakenly turned over evidence to Patty, who didn't realize what she had all these years, then yes, this was going to be a problem. Even though Ben filed a motion to quash both the warrant and the complaint, a judge would have to hold a hearing. That was going to take a bit of time, at least a week, possibly longer. She knew how to stall when she had to stall. Just like all lawyers knew the drill. Buying time for your client was what it was called.

Kala's fingers continued to drum on the desk. She looked up when Linda appeared with a fresh cup of coffee. Hawaiian

Aulani coffee, the only kind she drank. It smelled heavenly. And it tasted pretty damn good, too.

"Patty called, she's on her way. She said Nick is being ornery and cantankerous. Actually she said he's being a pain in the ass. He wants to do things he can't do, and he's taking his irritation out on everyone. Just so you know. By the way, Kala, in all the confusion of your unexpected return, I didn't properly thank you for that exquisite French perfume you brought back for me. Jay loves it."

Kala smiled. She loved buying presents for people, especially people she loved.

"I'm getting married," she blurted.

Linda blinked, then blinked again. "That . . . that's great, Kala. When?"

"When this mess is all over. I'm retiring to Hawaii. Ben is going with me. The truth is, I asked him to marry me, and he said yes. It . . . it was one of those serendipitous moments, if you know what I mean. It's going to be a traditional wedding. A luau, and I'm going to wear the traditional garb and do the hula in a grass skirt. The bride has to make the skirt and top herself out of leaves and . . . and stuff. A crown of flowers, too. Do you think I'm too old for all of this?"

"Hell no! Why would you even say such a thing?"

"Well, because of my culture. You absolutely cannot live in sin, so I have to get married. Ben is okay with it, but he said he is not going to wear a loincloth—that's part of the tradition. Of course you are all invited. The whole office. We can charter a plane or something."

Linda laughed until tears rolled down her cheeks. "Is this a secret, or can I tell everyone?"

Kala rolled the question around in her head. The more people who knew would be good because . . . because then she wouldn't change her mind. If no one knew, she could say she had a senior moment and hadn't known what she was doing when she had proposed to Ben. "Tell everyone," she said in a strangled voice.

So it was official. She was getting married.

Kala's mind started to wander as she stared out the window. Life in Hawaii with Ben. Slow and easy. Family, all the little nieces and nephews to see, long walks on the beach. She would have all the time in the world to do . . . nothing. Maybe, maybe, she could open up a storefront law office and work when she wanted to. Everything would be pro bono. Years and years ago, she couldn't remember how many, she'd taken the bar in Hawaii and had a license to practice there. She'd renewed the license faithfully every single year. In fact, she'd just paid to renew it in the early spring. Maybe Ben would be interested in joining her fledgling little firm.

Kala thought about her homeland. Warm golden sun almost every day of the year, gentle breezes, the sparkling blue Pacific, finer in color than any sapphire, the scent of plumeria, which she dearly loved, everywhere. All the doors and windows in her house would be open all day and into the evening. The sheer curtains would billow inward, carrying the rich scent of the flowers indoors. Paddle fans would whirl quietly. What was not to love about that scenario? Absolutely nothing. She had enough money banked that she'd earned on her own that she never needed to worry about a thing. She had no bills, and she was certainly more than solvent, as was Ben. She wasn't even counting the monies that went into her brokerage account from the family coffee business. Time to give back. She could do that. She corrected the thought. She *would* do that.

That thought took her down a different road. What was going to happen to Sophie Lee when this was all over? How would she spend all her money? Would she ever recover from those ten years in prison? Sophie would have Patty and Nick. Her heart told her somehow, some way, Sophie was going to end up with Nick, and Nick would make her world right again. With Nick and Patty at her side, Sophie would take her place in the world again, Kala was sure of it. And taking her place in the world had nothing to do with money. "And that,"

Kala muttered aloud, "you can take to the bank. Sophie Lee is not about money, never was, never would be."

Kala looked up to see Patty standing in the doorway. She smiled. "I was . . ."

"Woolgathering?" Patty smiled in return.

Kala nodded. "In a manner of speaking. We need to talk, Patty. Come in, take a load off. First, though, how's Nick?"

"Welcome home, Kala. It's nice to see you sitting at your desk again. Nick is cranky. You know men. He has some pain but refuses to take any pain meds. He's going to tough it out. He tries to do more therapy than the doctors want, hoping that will speed up the healing process. Men can be stupid sometimes. That's the good news. The bad news is his other hip is not good. He says his career is over if he has to have his other hip done. That's not quite true, he actually said that his career is over *now.* He's angry with his doctors, and he has a slew of them. None of them will commit to anything, so, of course, like any other stubborn guy, he's thinking the worst.

"Between you and me, I think his days as a professional golfer are over. He'll be able to play recreational golf, but no more grueling ten-hour practices, and no more tournaments. There go all his endorsements, but he isn't even worried about that. All he keeps saying is he's washed up at the age of thirty-four.

"One good thing is he has no money worries. He's made some wonderful investments, and he's always been frugal. They taught us that at the orphanage. He has those two golden retrievers that are at his side night and day. They're good for him. He walks them religiously, and that'll keep him active. He's going to be fine physically. It's just going to take some time. All he really wanted to talk about was Sophie. I couldn't tell him anything positive one way or the other. I did share what we have and what we hope to do. That seemed to please him, but he wants it quicker and faster. What can I tell you, Kala, he's a guy."

Kala smiled. "Enough said. I want you to think back to the day you and I went to the precinct to pick up Sophie's belongings after her sentencing. Do you remember that day?"

Patty squeezed her eyes shut to ward off the burning in them. "I remember," she said softly. "Why are you asking?"

Kala explained about Spenser's lawsuit and the search warrant. Then she told her about the check that was supposed to arrive via Spenser's hand tomorrow at ten. "Tell me what you remember about that day."

"I met you there because you had to go to court that morning to file something, and you were going to be cutting it close by going with me. We went to this . . . it looked like a dungeon to me at the time, and you signed off for Sophie's personal effects. You explained to the cop on duty that she was to give me the stuff as you had to head to court. The officer said okay. You left, she went to get it, and came back with a box. She opened the door of the cage where she was sitting, handed me the box. She asked if I wanted to look at it, and I said no. I never did look at it, Kala. Was I supposed to? Is something missing? Sophie didn't have a whole bunch of stuff, you know. She was even more frugal than Nick. She only had a few changes of clothes with her at the Stars' and would come back to the apartment on her days off, do her laundry, catch up with me, then head back. Now that we're talking about it, I do remember thinking the box was kind of heavy, but I wasn't in any frame of mind that day to want to . . . you know, look at her things. I just couldn't cry anymore."

Kala nodded. "I understand. Where is that box now?"

"You know what, Kala? I don't know. I don't mean that it's lost or anything like that. Nick and his friends moved me out of Sophie's and my apartment that very same day. They put me into an investment house Nick had just purchased, and I bought it from him. He holds the mortgage on it. You've seen it, it's small. Not a lot of storage, normal closets, no basement. But to answer your question, it's either in my garage or at Nick's. He took the overflow to his house because it's bigger, and he has a three-car garage. By overflow I mean all my research from the paper. I had like fifty boxes of stuff."

Kala nodded again, and said, "We need to find that box and go through it."

"Well, there's no time like the present. Let's go and give Nick a thrill, two visits in one day. I say we make him give us lunch, too. It will give him something to do. I'll call him and tell him we're on our way."

"Now, that sounds like a plan," Kala said happily as she got up to follow Patty out of the office. She called out hers and Patty's plan to anyone listening.

Kala rather thought they were on a roll.

Chapter 18

RYAN SPENSER TOOK ONE LAST LOOK AT HIS REFLECTION IN THE mirror of the men's room. Time to beard the lion. Such a cliché, but of late his life seemed to be one huge cliché. Once he had been the media's darling. Today he was *The Devil.* Right or wrong, he knew that his goose was cooked. There was no way he could recover politically from the slaughter he was going through. Another cliché. If his father had his way, he'd fry his ass. Was that a cliché? He didn't know or care.

No way was he going to walk away from any of this. No way in hell. Well, goddamn it, his conscience was clear. He had presented what he had to a jury and a judge. He turned the ball over to them. And now here he was as *The Devil.* He stared hard at his reflection. He'd lost weight, his summer tan was fading. He almost looked ghostly. His Armani suit hung on his big frame. A month ago, he'd looked smashing and debonair in the seven-thousand-dollar suit. A real Renaissance prince to be sure.

Spenser slammed his way through the door. His feet picked up speed as he strode down the marble hall to the EXIT sign, where reporters were waiting for him. He knew they were out there—they'd been dogging him for two weeks. No reason to think they wouldn't be there again. Look like a winner, and you are a winner—his father's favorite bit of advice. Look like a loser, and you are a loser. "Bullshit," he muttered under his breath.

He was on the courthouse steps in the bright sunshine. He wished he'd thought to keep his sunglasses out, but they were in his briefcase. The aviator shades, in his opinion, made him look like movie-star material. If he was guilty of anything, it was of being vain. And he looked like a washed-up movie star.

There were just four reporters trailing him. More proof that he was a has-been. Right then, right that very second, he thought he would sell his soul to the devil if he would magically be given a smoking gun. He felt sick to his stomach as he stood tall and waited for the onslaught of questions. All of which he would respond to with, "No comment at this time."

The four reporters shouted their questions, talking over each other.

"Is Sophie Lee going to get the payoff she deserves?"

"How do you feel about that payoff? Do you feel guilty?"

"What's your feeling on Kala Aulani these days?"

"You still going to try to run for governor?"

"Where is Sophie Lee?"

"Do you have any proof Kala Aulani stole evidence from the evidence locker?"

"Did you lose weight, Mr. Spenser? Is that Armani you're wearing?"

"What's the Speaker of the House saying about all this?" Then, as an afterthought, "What is your uncle the governor saying?"

The questions kept coming. Spenser felt sick to his stomach. He tried for a smile, but it was sickly at best. "I'll have a statement shortly. You know I can't comment on an ongoing situation like this. Now, if you'll excuse me, I'm already running late."

"Where are you going, Mr. Spenser?"

He wanted to say, "Home to lick my wounds," but he clamped his lips shut. They'd all know soon enough where he was going because they'd follow him.

"I'm going home because it's the only place I can work uninterrupted. I owe the taxpayers my time, and I can't fulfill my obligations if I'm constantly interrupted. Please, show some respect, okay?"

Finally, finally, he was in his car, a Mercedes 560 SEL convertible. It was blistering hot inside the small car, so he removed his designer jacket, jerked at his tie, then rolled up his shirtsleeves. Hot air blasted from the AC unit. Within seconds, he was drenched in his own sweat. He longed for a drink and a cigarette. He never smoked in public, but he did at home. And then he sucked on mints. Ten minutes and he'd be home and he could indulge himself. Just ten more minutes.

It wasn't ten minutes but seventeen minutes because somehow he managed to hit every red light on the way home. He roared his way down the ramp, waited impatiently for the guardrail to rise, then raced up to the fourth level of the garage. He hopped out of the car, grabbed his jacket and bulging briefcase, and headed for the private elevator that would take him straight up to his penthouse apartment.

He always enjoyed coming home to his apartment. He loved it there, with the panoramic view of a town he loved, the town he'd sworn to protect as an officer of the court. And now that same town was out to skin him alive for doing his damn job. Where the hell was the loyalty? Where was the goodwill? Not liking his thoughts, Spenser walked around his spacious apartment, his eyes half seeing the furnishings, the other half somewhere else.

He never told anyone, but he had decorated the place himself. Everything was stark, black and white. Because that was the way he thought, either something was black or it was white. Either there was proof or there was no proof. End of story. Period. Chrome and glass with colored Jackson Pollock prints on the walls that added color. He always had fresh flowers delivered every other day. He liked flowers for some reason. He looked around; the place looked like a war zone in

Beirut, with papers and files and folders everywhere. He'd given Yolanda, his housekeeper, a six-week paid vacation to visit her family in Guatemala to get her out from under his feet. Besides, he liked to reward loyalty, and Yolanda had been with him from day one. She'd certainly have her work cut out on her return. Which, in turn, would require an extra bonus.

Spenser stomped his way into his bedroom. He eyed the messy bed, the clothes he'd dropped wherever they fell. He wasn't a slob by any means, but, over the past weeks, all desire for neatness had vanished. His bed linens needed to be changed, he needed clean towels, and he needed to do his laundry and hit the dry cleaners. Maybe he could call them, and they'd pick up his things. Well, he knew how to clean and make beds. It was the first thing that had been drilled into him at boarding school. Just because he knew how to do it didn't mean he liked doing it.

Spenser shed his clothes, donned a pair of creased shorts and a snappy white T-shirt that said he loved Atlanta. Which he did. An hour later, his bed had fresh linens with hospital corners, his towels were in the washer, his dry cleaning sat in a bag by the front door. He forgot his desire for a drink and made coffee. While he waited for it to drip into the built-in coffeemaker, he eyed Yolanda's favorite kitchen tool: a Crock-Pot. He needed to eat some nourishing food, and there was no way in hell he was going to go out to a restaurant, where people would gawk at him and whisper all kinds of things about him out of earshot. He opened the freezer, took stock of his food supply, and yanked at several different packages. He unwrapped everything and dumped it into the Crock-Pot, along with some chicken broth, some seasonings, then put the cover on it. Done.

Spenser wondered if his father had ever eaten anything out of a Crock-Pot. Unlikely. His father had a gourmet palate, unlike his own. Thanks again to summer camps and boarding school. He'd grown up on mac and cheese, stews, spaghetti, and anything that could be cooked in one pot. And he liked it. The only thing he and his father had in common was their appreciation for fine wine. He realized in that moment that he really didn't like his father very much. Hell, he didn't like him at all. He didn't much care for his socialite mother, either. How could he? He had never been around them long enough to form any kind of attachment when he was a child.

The coffeemaker made one last cheerful gurgle, then went silent. Spenser peeled a banana and forced himself to eat it before he poured and carried his coffee into the living room. He brushed aside papers, set the cup down, and let his mind race. He needed to come to terms with what was staring him in the face, and he needed to do it *now.*

Spenser let his mind go back ten years in time. The police had called his office the moment they realized Audrey Star was dead. His office was always the first notified when a high-profile case came into being. He had dropped everything and raced to the Star mansion. He knew within seconds that this was the one big case that could make or break him. The media were everywhere, twenty-four/seven. He'd lost count of the interviews he'd given, always careful to speak the truth and to stay inside the letter of the law.

Spenser remembered his first thought when he entered the death room and saw the pretty little nurse, the dead woman who wasn't so pretty in death, and the handsome husband. Triangle. Money. The husband was going to inherit the Star fortune. Sadly, to his dismay, he soon found out that wasn't the case since Star had already had the fortune, and it had been turned over to him long before the wife had her tragic accident. It was still a triangle. A love triangle. Pretty young nurse with stars in her eyes, a handsome man, and an invalid wife. Anyone with half a brain would have thought the same way he did at the time. He'd burned the midnight oil, getting by on as little as two hours' sleep a night in his quest to get to the truth.

The pretty little nurse had a squeaky-clean background.

Orphan, friends in the city, put herself through nursing school, sterling affidavits from friends and teachers, glowing testimonials from those do-gooder nuns at St. Gabriel's. It wasn't computing.

He'd interviewed Adam Star personally at least a dozen times before the trial. He was adamant that there was nothing going on between the nurse and himself. Spenser actually believed him. He tried another tack: Sophie Lee was enamored of her boss, a secret love crush. Star had scoffed at that. Sophie Lee, he said, had always been professional. He'd gone on to say he never understood why she'd stayed on because his wife was so verbally abusive. Until Sophie came, they hadn't been able to keep a nurse more than a week. Star had said he actually asked her why she stayed, and her response had been, "Your wife needs me. She needs a constant. They're just words, Mr. Star, and they're a result of her medications and being an invalid with no hope of recovery." Star had gone on to say, because of her dedication, he always gave her a bonus in her paycheck to show his appreciation. She always thanked him and said it wasn't necessary. Star said no one, and that included Spenser, could ever convince him that Sophie Lee had killed his wife.

"Well then, Mr. Star," Spenser had said, "that just leaves you as the guilty party."

"Prove it," had been Star's challenge. He lawyered up with eight-hundred-dollar-an-hour lawyers; not one, not two, not three, but four of them. Within hours of Audrey Star's death, he had the mayor, the chief of police, and everyone else with a title in the state of Georgia covering his back. Star was right, there was no hard proof, not so much as a shred. So, Spenser concentrated on Sophie Lee and his theory of a secret, unrequited, one-sided love affair. It was weak, and he knew it, but he ran with it anyway because he had nothing else to go on. There was a dead woman who demanded justice be served, and he had to serve Audrey Star.

The medical laptop computer that belonged to Dr. Hershey Franklin had yielded nothing. On his daily visits to check on his patient, Dr. Franklin had typed in his orders, and Sophie Lee initialed them. She recorded everything on the computer every fifteen minutes, even Audrey Star's abusive comments. Kala Aulani had argued to the court that those entries were all the proof a jury needed to show that Sophie Lee was a dedicated nurse.

Sophie Lee had arrived with her own outdated, beat-up, secondhand laptop, Adam Star had said. But when she realized she didn't need it, she'd taken it back to her apartment. He'd confiscated that, too, but there was nothing on it to incriminate Sophie Lee. Then he had decided maybe it was a conspiracy between the doctor, Star, and the nurse. Well, that had been a shitstorm to equal no other. Franklin's lawyers had come on like bulldozers and he had to back off that theory and actually offer an apology to the doctor. That left him with Sophie Lee and his unrequited-love theory. Audrey Star was dead, and if her husband didn't kill her, that left only Sophie Lee. All he had to do was convince a jury of Sophie Lee's peers that she was guilty. And he had successfully done that.

Had Sophie Lee killed Audrey Star? In his heart of hearts, he didn't think so. What he personally thought did not count in a court of law. Spenser thought Adam Star had killed his wife. He just couldn't prove it. He had hoped, in the dark and silence of this very apartment, late at night, that Adam Star would own up to what he had done at some point. But he never had, so he gave the case everything he had, and Sophie Lee was convicted.

Okay, that was his side of things. Spenser finished his coffee, trotted out to the kitchen for a refill, and brought it back. He rummaged until he found Kala Aulani's opening statement. He read it, reread it, then read it a third time. What jumped out at him were the words: Audrey Star had kept a journal. He'd grilled Adam Star about the journal—Star had referred to it in old-fashioned girly terms as a diary. On the stand, Star had said his wife kept a diary long before he had ever met her, and that she continued to write in her diary during the good years of their marriage, and as far as he knew she hadn't done it since the accident. Then he had corrected himself and said maybe she had kept one, but if she did, he didn't know where it was, and no, he had never felt the need to pry into his wife's secret thoughts. In her deposition, Sophie Lee said there was such a diary but she referred to it as a journal and that Audrey wrote in it on her "good days." She said Audrey kept the journal either under her pillow or in the drawer of the night table that she could reach by the side of her hospital bed. She said also in her deposition that Audrey used to clip articles or things of interest out of magazines, again, on her "good days," and kept them in the back of her journal or would tape them to pages in her journal.

Spenser's instincts back then had been on the money, but the suits who charged $800 an hour had successfully gotten Star out of it, leaving only Sophie to prosecute. The son of a bitch had never confessed until he himself was dying. He wondered how those eight-hundred-dollar-an-hour suits were sleeping these days. No better than he was, he hoped.

A warrant to search the Star mansion and Sophie Lee's apartment did not turn up a journal, a diary, or even a notebook. At trial he had hammered home the point that only Sophie Lee had direct knowledge of the journal and that she had gotten rid of it before the fateful day she'd decided to kill her patient. On the stand, Adam Star had openly scoffed at that suggestion, and for his point of view, he had been declared a hostile witness.

So where in the damn hell was the journal? Sophie Lee had been adamant about there being one. Adam Star, hostile witness or not, had backed up the fact that his wife had indeed kept a journal, though he thought she only wrote in it on her good days. Previous nurses who hadn't wanted to get involved in a messy murder trial had selective memories. A few nurses said they thought Mrs. Star wrote in something from time to time, others said absolutely not, the patient just watched television.

Spenser realized his career was over regardless of what he did from that point on. He had cut corners, but always in the interest of justice. He did what he had to do. To the best of his knowledge, he had not broken a single law. All those other cases he'd prosecuted were now going to come back and haunt him. The lawyers would nitpick every little goddamn thing they could. The cases would be tied up in the courts for years and would probably never end. Unless he could find the damn journal. If he couldn't find it ten years ago, how was he going to find it now?

He wasn't. That was the bottom line. As much as he wanted to believe Kala Aulani had it, he knew she didn't. If Sophie Lee had it, she would have turned it over to her attorney. That just left Adam Star. And Adam Star or Adam Clements, whatever the hell his name ended up being, was now dead. Unless Spenser could find a direct line to hell, he was never going to locate the journal.

Spenser sniffed the aromas wafting out of the kitchen. He hoped the mess in the Crock-Pot turned out to be as good as it smelled. He forced his thoughts back to the matter at hand. And that's when he had his *epiphany*. Did he have the guts to act on it?

Spenser leaned his head back and closed his eyes and thought about Sophie Lee. Maybe, just maybe, he could salvage this whole disaster.

Sophie Lee walked on the beach with Sula at her side. She felt better than she'd ever felt in her whole life. Kala had called and said the state of Georgia was going to meet Kala's demands. She was going to have so much money she wouldn't know what to do with it. They were wrong. She knew exactly what she was going to do with it, and with the Star fortune, too.

She absolutely loved it in Hawaii. As each day wound down, she thought more and more about making the island her home. If she needed a stateside fix, she could always head for the mainland.

Sophie was tanned and toned, the muscles in her legs and thighs like steel with all the sand walking she'd done these past weeks, ten miles in the morning, ten miles at night. She had developed superior upper body strength, what with all the swimming she'd been doing. The swimming pleased her more than anything. She'd conquered her fear of the water, thanks to Sula, who swam with her every day as she perfected her breaststroke. If ever there was a time to take on the world and Ryan Spenser, this was the time. But did she really want all that upheaval in her life? She simply didn't know.

But did she really want to let it all go? Wasn't that why she had a lawyer? You couldn't unring the bell, everyone knew that. Whatever, if anything, was going to happen to Ryan Spenser would happen regardless of what she and Kala would decide to do. In the end, Kala could take care of all that. All she wanted now was to get on with her life. More to the point, make a new life for herself. If she elected to live in the past, she'd never move forward. All that was important to her these days was that the people she loved and cared about the most finally had hard and fast evidence that she hadn't murdered her patient. *That,* she had decided, was enough for her to start to lay the groundwork to begin a new life. She could do that, too. She was mentally and physically strong and getting more so with each passing day.

The only thing that remained to plague her was Audrey Star's missing journal. Adam Star must have taken it and hidden it somewhere. She realized they would probably never know what had happened to it. It was strange, though, that Adam had not mentioned it in his deathbed confession. Was it that unimportant, or was it too important to talk about? The point was moot now, she assumed, with both Audrey and Adam dead.

The sun was starting to go down, so Sophie turned and headed back to the house where she was living. She was tired, but it was a good kind of tired. In her whole life, she had never gotten this much fresh air or exercise. She poured herself a big glass of pineapple-mango juice and got a chew bone for Sula before she headed to the lanai, where she collapsed onto a flower-patterned lounge chair. Sula hopped up next to her and curled up in the bend of her knees.

Sophie clicked on the remote, and the news came on. She watched it, paying attention to what was going on locally. Then the newscaster switched to the national news, and she watched Ryan Spenser outside the courthouse. He looks terrible, she thought.

There was something different about him, though. Was she mistaken, or was the man being humble? She was mistaken; Spenser didn't know the meaning of humble. Or did he? Only time would tell.

Sophie had no idea how close to the truth she was or how soon everything would be resolved, one way or the other.

Chapter 19

"THIS IS REALLY A SNAPPY LITTLE CAR, PATTY," KALA SAID, GETting out of the two-seater and smoothing down her skirt. "I like it."

"I like that it's affordable. Nick got it for me. I don't mean he paid for it—I'm paying for it—but he got me a rock-bottom price on the deal because of his endorsement for Ford. Gets great mileage. I just love red. I feel important for some reason. I never ever thought I'd be driving a racy convertible. Guys really look at you when you drive a convertible, did you know that?" Patty grinned.

"What does Jed think about that?" Kala asked.

"Jed's cool with it. He's cool with everything. That's why we get on so well. He's a great lawyer, Kala. He cares about his clients. He really does."

"I know that. Why else do you think I hired him? He does more pro bono work than any other lawyer in this town. You know," Kala said, looking around, "I've never been here to Nick's house. I don't know why, but I thought, considering his golfing status and all that, that he would live in some fancy gated community."

Patty laughed. "That's what everyone says. He's no snob. He is who he is, and, guess what? He mows his own grass, too. Last year he painted the house. Jed and I helped him. You could do Nick the biggest favor in the world if you'd tell him where Sophie is so he could call her. He's in love with Sophie—you do know that, right? Always has been, from the time we were little kids. I think Jon was in love with Sophie, too."

"I know. I will tell him, but just not yet. Sophie is still in a fragile state. I don't want anything to go awry. He can handle a few more days of not knowing. You said something about lunch, right? I hate to admit it, but I'm starving. Nick won't give us yogurt, will he?"

"No. But I think lunch will probably be a bit of a surprise. We didn't give him all that much notice. And he's also a tad upset with you because you won't tell him where Sophie is. Just so you know.

"Come on, let's walk around the back. He likes to eat out on his patio. Nick is an outside kind of guy." Patty shouted a greeting as she turned the corner at the end of the house. "We're here!"

Two magnificent golden retrievers bounded over to Kala and Patty, then skidded to a stop. Both held up their paws to be shaken. "Kala, meet Jam and Jelly. Girls, this is Kala." The dogs sniffed Kala's shoes; then, satisfied that she was a friend, they trotted over to their master, who held out his hand to Kala.

"Nice to see you again, Kala. Where the hell is Sophie?" he barked.

"Safe," Kala barked in return. "Now that we've settled that question, what's for lunch?"

Nick, all six feet four inches of him, stared at Kala to see if she'd say anything else. "Okay, as long as she's safe. As to what's for lunch, help yourself," he said, as he gingerly lowered himself to a padded chair."

"Oooh, this looks good," Patty said as she popped covers from the bowls on the table. "Ah, the famous Mancuso salmon salad straight off the grill, garden salad, fresh from your garden over there at the back of the yard, warm rolls that you did not make from scratch, and the leftover rice pudding complete with raisins that you made last night. Homemade sun tea. A feast, Nicky. Served on fine plastic plates that are disposable." Patty giggled. In spite of himself, Nick laughed heartily.

Kala loved the sound of Nick's laughter. It reminded her of Ben.

"Nick has a rule," Patty said as she loaded up her plate. "We can't talk about why we're here while we eat. Bad for the digestion, he says. We can talk about anything else you want to talk about. I'll go first. So, Nick, how are your pole beans doing? Looks like you have a bumper crop of tomatoes this year. When do you have time to do all the weeding and stuff?"

Nick suddenly looked embarrassed. "I got the garden planted, then I couldn't bend down to do all the weeding, so one of the kids down the street comes by a few days a week to do it, and he gets all the vegetables his mom can use. It works for both of us. He's only ten years old, and his name is Jake. The dogs love him."

"You left off the part where you've been giving Jake and his mom and dad golfing lessons. For free!"

"Yeah, that, too," Nick muttered.

"And he's shy, too," Patty needled.

"Free's always good. I like free anything," Kala said, stuffing her mouth. "And this is one of the best lunches I've had in a long time. Thanks for taking the time to make it for us on such short notice."

Always painfully honest, Nick's response came as no surprise. "I only did it hoping you'd tell me where Sophie is."

"I know," Kala said quietly. "I guess we're done eating if we're talking about why we came here. We need to find out where Sophie's belongings are. Patty seems to remember you taking her overflow. If you tell us where to look, we'll do it."

"What exactly are you hoping to find? All the overflow is in the garage. Patty's boxes are clearly marked. I'd offer to help you, but I'm still not allowed to lift anything."

"We're looking for whatever we manage to find, which I'm sure is going to turn out to be nothing, in which case we're getting ourselves worked up over nothing. But we have to cover all our bases," Kala said. "Do we have to clean up?"

"Well, yeah," Nick drawled.

Quicker than lightning, Kala and Patty had the table cleaned and everything back in the kitchen. The only thing remaining on the table was the pitcher of sun tea, a bucket of partially melted ice, and their glasses.

The dogs remained under the shade of the huge umbrella as Nick led the two women through the kitchen and the door leading into the garage.

The garage was as neat and tidy as the rest of Nick's house, at least what Kala could see of it. Unusual for a bachelor. But then she already knew that Nick Mancuso was a "what you see is what you get" kind of guy. No pretentious airs here. She liked that.

It took a good thirty minutes of shifting and stacking and replacing boxes before they found the yellow box Patty had carried out of the precinct ten years ago. She pulled it out to the middle of the third bay and squatted. "You want to open this, Kala?"

She did, and so she squatted alongside Patty. Nick remained standing.

Kala took a deep breath and let it out with a loud *swooshing* sound. "Here goes!"

Nick and Patty watched as Kala removed the items, one at a time. She felt choked up and knew the others felt the same way. It was almost sinful to be touching Sophie's things this way. The clothes she'd had with her at the Star mansion, her plastic bag of toiletries, her purse, the things taken from the apartment. Kala sniffed. "It all smells faintly of lavender."

Patty smiled. "We used to make our own dusting powder.

The nuns showed us how to do it when the flowers bloomed in the spring. Sophie loved the scent, said it was so fresh and clean smelling."

Kala nodded. She found it sad that these two remarkable women, Sophie and Patty, had made their own dusting powder. She thought then about how much money she'd spent on the French perfume for all the girls. She wished now that she hadn't done it. "Okay, here's her laptop. You recognize it, don't you, Patty?"

"Yes, it's Sophie's. What else is in there?"

"Another laptop. It says it is the property of Dr. Hershey Franklin. Okay, what this tells us is, the officer on duty that day gave you, by mistake, the stuff in the evidence locker as well as Sophie's personal effects. I'm sure it was an honest mistake on the officer's part, and one no one would have caught except for the mess we're in now." Kala rocked back on her heels and stared at the contents. There was no smoking gun in the box. Nothing of any importance that could help her, or Ryan Spenser, for that matter.

"Nick, do you have an extra box somewhere to put Sophie's things in? As an officer of the court, I have to return these things to the police precinct."

"No spare boxes, but here's a plastic bag for Sophie's things. You can leave them here until she gets back. She is coming back, isn't she, Kala?"

"That's entirely up to Sophie, Nick. If she elects not to come back to Atlanta, I'm sure she'll welcome you wherever she decides to put down her new roots. I wish I could say differently, Nick, but I can't. Sophie's been to hell and back, we all know that. If I were standing in her shoes, I'd want to put as much distance between me and this place as possible. But, that's me. I'm not Sophie."

Kala was on her feet, and Patty was holding the evidence box. "I guess we should be on our way. Thanks for lunch, Nick," Kala said. "I really enjoyed it."

Kala watched as Patty stood on her tippy toes to hug Nick. She smiled at the way he hugged her back. Kala decided at that moment that there was nothing better in the whole world than true friendship. She smiled all the way out to the car.

Nick waved good-bye. The goldens barked joyously, now that they had their master all to themselves again.

"Tell you what, Kala, I'll drop you off at the office, then swing by the post office to pick up your mail. It's just a few doors down. Do you want me to pick up Ben's mail, too? If so, I'll drop everything off at your house, and tomorrow we can take the box back to the precinct. Does that work for you?"

"Do you mind? Yes, pick up Ben's, too. I'll call him and tell him not to bother. He gets so cranky when he can't find a parking spot."

"Then we have a plan, my friend."

Forty minutes later, Patty Molnar gasped at the huge sack of mail the postal worker dragged to the door. "Do you think you or someone could carry that out to my car? I'm sorry, I had no idea there was so much, or I would have brought someone to help me," she apologized.

"No problem. Anything for a pretty girl on this fine summer day. Gets me outside for ten minutes. Just show me where your vehicle is."

"I got lucky today; it's parked right in front." Patty held the door, then followed the burly man out to her Mustang. Patty just loved her Mustang, particularly the true candy red color. Nick drove an identical car, but his was black. She had the top down now and loved driving with the wind in her hair and face.

"You wait right here, miss, and I'll be right back with the other bag."

"What other bag?" Patty asked, dumbfounded that one person could get so much mail in three weeks. Kala, Patty decided, must be on someone's junk mail list.

"The judge's mail that we've been holding. He called earlier and asked to have it ready along with Miss Aulani's mail. He just has a quarter of what's in this bag," the postal worker added, pointing to the canvas sack in the Mustang's trunk. "You have to return the sacks, in case you didn't know that, or else leave them by your mailbox, and the mailman will pick them up and return them. I'll be back in five minutes, have the judge's mail right by the door. The judge doesn't have a whole lot of patience, so I got it ready soon as he called."

Patty leaned up against the back fender of her little sports car. She looked around at all the normal people—at least they looked normal to her—entering and exiting the post office. None of them looked like they had the problems of the world on their shoulders, which was exactly how she felt right now, this very moment. She almost wished she could turn the clock backward, back before Adam Star had made his confession. But back in time only if Sophie had been released and they had all picked up their lives and moved forward. Well, that wasn't going to happen, so she had to deal with the here and now.

As Patty waited for the postal worker to bring the judge's mail sack, she wondered if tomorrow, when Ryan Spenser showed up with the check for Sophie from the state, she would think or feel differently. She also wondered how much attention the *Atlanta Journal-Constitution* would give the check. Would they downplay it? Such a silly thought—of course they would. Well then, she would just have to make sure the media was up to snuff. She made a mental note to place a few calls the moment she returned to the office.

Patty had been so engrossed in her thoughts that she hadn't even seen the postal worker dump the small canvas bag in her trunk. She offered him a generous tip, but he refused, saying he was just doing his job. He snapped the trunk lid down and gave her a cheery salute before he walked back into the post office.

Even though it was a few miles out of her way, Patty drove to Kala's house, where she backed her car up against the garage and tugged and pulled until she got the canvas bags of mail out of her trunk. The box of Sophie's belongings was set down next to the sacks of mail. It was a good neighborhood, and there were NEIGHBORHOOD WATCH signs all along the streets, which meant that the neighbors kept a sharp eye out for vandalism. She called Kala to tell her what she had done and to let her know she was headed back to the office.

Patty made good use of her time as she drove back to the office. Why wait to do something if it could be done *now*? At the first red light she came to, she yanked out her cell phone and called her friend at Fox News.

"You didn't get this from me, okay? I don't want anyone knowing I'm your source." She prattled on, pleased with herself that her friend would get a jump on everyone else. With a promise that her news would be at the top of the hour, starting at 5 P.M., Patty broke the connection. Should she or shouldn't she call CNN? In the end, she decided not to make the call even though her contact at CNN was as much a friend as the reporter at Fox. Better to stay loyal to Fox News. Fox had been the only network that had stood by her when the *AJC* fired her. And that, she knew, was because of her friend. Loyalty demanded loyalty.

Chapter 20

KALA SAT OUTSIDE ON HER TERRACE AND STARED AT THE POTTED plants that were once colorful and lush but were now yellow and brown, with no hint of a bloom anywhere. Well, it was her own fault. She hadn't told the guys who came by to look after Shakespeare to take care of anything else. And they had taken her at her word. She closed her eyes as she thought about her lanai back in Hawaii and how Mally pruned the flowers, sometimes with manicure scissors. She couldn't ever remember a yellow leaf anywhere on any of the plants. Mally simply would not allow it.

The overweight, oversized cat climbed up on her lap and settled himself. He purred contentedly, his own morning symphony. Stroking his thick fur, Kala smiled as she wondered how he would like living in Hawaii.

Even though it was almost time to head for the office, Kala remained fully relaxed. As long as she was there for her ten o'clock appointment with Ryan Spenser, she still had time to sit right where she was. It wasn't too hot yet, but the heat would be unbearable in a few hours. Earlier, she'd heard on the news that it would be in the mid-nineties, with 100 percent humidity. She didn't mind the heat, but she hated the humidity, mainly because her hair frizzed up. Maybe she should think about cutting her tresses, but long hair was a Hawaiian tradition.

Last night, before she'd gone to bed, she called Sophie for their daily check-in, and Sophie had been getting a haircut, courtesy of a cousin, out in the lanai. Sophie had gone on and on about the cousin saving the twelve inches of hair she cut off to donate to cancer patients for wigs. She said she now had golden highlights in her hair, a fashionable cut, which the cousin called a skullcap haircut, meaning Sophie's hair was clipped short so it could curl naturally. "I look smashing, Kala," Sophie had said, giggling. "And you know what else, Kala? I think I could enter a swim contest and have a good showing. I took it as a real compliment when Kiki said I could swim almost as well as he could. His arms are longer than mine, and so are his legs. And when I gave him a lei I made, he said it was as good as the ones Mally made."

"I'm so happy to hear that, Sophie. You've come a long way in a few short weeks. I'm very proud of you. Just a few more days, kiddo, and you can do whatever you want to do. Just be patient, okay?"

"I am. I am." Sophie's voice had turned serious at that point. "I'm not sure I want to leave here. I love it here. Do you think maybe I was meant to come here and stay?"

"Only if you stay for the right reasons. If you're planning on staying to hide out, to feel safe and secure, then, no, that's not a good reason. You have to make your way back into the world you left behind. Slow and easy, honey."

Kala stirred then; the cat hissed and climbed down off her lap. "What? You thought I was going to sit here all day and listen to you purr so I fall asleep? I have things to do and places to go, Shakespeare." And she did have things to do and places to go.

"Now I have cat hair all over me," Kala grumbled as she carried her breakfast dishes into the kitchen, the huge cat behind her. She quickly ran what she called her cat roller over her clothes to remove the cat hair. "I'm good to go, Shaky. You be a good boy till I get back, and do not, I repeat, do not, shred those new curtains. If you do, you are only getting dry cat food from here on in. You need to go on a diet anyway."

The monster cat, not liking his mistress's tone, hissed, his favorite thing to do, and sashayed his way into the living room and his favorite chair, where he would sleep until Kala returned home—unless, of course, the new curtains became irresistible.

Kala looked at the clock. She had plenty of time but only if she hit all the green lights. Well, if she was late, she was sure that Spenser would wait for her. Purse on her shoulder, briefcase in one hand, car keys in the other, Kala entered the garage through the kitchen door. "Oh, crap!" she said, as she saw the sacks of mail and the evidence box waiting for her. She'd have to drive the SUV, which was sitting in the driveway, instead of her little convertible. She gathered up the evidence box Patty had left along with the sacks of mail and dumped the box on the passenger side of the SUV. She closed the door, wincing at the sight of the mail bags. Maybe she'd get to them over the weekend. If not, oh, well. Life wouldn't come to a standstill if she didn't, that was for sure.

Thirty minutes later, hitting the traffic lights just right, Kala parked her SUV and made her way to her offices without seeing even one reporter. As always, the firm was a beehive of activity. She waved to everyone and headed down the hall to her office. She passed Patty, two of her temporary investigators in tow.

"She does look like a powerhouse," one of the two said.

"It's true, then, that she does wear a white hibiscus in her hair," his female counterpart said in awe. "White is for victory, and red means she's going to war. Right, Patty?"

"You got it! Today is a victory day for her and this firm, and especially for Sophie Lee."

Patty wished she'd made that particular meeting for a little later so she could witness Ryan Spenser's arrival. Oh, well, she'd hear about it, she was sure, in glorious detail, from

Linda. She closed the door, sat down, looked at her two novice investigators, and said, "Talk to me."

The blonde, whose name was Beth, said, "You aren't going to like what we have to tell you, but here goes. Bill and I," she said, indicating her partner, "picked Ryan Spenser to investigate. We did Webcam interviews, Skype, and some personal interviews, plus what we were able to pluck off the Internet. We drew up a report, but we can brief you now. Ryan Spenser is as clean and white as the driven snow. That's the bottom line. Now, we'll go backward in time to when he was born."

Bill looked down at his notes. Mother's name Adelina Avery. She was a debutante, never worked a day in her life. Family money came from tobacco. She inherited, along with her brother, a fortune. She married Ryan Spenser Senior at the age of eighteen. Ryan senior's money came from cotton and tea. An excellent merger. Ryan Junior is an only child. Nurses and nannies until he was six. At age six and one half, he was sent to an all boys' school. You know the kind, with a headmaster, et cetera. He came home holidays and summers, and in summers was sent to camp until it was time to go back to school. Holidays were whatever the nurses and nannies could conjure up for him. Parents were usually off somewhere during holidays. Ryan was left to himself. He had no friends at his home base, the Spenser plantation. No cousins to play with. The nanny and staff were all he had in the way of affection and nurturing. His very first nanny is in an assisted-living facility, and while she might be old and frail, her memory is very sharp. The way she summed it up was, the little tyke had a boatload of love and affection and no one to give it to. She said he was an obedient and kind little boy. She said to this day Ryan Spenser sends her birthday and Christmas cards and gifts. And he goes to see her at least twice a year, usually around Mother's Day. And, of course, he always brings a gift. He takes her out to lunch in her wheelchair and they spend a pleasant day. She says she *thinks* he pays for part of her care at the facility but isn't sure. She said she made sure that, when Ryan was home from boarding school, the staff always put Ryan first on their agenda. And, of course, she did the same. As he grew older, nothing changed except that the parents wanted to terminate her employment, but young Ryan would not allow it.

"She also said he called her in the dayroom—that's where the residents can receive phone calls—last week, and told her not to believe anything they were saying about him on television. She said she assured him that she already knew he did none of the things he was being accused of. That's pretty much all she had to say. Her name is Margaret Tynedale, and she allowed young Ryan to call her Mama Margie while he was in her care. He still calls her that to this day. Oh, one other thing. She said she stayed on at the Spenser mansion until young Ryan turned eighteen and went off to college. Then the Spensers retired her with a very nice pension."

Patty digested what she'd just heard. "Doesn't sound like our boy had a very nice childhood."

"She said something else, too," Beth interjected, looking at her notes. "Miss Tynedale said from the time she started working for the Spensers until Ryan turned eighteen, the boy's parents never spent more than twenty-four hours with him during any given year. That's in a *year,* Ms. Molnar."

Bill picked up. "We did a Webcam with a few of his friends, who turned out to be more acquaintances than friends. And all three said Ryan had no close friends—you know, the kind that hang out getting a beer or going to ball games. Always a gentleman, dated but nothing serious. Helped tutor a few students who needed outside help. For free. No one had a bad thing to say about him."

It was Beth's turn again. "The same thing at law school. Graduated second in his class, summa cum laude. No family members attended any of his graduations. I verified that with Miss Tynedale, and she said it was absolutely true, but she said that she and the staff always made sure to send cards and a gift."

Bill shuffled his papers, and said, "When he passed the bar, he applied for a job at the District Attorney's Office, and they snapped him up. His father was already in Washington by then, and his mother was more distant than ever. The father wanted him to set up a white-shoe firm in the District of Columbia and become a force for politicians. Ryan would have none of it; he wanted to live and work in Georgia. His trust fund kicked in when he was twenty-five. He bought himself a penthouse apartment and a sports car, and sent Miss Tynedale on a two-week Caribbean cruise."

It was Beth's turn. "There was never a hint of scandal with Ryan. As far as we could tell, he never made a trip to Washington to see his father. Never. He also, as far as we could tell, never returned to the Spenser mansion, even on holidays. One of his staff said he was a workaholic. He had a few short-lived relationships, nothing serious."

Bill closed one notebook and opened another. "Though most of his staff do not like the guy, they had to admit that he was a hard-ass but fair. Getting praise or a compliment from him was like pulling teeth. He liked to win, and when he lost, he pored over the transcripts for days, trying to figure out what had gone wrong and whether he could correct it in the future. He was vain as hell, liked publicity, and as everyone knows, was good before the camera. Outside the office, he was a very charismatic guy, and the media loved him."

Beth leaned back in her chair. "This is the part you really are not going to like. No one knows it but Miss Tynedale and a few board members of a club he started up. He started a camp for underprivileged children. We checked this out six ways to Sunday, and it's all on the up and up. The camp runs from May till the middle of September. He goes to the camp every weekend unless he's in the middle of a trial. He does his share, helps cook, gives swimming lessons, is a big brother to all the boys. This is the best part, though. The counselors are all older women, motherly and grandmotherly types who tuck the kids in at night, read stories to them, and generally act as mothers and grandmothers away from home. The kids, I was told, eat it up like they are starved for love and affection. One of the groundskeepers said they're going to expand the facility, starting in September, when the camp closes.

"Needless to say, no one had a bad word to say about Ryan Spenser. The thing is, this camp is a secret. We both went back to talk to Miss Tynedale and asked her if she knew about it, and she said yes, but Ryan had sworn her to secrecy. She cried when she said she wished she could have been a grandmother to all those lost little children. She also said Ryan took her out there last year, on Memorial Day, so she could see the first batch of kids. She said she loved every minute of that all-day visit and didn't want to leave. She said Ryan was so good with the kids, had the patience of Job."

"And that's *all* you guys got, just all that *smothery* good stuff?" Patty asked, outraged that nothing bad was in the report.

There was a definite chill in both investigators' voices when they said maybe it was because there wasn't anything bad to find, and Ryan Spenser wasn't the devil he was being made out to be.

They said the words with such conviction, Patty winced, setting her back on her heels. She had to wonder if maybe the investigators were right. She forced a smile on her face, thanked them, and dismissed both of them. "See if the others need any extra help and pitch in if they do. Leave your reports."

The chill stayed behind as the two law students left the office. Patty felt lower than a skunk's belly for a few minutes. She read through the reports, speed-reading natural for her. Then she looked at the clock and realized she had a few minutes until Ryan Spenser was due.

Patty ran down the hall to Kala's office. She slammed

through the doors, and said, "Read all of this before you meet with Spenser, okay? Stall him if you have to but, Kala, you need to read this."

Kala reared back in the chair with its cracked leather. Her eyes narrowed as her fingers went automatically to the white hibiscus in her hair. "I'm not going to like this, am I?"

"No, Kala, you are not going to like it."

Chapter 21

LIKE PATTY, KALA WAS USED TO SPEED-READING. SHE WENT through the investigative report quickly, digesting the gist of it all, then went back and reread what she'd breezed through. If all this was true, and she had no reason to believe it wasn't, Spenser certainly kept his real persona under wraps. She thought about the picture of the two of them in the ornate frame he'd given her for her retirement party. She wished now that she hadn't thrown it away. Maybe it was still in the trash basket. She made a mental note to check on it since she wasn't big on emptying wastepaper baskets.

What to make of this? Spenser had two lives. His personal one and his professional one. Well, most people did. So what? He'd still put Sophie Lee in prison for life without the possibility of parole. That was what *So what?* meant. The wind taken out of her sails for the moment, Kala got up and walked over to the window. There was no stellar view, just the street and a portion of the small parking lot that carried through to the entrance of the underground parking garage.

Kala turned around and looked at the white hibiscus bloom she'd tossed on her desk. She walked over, picked it up, touched the petals, then dropped it in the wastebasket.

Rarely was Kala unsure about anything, but at that moment she didn't quite know what to think, or even feel, for that matter. She looked at her watch and walked back to the window. Spenser was late by five minutes. Maybe he was going to be a no-show. Unlikely, but a possibility. She wondered if she'd missed him until Linda poked her head in the door to say that Mr. Spenser was in the waiting room.

With an edge to her voice, Kala said, "Show him in, Linda."

"He looks different today, Kala. Can't put my finger on it, but he doesn't look . . . I don't know, maybe *cocky* is the word I'm looking for. Hey, what happened to your flower?"

The edge was still in Kala's voice. "Just show him in, okay? Bring us some coffee and sweet rolls if you don't mind. Make the plate look pretty."

"Yes, *ma'am*!" Linda said smartly, not understanding what was going on. Sounded like a party, and everyone was going to make nice.

Kala was still standing by the window and remained there until Linda opened the door to usher Ryan Spenser into the room.

The two attorneys smiled at one another and shook hands. Kala motioned to a cozy seating corner. "I guess we both know why you're here today, Ryan. This might be the mother I'm not in me, but are you okay?"

"No, actually, I'm not okay. Listen, how do you feel about going somewhere with me for a half hour or so? I'd like to buy you a cup of coffee. I want to talk to you about something, but not here." Before Kala could respond, Spenser withdrew a white envelope from inside his jacket pocket. He laid it on the coffee table that separated the two chairs.

Like she was going to go anywhere with Ryan Spenser. "Sure, what do you have in mind?"

"Well, the breakfast rush is over just about everywhere, so how do you feel about two doors down at Logan's? If you don't mind, let's take the back exit."

"Sure, no problem," Kala said as she reached for her purse. "Is this going to be inside or outside?"

"Whatever we can make work for us. I don't want to be swamped with reporters."

"We have a little eating area outside behind the building. Tenants go there to eat their bag lunches or smoke a cigarette. Do you think that would work? The reporters won't know we're there, and before you came, I asked for coffee and pastries to be brought to my office."

"That's fine. Actually, that's the best solution of all."

The EXIT sign was just a short distance from Kala's office. The office boy held the door for Kala and Spenser. "Tell Linda to bring the coffee and pastries outside to the eating area, okay, Bobby?"

"Sure thing, Ms. Aulani."

On the way down the five flights of steps, Kala called comments over her shoulder. "I was never very good at cloak-and-dagger stuff, Ryan. Do you mind telling me what this is all about? I sure hope you aren't going to tell me that check vaporized or something. Or that it's short of what we agreed on."

"I'm not going to tell you that, Kala."

At the bottom of the steps, Spenser looked around at the profusion of colorful flowers and pruned shrubs and the brightly colored picnic tables that were empty at this hour. "It's pretty here. I had no idea this area was even here."

"The tenants are responsible for maintaining it. We take turns on a monthly basis. I like to come out here late in the afternoon and just sit with a cold glass of ice tea."

Bobby, the office boy, was right on their heels with a heavy tray. He placed it in the center of the bright yellow picnic table. Kala blanched when she saw the small bud vase with a white hibiscus. Quicker than lightning, she plucked it from the bud vase and tossed it into the shrubbery. She tilted her head to the side as much as to say *your turn.* Damn, she wished she hadn't read that investigative report, wished it more than anything in the world just then.

Ryan Spenser took the initiative and poured the coffee. Kala noticed the slight tremor in his hand. He looked at Kala, and said, "I had an epiphany last night."

Coffee cup midway to her lips, Kala froze. Of all the things she was expecting to hear, this was not it. She let her eyes express her questions.

"Look, Kala, I'm not . . . I'm not what you think I am. The media . . . early on, they made me out to be this . . . shark or barracuda, some kind of legal killer. At first, I was kind of flattered. Then it was just too much trouble to back it all up. What I am trying to say here is that I did not railroad Sophie Lee. I did not falsify anything. I prosecuted the case the way I would have prosecuted any other case. I gave it a hundred and ten percent. That extra ten percent was jammed down my throat by the powers that be because Audrey Star was such a high-profile figure.

"I never personally believed Sophie Lee murdered her patient. As we both know, the law doesn't care what I think. The law is made up of facts. Personally, I always believed it was Adam Star who killed his wife, but I did not have a shred of evidence to prove it. The only person that left was Sophie Lee. I cut you all the slack I could, Kala, hoping as a defense attorney you could do things I couldn't do inside the law, but you didn't come up with anything either."

Kala sipped at her coffee, knowing that what Spenser had said was the truth.

"The mayor, the police chief, and the governor—yeah, my uncle—were on my ass, up my ass, in my face twenty-four/seven to convict *somebody*. Audrey Star had the right for justice to be served. The board of directors for 'Everything Star' brought some heavy artillery to the table. In the end, it was all dumped on me.

"I know this is all old hat to you, Kala, but I went with the facts. In the end, a jury of Sophie Lee's peers found her guilty. No, I did not sleep for weeks after the verdict and for months after the sentencing. If it's any consolation to you, I was as convinced in my own mind as you were of Sophie Lee's innocence. I kept sending you, anonymously, points of law when you were drafting your appeals. I thought they would work, and I was devastated when you lost both appeals."

"You! You're the one who sent me those . . . points of law? I never—Oh, dear God! I used all of them. I thought it was some judge that Ben knew. Thank you, Ryan."

Ryan shrugged.

"One other thing. Not that it's important, but my secretary said it was presumptuous of me to give you that picture of the two of us at your retirement party. The day they took that picture of the two of us was one of my proudest moments. I was there with the great Kala Aulani. I just want you to know I went to six different stores, looking for just the right frame." Ryan grinned ruefully.

Kala felt sick to her stomach. She had to find that picture. Even if she had to go to the city dump site and dig through all the trash. "I appreciated it, Ryan," she fibbed. "Six stores, huh?"

Spenser laughed. "It might have been seven, and I'll have you know I wrapped it myself. Anyway, back to the moment at hand. I had this epiphany last night, and I couldn't wait to get here this morning. Listen, Kala, let's work together on this. My career is over no matter what happens, and that's okay. When I leave here, I want my record to stand for itself. And right now, I want to assure you that all of my old cases are solid; those lawyers are doing nothing but wasting time, manpower, and money. Say what you will about me as a person, but as a lawyer, you won't find a better one—except maybe you. I would never, ever, shortchange justice."

Kala believed him. Damn. Now she really did have to find that picture. "So what was the epiphany?"

"More coffee?"

"Yeah," Kala said, holding up her cup. Spenser's hand was now rock steady.

"I don't think Adam Star, or Adam Clements, or whatever

name he went by, killed his wife. *I think Audrey Star killed herself.* I can't prove it. Can you? Between the two of us, maybe we *can* prove it, and I can ride off into the sunset knowing I helped Sophie Lee. Legally."

It wasn't often that Kala was at a loss for words, but she was at that moment. She flapped her arms like a fish out of water as she stared at Spenser. Again, her expression was full of questions.

"I know exactly how you feel, and that's how I felt last night. I went through every goddamn word of the trial transcript. Word by word. I was looking for my own failure, your failure, and it wasn't there. It simply was not there. That just left testimony. Adam's, to be precise. He said from the git-go that he did not believe that Sophie Lee killed his wife. He was her staunchest supporter. Sophie, even though you didn't put her on the stand, backed him up, too. She said there was never a time when he could have killed his wife. You said it yourself, Kala, in open court. I don't think you believed it then, and you didn't believe it all these years until the day Adam showed up in your office. Right or wrong?"

"You're right. So if your theory is right, how do we go about proving Audrey Star killed herself?" Kala demanded. Now that was something she had never even considered. Some attorney she was.

"I don't know. I was hoping you would have some ideas. Was there anything in the evidence locker?"

"No. And let's set the record straight on that. I did sign the stuff out, but I left before it was turned over to Patty Molnar. I had a motion to file in court and didn't want to be late that day. We picked it up yesterday from Nick Mancuso's garage, where Patty had it stored. She never looked inside the boxes, and it's our theory that the rookie assigned to the evidence locker that day is the one who made the mistake. It would have stayed a mistake if you hadn't gotten all uppity and threatened to sue me."

"I was just busting your chops. It was a threat, nothing more. I wouldn't have gone through with it. I'm sorry about that, I really am."

"Well, thanks to Ben, it worked out okay. We went through it thoroughly. The box is in my office, and you can take it with you when you leave."

"Kala, how is Sophie Lee? I'm not asking out of idle curiosity. I actually care how she is. I am personally willing to do anything I can to help her. All you have to do is tell me what that would be. I don't know if you'll understand this, but even though I did nothing wrong, I still feel guilty for robbing her of her best years, her youth."

"You know what, Ryan? I think Sophie knows that. I'll pass it on. Just don't prick my bubble and tell me that check you left on the coffee table is no good."

"I wouldn't do that, Kala. It's solid gold."

"Well, in that case," Kala said, texting Jay, "I'm going to have Jay deposit it."

"The quicker the better," Spenser said, getting up off his chair and walking over to the bush that held the hibiscus and handing it to her. Then he sat down and reached for a sugary pastry. He laughed when Kala stuck the flower behind her ear.

"So, partner, what's our next move?" Kala said, before she jammed one of the sticky buns in her mouth.

Patty Molnar stood by the window, her back to Rob Pope and Bonnie Garrison as they reported in on Audrey Star and her husband, Adam. She only heard half of what they were saying because she was so intent on watching Kala and Ryan Spenser down in the little garden where they were sitting. What was going on? They looked to her like they were suddenly new best friends. Her reporter's instinct kicked in. Something was up. Even from where she was standing, inside the building, she could smell it, feel it in every bone in her body. What? Did it have something to do with the evidence box? Had she missed something? Well, if she missed it, then so did the others.

Patty blinked when she saw Spenser get up and pick a white flower from the bushes and hand it to Kala, who then stuck it in her hair. What the hell did that mean?

Now she was cranky. She turned back to her two investigators, and said, "Okay, this is all really good. Thanks for getting on this so fast. Just leave me your reports and check with the others to see if they can use any extra help. I'll call you later this evening."

Patty wandered back to the window, the thick file in hand. She needed to go somewhere quiet and read through it before she handed it over to Kala. What *were* they talking about down there?

Out in the hall, Patty ran into Jay, who had a jubilant look on his face. He waved a white envelope under her nose. "I am on my way to the bank with ten million dollars. I have never seen ten million bucks in my life. Do you want to see it?"

"Sure, why not? Show it to me," Patty said. Jay showed her. She was not impressed.

"Big deal. It's just a bunch of zeros. What's going on with Kala and Spenser? I could see them out the window. They suddenly look like best buds."

"I have no idea. Some kind of plan, I guess. How's the investigating going? You getting any dirt, any smoking guns or secrets?"

"It's all right here," Patty said, waving the papers in her hand. She wondered if it was wishful thinking on her part.

Chapter 22

PATTY WALKED BACK TO THE LITTLE OFFICE THAT HAD BEEN ASsigned to her at the rear corner of the building. Before she settled down to sift through the reports in her hands, she went over to the window. Kala and Spenser still looked like they were having a very intense discussion. She figured it all must be good for Camp Aulani since Kala had stuck the white hibiscus in her hair. To Patty, that had to mean Ryan Spenser was no longer Public Enemy Number One. But how and why was it happening? She hoped Kala would call a meeting once Spenser left and fill the staff in on what was going on.

Back at her desk, Patty separated the interviews, two for Audrey Star and two for Adam Star. The female version and the male version of an investigation. She marveled at the tidy reports and the thoroughness. Well, the two law students turned investigators were just a hair away from becoming full-fledged lawyers, so they knew a thing or two about thoroughness when a client's well-being was hanging in the balance.

Patty started with Rob Pope's report first. A male's perspective always intrigued her because, unlike women, the males left out the little things that sometimes had a way of making an entire case; then there was that aha moment when the lightbulb went on. Patty rifled through the pages and had her aha moment herself when she saw that Bonnie Garrison's report was eight pages longer than that of her partner Rob.

Before she settled down to read, Patty headed to the kitchen for a fresh cup of coffee. Back in her little nest, she got comfortable. Who first, Audrey or Adam? She flipped the pages and went with Audrey. After all, Audrey Star was what this was all about.

Patty read steadily, marking sentences, sometimes whole paragraphs, with a yellow highlighter. When she was finished, she read the summary and was pleased with the information Rob had submitted. What intrigued her most of all was the final sentence, which was a question: "Where are Audrey Star's journals?"

Audrey Star had been born to Edith and Henry Star on August 7, 1965, in Marietta, Georgia. She weighed in at seven pounds, nine ounces. She was an only child. Her parents died in a boating accident when she was nineteen. The Star fortune was held in trust for her until she turned twenty-five. At that point, she had one aunt on her mother's side and two uncles on her father's side. All were deceased now. No cousins to be found anywhere. Nannies and various caretakers over the years were all deceased. Audrey was a pleasant child and went to private schools, young ladies' finishing academies, "whatever they were," Rob had written. Her early academic reports indicated that Audrey Star was *slow.* She showed no interest in the three R's or anything else, such as spelling, science, or geography. She "failed" every psychological test she was ever given. One brave soul, a psychiatrist named Arnold Rosenberg, had brazenly stepped up to the plate and written that Audrey Star's mind had never progressed past the age of sixteen. That same brave soul went on to say that Audrey Star was functionally illiterate though one could understand what she wrote despite the misspellings and total lack of grammatical structure, and that she worked very hard to cover up her deficiency. Because she was so bad with numbers as well as monies, she had credit lines out the wazoo, and all she had to do was sign her name, which she was able to do with no problem.

Patty closed her eyes for a moment as she tried to recall if any of this had come out at the trial. She had no recollection of it at all, so obviously it had not come out. Was that because Spenser didn't root around in Audrey's past because she was the victim or because he didn't know where to look? Or maybe the Star people put a lid on the information they were willing to divulge. Patty wondered if Adam had known all these details. If he had, he'd never shared them with anyone, at least not to her knowledge. Then how was it two third-year law students, a.k.a. investigators, were able to find all this information?

Patty scribbled some notes to herself. Ten years was a long time, and maybe the people who did finally talk were aware of Sophie Lee and wanted to right some wrongs? People? So far the only live person who had talked was this Dr. Rosenberg. Where that kind of thinking would take her, Patty had no idea.

Rosenberg, she read, was the doctor who had informed the board of directors of Star Enterprises that Audrey was not mentally capable of handling her fortune and that a trust lawyer was needed to oversee Audrey's fortune. Things went smoothly when that was done, with Audrey flitting all over the globe partying and enjoying herself until the day she met Adam Clements. A note in the margin, handwritten, forced Patty to turn the paper sideways to read it. Audrey stayed under the care of Dr. Rosenberg until the day she died. Rosenberg was the only person Audrey let it all hang out with. She understood when the good doctor told her she wasn't on par with other people her age. He encouraged her to keep a journal, and only he and she would be privy to it. If she felt she didn't want to voice something, she'd write it and let the doctor read it. He had to explain to her dozens of times about patient-doctor privilege. Audrey saw him on the average of twice a month and stayed in touch if she was traveling the world. Along the way, there were many one-night stands, short relationships, and several broken engagements. Men used her. However, she was never brokenhearted when a relationship ended. She simply moved on to the next man waiting in the wings.

Patty turned the page and saw a short report from someone named Derek Saxton. Rob Pope penciled in a note saying, "This guy's summary is pretty much what all the guys said in regard to Audrey Star. She was coy, kittenish, often resorting to baby talk to get her way. She was easy on the eyes and didn't mind spending money—not that I was a gigolo, mind you," Saxton said. "But I did appreciate the pricey gifts. Who wouldn't like a Maserati?" Audrey was incapable of carrying on any kind of meaningful conversation even if it was about the weather. She liked to be complimented on her clothing, her hair. She was just okay in bed but really didn't like sexual intercourse. She did like to cuddle and talk about *someday*. She was a terrible driver, had had numerous accidents, smacked up or totaled more than a dozen cars, until finally the DMV revoked her license, and she had to resort to a chauffeur. From time to time it was known that she did take a car on the road and drive with no license. Even the threat of being arrested didn't deter her. She knew the Star powerhouse of lawyers would get her off anything that caused her even a moment of trouble.

When Audrey met Adam Clements, she fell in love with him. Adam Clements, Audrey told Rosenberg, was the answer to all her prayers. He could take over her fortune because he was an investment banker. She asked him to marry her, and he accepted. He did put up some resistance when Audrey asked him to give up his job and stay home with her or travel the world, just the two of them. Adam had many sessions with Rosenberg. He knew what he was getting into when he married Audrey. Sometimes they were more like two kids, brother and sister; other times they actually acted like a married couple. Rosenberg said it was a very strange relationship but that it worked for the two of them. He said Adam was a decent human being, and he tried to help Audrey. He'd take her on nature outings since he liked the outdoors. He taught her how to swim. He'd read to her by the hour. She particularly liked political thrillers for some odd reason. With Adam around twenty-four/seven, Audrey gave up for the most part her facials, her hair and nail salon appointments, and her daily massages because Adam said she was beautiful enough without all those "trappings." They did extensive traveling, with Adam showing her other ways of life and what other countries and their people were like. Even though she'd already traveled to those other countries, she had only experienced the party aspects of the cultures. She particularly liked Africa and its people for some reason and made many trips there.

Patty stopped reading, rubbed her temples as she tried to picture the life Audrey Star had led. She got up and walked over to the window. Kala and Spenser were still talking. *About what?*

Patty skimmed through a stack of photocopied articles that Rob had included in the file. She went back to Rob's typed report. Dr. Rosenberg had retired a year ago and was dividing his time between Georgia and Vermont, where he went every summer to escape the heat. "He said he had just returned to Georgia a week ago to testify in a court case and was headed back to Vermont the very day we spoke to him," Rob wrote. He would be there until after the leaves turned, then come back to the South for the winter months. He said his wife, who had passed away three years ago, was from Vermont.

He said he was shocked, actually the word he used was *stunned,* when he heard that Adam Star had confessed to killing Audrey. He said in all his counseling sessions with Adam, he never saw one scintilla of violent potential in the man. He said that, in his opinion, "Adam was simply not capable of murder."

Rosenberg said his services were terminated at Audrey's

death. He said he was given a magnificent bonus for his years of service to Audrey. He followed the trial, testified, and was represented by the Star legal team. At that time, his wife became ill, and he cut back on his practice to spend more time with her. When asked if he had an opinion on Sophie Lee's guilt or innocence, he said that he did not.

More articles were stapled to the file, articles of Rosenberg's testimony and the ongoing daily trial reports. And then Patty reached the end of Rob's report. Her eyes were glued to the last sentence: *"Where are the journals?"*

Yes indeed, where were Audrey Star's journals? Especially the last one.

Patty got up again and walked to the window. Kala and Spenser were still talking. She stood at the window for a good ten minutes, her thoughts all over the map. As the personal representative of Adam Star's estate, Kala had to have a key, or could get one, to the Star mansion, where Adam and Audrey had lived. Maybe it was time to send in a search team to see what could be uncovered. She was sure the police had done it ten years ago, but this was now. The journals could have been secretly removed, then brought back after the trial. It was just a thought but a thought that wouldn't go away. Because the thought wouldn't go away, Patty knew she was onto something. Plus the fine hairs on the back of her neck, always a warning sign that she should pay attention, were tingling.

As soon as she was finished reading Bonnie's report, she would ask Kala, if she ever finished talking to Spenser, if she could go to the house and search it. The thought excited her. Maybe Nick would go with her. It would make him more a part of what was going on. She knew he felt left out—he said so on a daily basis. The thought was so strong she picked up her cell phone and hit the speed dial. "Come over here, Nick. By the time you finish your PT, Kala should be back inside, and we can leave. Unless you have something else planned for your day." Nick assured her he would be there with bells on. Patty thought he sounded as excited as she felt.

Patty looked at the time on her watch as she started Bonnie's report. It was almost identical in content to Rob's but with what Patty called a few more female details. Audrey was addicted to designer clothes, went to all the Paris fashion shows, and bought tons of clothes. At her death there were racks and racks of clothes in her many closets, a good many with the price tags still on them. She also liked expensive jewelry and had millions of dollars in gems, most of which was kept in a safe-deposit box, although she kept a goodly amount at home in a wall safe. The combination was enclosed in the report as well as the location. "I got this from the police report," Bonnie had penciled in the margin. Dr. Rosenberg said Audrey had six different engagement rings, all emerald cuts. He said he had told her she should return them to the various fiancés but she'd said no, they were given to her, and she was keeping them. When he told her that wasn't the proper thing to do, she said she would think about it, and maybe she would return them. She never did, to his knowledge.

Dr. Rosenberg said it always bothered him that Audrey used to like to play dress-up in fancy high-end clothing with lots of feathers and boas and the like. She'd spend thousands of dollars on stuff, play with it, then discard it. He went on to say Audrey, when she would return from a trip, would plan a dinner party but not invite anyone. When it was time to sit down to eat, she would call all the staff to eat with her. When he asked her why she did that, she said because no one loved her, and as long as she was paying the staff, they would love her.

Dr. Rosenberg said Audrey Star was one of only four failures in his career. He simply could not break through to Audrey. Audrey Star was never a happy child or a happy woman. However, he said, when she married Adam Clements, she was content. When she insisted Adam change his name to Star, Adam pitched a fit and said no. Audrey went into a deep depression followed by many sessions for the both of them with

Dr. Rosenberg. Adam finally gave in when he saw that was the only way to lift Audrey out of her depression. That very day, Audrey bounced back, giddy as a little girl. She immediately called in a team of decorators and decorated the mansion with stars. She called Adam and herself the Two Stars who lived in the Star mansion.

Patty started flipping pages, then she went to the trial transcript. There was nothing about the Star mansion decor anywhere that she could see. She would have remembered that. "Oh, baby, you were one sick puppy, and to think they locked up Sophie!"

What she was reading was so unnerving, Patty shoved the papers away and got up to walk down to the kitchen for another cup of coffee she didn't need or even want. She saw Kala pouring herself a glass of juice. "So what, now Spenser is our new best friend?" Patty all but snarled.

"Close, but not quite best friends. Yet. Remember what I've said all along. Things are not always what they seem. How did your people do with the interviews on Audrey and Adam Star?" Kala asked.

"They're very enlightening, to say the least. Do you have a key to the Star mansion, Kala?"

"As a matter of fact, I do. Clayton Hughes sent it over about a week ago. Why?"

"I'd like to take Nick with me and go over there and search the house for the journals. Are you planning on staying here at the office?"

"I am, why?"

"Then I'll give you the reports on Audrey and Adam, and you can read them while we're gone if you say it's okay to go over there and poke around."

"I don't see any reason why you can't do that. Come back to my office, the key's in my desk. Bring the reports with you. You okay with the way things are going with your investigators, Patty?"

"Yes, I am. You're going to find them very interesting. I didn't finish Bonnie's, but I'm sure it's just clarification of what Rob had in his report. You know as well as I do that women see things differently than men. For some reason we pick up on the nuances, and sometimes that can be crucial, which really isn't the case here, but I do question why neither side hit a home run with Dr. Rosenberg. With what's in this current report, it seems to me he's a key player."

"Not at trial. Audrey was dead. She wasn't on trial, Sophie was on trial, and Dr. Rosenberg was represented by the Star legal team. Patient-doctor privilege. Audrey Star was well represented by her team of medical doctors, all high-dollar specialists from all over the world. Dr. Rosenberg merely testified that Audrey had good days and bad days and on her bad days was depressed but easily cajoled out of it by her husband. End of Dr. Rosenberg's testimony."

"Yeah, well, wait till you read this report. Wonder why he talked so freely to Rob and Bonnie now."

"Probably because Adam is dead now and a wrong has been righted with Adam's confession. Doctors are like us lawyers, Patty, we take an oath. For all we know, Adam had some kind of agreement with the doctor that said after his death, he could spill his guts. I'm just guessing here because I don't know. Didn't your people ask him?"

Patty shrugged. "I'll go get the report and wait in the lot for Nick to pick me up. I'll check in when we're done. Is there anything in particular you want me to look for while we're there?"

"Anything that screams my name, snatch it up. This is a hot potato, isn't it?"

"And it's getting hotter by the moment," Patty called over her shoulder as she ran to her little office. She was back in minutes with the report. She accepted the key to the Star mansion, which was on a curly purple wrist chain. Patty blew her boss a kiss and raced for the stairs that would take her outside.

By the time Nick pulled up in his convertible with the top down, Patty was drenched with her own perspiration. "You need to put the top up and the AC on full blast, or I'm going to explode. What took you so damn long?"

"I had to get gas. This car does not run on empty, you know."

It was a running battle with the two of them, with Patty saying to fill the tank when it was a quarter full, and Nick saying his car buzzed when he was down to his last five gallons.

Within minutes, the canvas top curled upward and the AC started to spew cold air. Patty fanned herself with her hands. "You know where to go, right?"

"Yeah, I dropped Sophie off a few times. What's up?"

Patty told him about the reports as well as what Kala had said before she handed over the key. "I hope I'm not wrong, Nick, but I think Dr. Rosenberg is a key player here whom no one explored, or if they tried, were thwarted for their efforts. Money talks and bullshit walks, as Kala and Jay say constantly."

His eyes on the road, his hands gripping the steering wheel, Nick said, "Give me your definition of Audrey Star and don't stop to think about the answer before you reply."

"In my opinion, Audrey Star was mentally challenged and never progressed beyond the age of sixteen. No one wanted that information to come out. Even Adam, at the end when he confessed to murdering her, never said a word about her mental condition. Maybe it had something to do with the stockholders or something. I would imagine that stockholders have the right to expect whoever was at the head of a monolith like Star Enterprises to be of sound mind. It would be like Kala sending Bobby the office boy to defend a client on a murder charge. Bobby isn't qualified, and neither was Audrey qualified to run Star Enterprises even though she was the CEO and president. It was in name only. She signed her name.

Seems she was real good at that. Hey, what do you want from me, Nick? I'm a reporter, not a shrink."

Nick shrugged. "Do you think we'll find anything?"

"No. Well, maybe. It would be nice, though, if we did. Adam lived at the house until the last two weeks of his life. He might well have hidden something in the house, like Audrey's journals. But would he have left them there to be found, knowing when he entered the hospital he wouldn't be getting out and going home? I'm thinking the way he saw it was he'd confessed, and that was the end of it.

"If he ever did have Audrey's journals, he might have hidden them somewhere. I have not discounted in my own mind that Dr. Rosenberg might have them. For that matter, Adam could have hidden them in his locker at the country club where he plays golf. Or if he belonged to a gym, he would have a locker there and could have hidden them there. No one at the firm has gotten that far into this mess yet to have thought of that until today. For all we know, they could be hidden in the trunk of his car.

"Nick, let me ask you a question. Knowing Audrey Star's condition, knowing she knew she was never going to walk again, knowing everything she knew at the time of her death, what would she write in a journal? Her world was one room. She watched television, her husband read to her, a nurse took care of her needs. What would she write about? Why would she even bother to keep a journal? Before, yes, I understand the need to put thoughts to paper. I think those damn journals are suddenly a very big deal."

Nick took his eyes off the road long enough to give Patty a piercing stare. "What happens if we can't find them?"

"We have to find them. We look until we have to give up. That's the bottom line."

"Okay, we're here," Nick said as he put on his blinker and made a left turn onto a gravel driveway. "I hope you have the code to the security gate. Kala said the other day that all the staff are gone, even the gardeners."

"Four double zeros," Patty said. Nick punched in the numbers, and the gate slowly slid to the side. He drove through and continued on under the canopy of ancient oak trees.

It was a beautiful house, a huge Tudor with extensions that ran to the back of the house so as not to disturb the architecture. The shrubbery was dense and lush but overgrown. Flowers bloomed everywhere, but they were leggy and spindly and in need of water. The noonday sun glistened on the diamond-paned windows.

"It's pretty, isn't it, Nick? This is the first time I'm seeing it. But Sophie described it to me. She said it was a cold, strange house, beautifully decorated with costly things, but there was no warmth at all to it. Even if I didn't know the house was empty, I would still think so. It just looks like a shell to me even though I can see window treatments. Is that crazy or what?" Patty asked, getting out of the car.

"That's because you're a people person, Patty. But I understand what you're saying. It's almost like the house is shouting, 'They're all gone and they aren't coming back.' "

"I wonder what Sophie will do with it," Patty said.

Nick stopped in midstride. "If Sophie were to ask me for my opinion, I'd tell her to burn the damn thing to the ground."

Patty laughed, a bitter sound. "Funny. I was thinking the exact same thing. Maybe she could knock it down and make a little park with benches and flowers and stuff. A few statues, that kind of thing. A place where people could walk to in the evening after the sun goes down. Let's hope she asks for our opinions. Okay, here goes. Why do I feel like I should ring the bell?"

"Is that some kind of girl thinking? Just open the damn door already and get this show on the road."

Patty whirled around. "What's your problem, Nick? I'm getting sick and tired of your attitude. If you didn't want to come with me, all you had to do was say no. *No* I can accept. This surly attitude of yours of late is getting on my nerves. Do you want to sit out here on the swing and *talk* it out? We've done that all our lives, and unless we've been lying to one another, it always seemed to help. Why, all of a sudden, don't you want to talk about whatever it is that's bothering you? By the way, before I forget, it's my turn to take Jon home with me this week."

Nick walked over to the swing, noticed the patches of mildew, and perched on the very end. Patty leaned against the porch wall.

"They called me early this morning to tell me I have to have the other hip done, and the sooner the better. There goes my career. I thought I could handle it but . . . I'm not handling it. I have to be up front with all my sponsors, and the sooner the better on that, too. I'm washed up, Patty. Sophie isn't going to want some has-been like me. That's what's bothering me more than the endorsements and my career."

"Damn, you are one dumb sorry jerk, Nick Mancuso. Right this minute, I'm ashamed to even be talking to you. If you think even for a nanosecond that Sophie would feel that way, you're even more stupid than I thought. Don't say another word to me, Nick Mancuso."

"So you're telling me this is a guy thing?" Hope was in his voice, but Patty was heartless.

"I can't waste my time on stupid people like you. Now get off your ass and help me out here or else go home and I'll call a cab when I'm ready to leave. Don't you dare talk to me, Nick. I can't carry on a conversation with someone so stupid."

"*All rrriiight.* I get it. Look, see, I'm happy as a clam," Nick said, stretching his mouth out as far as it would go with his fingers.

"I'm sorry about your news. It's going to be whatever you make it to be, Nick. There are a million things you can do with your life. You're financially sound, and have your whole life ahead of you. Make it count. Do not whine anymore to me. We came here to do a job, so let's get to it."

Nick laughed. Patty could always shake him loose. He followed her into the house and gasped as loud as Patty did when they entered the foyer.

"Oh my God!" they both said in unison.

Chapter 23

Kala Aulani slapped the reports she'd just read down on her cluttered desk. She looked at the messy work space and wondered how it had gotten that way. She was retired, for God's sake. She felt like she was driving on a superhighway and boxed in by four eighteen-wheelers. She massaged her temples, hoping to ward off a headache she knew would sprout any minute. The urge to bang her head on the cluttered desk was so strong, Kala gave the cracked-leather chair she was sitting in a push. She slid backward.

She'd always been good at analyzing things, and people told her she had a keen analytical mind. Not that she was patting herself on the back. But, if that assessment was true, why couldn't she figure out this mess that was in front of her?

Ryan Spenser had been the surprise of a lifetime. A good one. She had never been one to judge a person quickly, and it had taken years to form the negative opinion she had in regard to Spenser. But just within the last few hours, she'd seen the real Ryan Spenser. A man whose ass was on the line. A man who no longer cared about his reputation and only wanted to help. All he wanted now was a life of his own choosing. And to help in whatever way he could. He was a strong ally. With the two of them on the same side, surely they could bring this whole sorry mess to a resolution.

He had guts—she had to give him that. For him to throw away his career, flip his father the bird, and stand tall with her was something she had never imagined he could or would do.

Kala pushed her chair forward, closer to the desk, the urge to bang her head gone. So was the throbbing in her temples. She picked up the report on Audrey Star and glared at it. She put it down and picked up the report on Adam. There wasn't all that much in Adam's report. Adam was a successful investment banker with the potential to move up the ladder. He was solvent, owned his own home and high-end car. Dressed well, had various relationships, none lasting longer than three or four months. Took a vacation twice a year. Nothing exciting there. He had a more than decent portfolio, was considered a good tipper. Kala yawned as she flipped the pages, hoping to find something that would leap out at her, but nothing did. Everything she was reading, she'd read in the report on his wife.

Kala squeezed her eyes shut. She wasn't buying Adam's confession, and Spenser hadn't bought it either. So, what did that mean? She and Spenser had both agreed that a boatload of guilt over Audrey's crippling accident was on the man's shoulders. But . . . and there was always a *but,* Spenser hadn't seen Patty's report on Audrey Star. Why didn't the prosecution go into Audrey's background ten years ago? More to the point, why hadn't she herself gone into it?

Kala turned her mind back in time. The best she could come up with was they had tried and were either stonewalled, or they decided the investigation was too costly since she was trying the case pro bono. But the prosecution had virtually unlimited resources; they should have done it. Were they stonewalled, too, by the Star flotilla of lawyers?

Even if either side had known, it wouldn't have changed the outcome of the trial. She was almost certain of that, but she was going to have to talk to Ryan again, and very soon, perhaps before the day was over. Her team had deposed Dr.

Rosenberg, who had said nothing like what she'd just read in the report. Then again, Audrey Star wasn't on trial. Sophie Lee had been on trial. Still, leave no stone unturned unless it cost too much money to turn over said stone.

Kala pressed a button on the phone console. "Ask Jay to come to my office. Linda, too."

Jay bounded into the room, followed by his wife. He grumbled the whole time about Kala's being retired and still showing up to work and screwing things up. Linda rolled her eyes, until Kala said, "Enough already! Tell me your best recollection as to why we never delved into Audrey Star's background ten years ago at trial."

"Because she was the victim. We did go into her background. She was a socialite, spent money like she printed it herself, partied around the globe, slept all day, and partied all night. She was addicted to manicures, pedicures, facials, massages, and loved to be pampered. She was engaged six times, kept the flashy baubles when said engagements were broken. She gave away her globe-trotting stilettos when she met and married Adam Clements. It was a happy union. Then she died by someone's hand. We said not by Sophie Lee's. Spenser said yes to Sophie Lee. End of story. And there you have my photographic mind at work."

"Jay is right. That's exactly how it happened. In his closing statement, Spenser gave a touching eulogy of Audrey Star, and the jury bought it," Linda said.

Kala blinked. "Well, then, read this report. Right now! I'll go get us some fresh coffee."

When Kala returned to her office fifteen minutes later, Jay was trying to argue with his wife, who was refusing to be baited. Kala set the tray down, poured out three cups of coffee, then took her seat. "Arguing is for fools," she said pointedly. "We need to have a discussion."

"I hope you aren't saying or thinking we screwed up—because we didn't. Rosenberg wasn't talking back then. And even if he had been, what difference would it have made? Sophie Lee was on trial, not Audrey Star." Jay's tone was so belligerent, Kala reared back.

"Well, it might have given us some more insight into Adam. We might have been more aggressive with him."

"And the judge would have slapped you down in a nanosecond. I remember the all-nighter we pulled back then, trying to decide how far we would get if we tried something like that. *You,* Kala, made the decision not to pursue it. We also had a money problem at that time."

Kala did remember that all-nighter. And Jay was absolutely right. She said so, gently, so as not to irk him even more. "I'll be out of your hair shortly, so stop complaining. Then you're going to really miss me, and you'll start calling me all hours of the day and night just to hear my voice. And guess what, Jay Brighton? I will not take your calls. So there!"

"That's not it at all, and you know it. You're forgiven. Did you call Sophie yet to tell her the check was deposited? And when are you going to tell us what happened with Ryan Spenser?"

"How about right now? I'll call Sophie later. She's probably still sleeping or just about to get up."

Linda settled herself more comfortably, and said, "Well, I for one am all ears. Shoot!"

"Yeah, tell us what the Great White Prosecutor had to say that took almost two hours. I can hardly wait to hear this," Jay said through clenched teeth.

Kala leaned back in the cracked-leather chair and brought the tips of her fingers together to make a steeple. "Remember how I always say nothing is exactly what it seems? Well, this, my dears, is a case in point."

"Yeah, well, I have one other point to make," Jay continued to grumble. "We should have all gone to the Star mansion with Patty and Nick. Five sets of eyes are better than two."

"Then who would run this very busy, thriving office?" Kala

snapped back. "Relax, if there's anything to find there, those two will find it. Trust me on that, partners."

Two hours later Patty sat down on the floor Indian style. "There's nothing here, Nick. This place is a nightmare. Any minute now, I'm expecting Merlin the Wizard to pop out and wave his wand. Can you imagine actually living here in this . . . this . . . ?"

Nick leaned up against a wall. "I think the word you're looking for is *nightmare.* And, no, you couldn't pay me to live in a house whose walls and ceilings are painted dark blue with gold stars. On top of all that, the furniture is covered with sheets. It's ghostly, to say the least. I guess the staff took care of everything before they closed up the house. I think you said this house is eight thousand square feet, and we've covered four thousand feet so far and found nothing. I'm game to continue, but I don't think we're going to find anything."

Patty shrugged. "You never know. They say if you want to hide something, hide it in plain view. This is the library, and I say this only because I peeked under the sheets draping the bookshelves and saw all those books. Adam must have been a reader, or else Audrey's parents were readers. Then again, they could have bought all those books from some vendor just to fill up the shelves. People do that, you know. They want to appear intellectual to their friends. We actually did a human-interest story on that a few years ago when I was at the *AJC.* The bottom line"—Patty giggled—"was if you gave any of those people a quiz on the books, they couldn't tell you a thing about them. It was stupid."

"Journals are books, aren't they?"

"Damn straight they're books," Patty said, leaping to her feet. A second later, the sheets were lying on the floor. "Well now, lookie here! And there's even a library ladder. I'll do the climbing, Nick."

"Don't worry, I'm not going to fight you for that honor. Are they listed in alphabetical order by author or title?"

"Looks like by author. Lots of first editions here. I see *Huckleberry Finn,* six different editions. *The Great Gatsby,* three editions. *Gone With the Wind,* three editions. Someone must have been a collector. Rare books are worth a fortune. Wonder if Adam read them to Audrey. Forget I said that. It was a stupid comment. The report said Audrey liked Adam to read her political thrillers. The spines haven't even been broken on most of these books."

Nick peered up at the top shelf. "If I remember correctly, *Huckleberry Finn* was written by Mark Twain, which was his pen name. His real name was Samuel L. Clemens. Those editions say Samuel L. Clemens. Don't you find that a little strange, my little reporter?" Nick grinned. "Think about Adam's last name. Isn't it Clemens?"

Patty was already on the ladder. "I think there's a T in his last name. But I get your point. I'll drop them one at a time, and you catch them, okay? Wow! Someone paid out a lot of money to have these bound in this luxurious leather, and the letters are all gold embossed. Nothing chintzy going on here, that's for sure."

"For sure," Nick muttered as he opened the first book. "And what we have here are Audrey Star's missing journals! Are we a team or what? You have to admit, this is pretty damn clever on someone's part, and my money is on Adam. I bet he did this for his wife as a gift or something. Maybe after her accident to perk her up or something," Nick said, pointing to the six books on the floor.

Patty nodded, beyond excited. "You take those three, and I'll take these three. From what I remember of the report, Audrey probably started writing journals around the age of sixteen, maybe earlier, can't be sure. Let's just find the earliest date and go on from there. What we're really looking for, though, is the last one, dated ten years ago, the year of her death."

They worked in silence, riffling through the pages, and finding a lot of the entries nothing more than chicken scratches. "She really couldn't write," Nick blurted. "This is like some pidgin English. But look how beautifully she writes her name. It doesn't compute."

"Rosenberg said she could sign her name for everything, which is what she did. I guess she had a lot of practice. I feel terrible pawing through this and talking about her like she was some dummy. She was a real person with limited abilities. This is really sad. What do you suppose was the attraction for Audrey and Adam? And don't say money."

"Maybe he wanted to help her, save her from herself. You said yourself there was never any scandal about the two of them until her car accident, and that wasn't a scandal. It was just a tragic accident that had its run of a week in the *AJC*. Fifteen minutes in the spotlight, then it's all forgotten by everyone except the parties involved, who are left to pick up the pieces."

"I guess that makes sense," Patty said, stacking the leather-bound books into a neat pile. Now what?"

"We keep searching until we see if there's anything else to uncover. This might just be the tip of the iceberg. Let's take another look at these books. Adam hid the journals in plain sight, so he might have hidden other things here as well."

Patty scanned the shelves until she came to the Js, then said, "You know what, Nick? You are an absolute genius. Look at this! Four books, bound in the same leather as the journals and written by someone named J. J. Jewel. Thick books, too, from the size of their spines. Bigger than your traditional hardcover book. More the size of a reference book. And look at this—they're hollowed out. Jewelry! Oh, this is some really gorgeous stuff! Look at the sparkle on these diamonds! Do we take them or leave them? I don't know much about costly jewelry since I never had any, but I don't think we should leave them since the house is empty, alarm system or not. What do you think, Nick?"

"I say we take them. Do you think Sophie will wear all this stuff?" Nick asked anxiously.

Patty glared at Nick. "Never in a million years. Sophie had a string of fake pearls and a bracelet she bought herself and, of course, her most treasured necklace, the locket you gave her. She never took it off until she was arrested. I have it to give back to her, and I bet that's the first thing she asks about."

Patty tried to hide her smile at Nick's sigh of relief.

"I think we can leave now. We found pretty much what we were looking for, the diaries and the jewelry. If Kala wants us to, we can always come back. I hate this place," Patty said, looking around. "I wonder why Adam never redid it after his wife died. Hey, wait a minute, I want to see the room where Audrey died before we leave, and no, I am not being morbid. I just need to see the layout. You want to come with me or wait here with our loot?"

Nick looked out the door at the stairway and shook his head. "I'll wait here. I can start taking all this out to the car if you like."

"Okay, good idea. Be back in a flash."

Upstairs, Patty walked down the hallway till she came to a suite of rooms that obviously belonged to Audrey. Minus the dark blue walls and all the stars, it would have been a beautiful luxurious suite. Patty thought she could probably fit her entire little house into just those two rooms.

Patty stood in the doorway and winced at the sight of the hospital bed. Adam had left it just as it was, right down to the rumpled sheets and light blanket on the bed. It looked to her like he had just closed the door and walked away. There was dust everywhere, the sheer curtains were gray and limp looking. A vase of what had once been flowers, which had petrified, sat on one of the night tables. She'd seen pictures of this very room at the trial, but seeing it in person was altogether different somehow. The pictures in court were of the furnishings and didn't show the bizarre walls and ceilings, with all the gilt stars of all shapes and sizes.

Was this room a shrine? Did Adam come in here and . . . do what? Stare at the bed? Did he close his eyes and see his wife propped up on the pillows wearing a pretty nightgown? Sophie had told her once that she had to change Audrey three times a day so that when her husband came to visit, she always had on a gown that was freshly ironed and scented with her favorite perfume.

Patty turned to look around the huge room. An ugly wheelchair sat in one corner. An artificial tree or plant of some kind partially hid the chair. The plant was thick with dust, almost obliterating the green color of the silk leaves.

A tear formed in the corner of Patty's eye. How sad all this was.

Patty walked around one more time, into the sitting room, the dressing room, the giant bathroom that was bigger than most people's living rooms, hoping to see something that would be of significance. There was nothing to see. Her shoulders slumped.

"Rest in peace, Audrey Star," Patty murmured as she closed the door behind her.

Out in the hallway Patty called Kala to report in. "Depending on traffic, we'll be back at the office in thirty minutes, forty-five if we hit the wrong lights. Have Bobby meet us in the garage with a dolly. The books are really heavy, and Nick can't lift them except one at a time. Saves us a bunch of trips if he can meet us."

Kala said she was excited with the news, and Bobby would be waiting in the parking garage. As always, she warned Patty, or in this case, Nick, to drive carefully.

Chapter 24

It was shortly past the noon hour in Hawaii. The golden sun was high in the cloudless blue of the sky. The brilliant sapphire ocean was calm as the tide rushed out. Even the sand glistened from the glorious golden sun as Sophie and Sula made their way back to the little house they shared. The warm breeze that caressed Sophie's body felt like a mother's gentle touch.

It took only minutes to make a sandwich and pour a tall glass of pineapple juice and carry it out to the lanai, her favorite place. She set down a small bowl of food for Sula to reward her for the ten-mile hike across the sand. The big dog ate daintily, then moved to a shady spot near where Sophie was sitting. They talked then, or at least Sophie did, and Sula listened.

"I have to say, Sula, I have never been more content than I am right now. However, I'm itching to get out and about. To see people, to say hello or smile at a stranger. I want to walk into a store, buy something even if it's just a trinket. Mostly, though, I want to buy a tube of lipstick. You probably don't know this, Sula, but girls need lipstick. Bright cherry red to go with my suntan. I never really had a suntan before I came here. I'd like to buy some mangoes on my own. I don't exactly have cabin fever, but I'm getting close to it. I'm starting to feel a bit like a prisoner. I know it was important for me to come here because I couldn't have handled the media circus back in Atlanta. I could now, though. I'm sure of it."

Sophie slid off her chair and sat cross-legged on the floor next to Sula. She stroked the big dog's head as she continued to prattle on. "Look at all the progress I've made since coming here. I can swim like a fish now, and I'm what they call toned. I learned how to do the hula. Even Kiki isn't laughing at me now. He said I'm just as good at it as all the cousins. I took that as a real compliment. And the leis I make are just as good as the ones the natives make. Of course, that's my opinion. I think, and again, this is just my opinion, but I've become something of an expert on Hawaii. I've read everything there is to read about this beautiful place. I know all about the flora and fauna. I know about the traditions. I could probably give a lecture on Hawaii if anyone were interested enough to listen.

"What all that means, Sula, is this. I'm ready to take my place in the world. My feet are more than ready to step forward. I miss people. Being alone is okay for a while, but now it's time to get on with life. I want to see Patty and Nick and Kala. I want to talk all this through one last time, so I can put it behind me."

Sophie leaned back against the chair and felt her eyes start to close. Only there in that island paradise did she nap or doze off in the middle of the day. She'd never taken a nap in her whole life.

That was when the cell phone on the table rang. Sophie blinked, got up, and flipped it open. She heard Kala wishing her a good afternoon. Sophie smiled because Kala sounded upbeat, and there was a smile in her voice. She hoped it was good news. She listened. A long time later, her face wreathed in a wide grin, she managed to say, "Are you telling me right this moment, I can hang up the phone and walk to town and actually go into a store? Okayyyy. And I can make arrangements to fly back to Atlanta tomorrow if I want to? I can even call Patty and Nick and talk for hours or until the battery on the cell phone goes dead? I can do all those things if I want to? What does ten million look like?" Sophie laughed when Kala said it was just a blue slip of paper with numbers on it.

Sophie continued to listen as Kala brought her up to date. They talked for another fifteen minutes before Sophie closed the phone and placed it back on the charger. She was so excited, she thought she was going to explode. She danced around the lanai, then ran out to the beach, threw her hands high in the air, and shouted to the world that she was free and alive and could do what she wanted from this moment on. She thanked God, the heavens, the universe, then sat down on the sand and cried like a baby. Sula was there in an instant, trying to lick away her tears.

Sophie wrapped her arms around the big dog as she continued to cry into the thick fur of her neck. "I can't leave you, Sula. What will I do without you? But would you be happy back in Atlanta?" Sula licked at Sophie's tears, then barked. "Does that mean you want to go with me?" The big dog barked again. "Maybe the cousin who owns you will sell you to me. I'm rich now, Sula. I'd give it all up if they let me keep you. Oh my God, oh my God! What day is today?"

Quicker than lightning, Sophie ran into the house to the kitchen, where a calendar hung on the wall by the back door. "Please, please, please," she said under her breath as her finger traced the days. What day was it? She didn't know. One day was just like the day before here, and it was hard to keep track of the days even if she tried. And she hadn't. She turned on the little television sitting on the counter. She clicked on the Fox network to see the time and date. She ran back to the calendar, her fingers marking off the days. "Yessssss!" she screamed at the top of her lungs. "Yes, yes, yes, a million times yes." She bent over to kiss the calendar. "I am Tuesday's child!" she continued to scream. When she was exhausted,

Sophie walked back to the lanai and reached for her cell phone.

"Kiki, it's Sophie. I have a question for you. And I need the answer today if possible. Kala just called me and said I can return to the mainland if I want to. I want to know if Sula's owner, your cousin, will sell her to me. I'll love her and take care of her like she was my own child. I'll pay him anything, anything, Kiki, if he agrees. I don't think I can leave without her. I know one thing, though. I'm coming back here, but I have to return home for a little while. You'll call him now? Good, good, I'll wait for your call."

Sula hopped up on the swing that every lanai in Hawaii seemed to have. She looked at Sophie expectantly, like she knew what was going on. Ten minutes later the phone rang. Sophie sucked in her breath and then let it out. She thought Sula did the same thing.

"My cousin said okay, and he wants no money," Kiki reported. "Just your promise to take care of his dog. His time on the mainland, he said, has been extended by three months, so it works out for all. He wanted me to ask you if you do move here, and he's here, will you allow him to see Sula, perhaps take her for a few days at a time?"

"Good Lord, yes. Whenever he wants. Absolutely. Assure him, okay?"

Kiki laughed. "I already did. I knew that would be your answer. Sula is yours, Sophie."

Sophie started to cry all over again. She broke the connection and hugged the dog so hard, Sula yelped.

What to do first? Shower, get dressed, go to town? Call the airlines and make a reservation? Sit there and continue to hug Sula? Call Patty and Nick?

Sophie stretched her neck to see the clock in the kitchen. It was just going on one o'clock. She could actually do it all in the next few hours. If she wanted to. Or she could sit with Sula and daydream the rest of the day away.

"Today is Tuesday, Sula! I told you all about Tuesdays when I first got here. I wonder if you understood me back then or even now."

Sula tilted her head to the side and barked.

"Girl, you are mine now. M-I-N-E! And your previous owner has visiting privileges. It doesn't get any better than that!" Sophie cried between her tears.

So many things to do. An hour ago she had nothing to do. Always do things in the order of importance, Sister Julie and the nuns had taught them. Sophie ticked off her small list as she mentally put everything in order. She smiled when she realized that Nick was at the top of her list, followed by Patty. Third on the list was walking into town, and last was making a reservation to go to the mainland.

Sophie positively itched to pick up the phone and press in the numbers Kala had given her. Her heart was beating so hard and fast she thought it would burst right out of her chest. It took her three tries before she was actually able to press the numbers that would connect her to Nick. She couldn't believe her ears when the call went straight to voice mail. Should she leave a message or not? She broke the connection. "Well, that was silly," she mumbled. She pressed the numbers again and this time left a short message. "Hello, Nick. This is Sophie. I'm sorry I missed you." She broke the connection a second time.

Sophie flipped open the phone again and pressed in the numbers for Patty that Kala had given her, with the same result, the call going straight to voice mail. This time, though, she was prepared. "Patty, it's me. Kala said it was okay to call. I'm sorry I missed you."

Well, that left the third thing to do on her mental list, taking her first walk into town. In order to do that, she had to go upstairs to take a shower and wash her hair. Tears rolled down her cheeks as she fled to the steps. "Everything happens for a reason," was something Sister Julie used to tell her.

Followed up with, "Ours not to reason why." So much for that little ditty, because she was questioning the why of everything of late, not just the missed calls to her best friends. At that moment, Sophie wondered why Kala hadn't given her Jon's phone number. Maybe he didn't have cell service in the jungles of Peru. She made a mental note to see whether, if she bought him a ticket now that she was rich, he would want to come back for a reunion.

In the shower, as she lathered up, she thought about all the things Kala had told her about Ryan Spenser. Then she thought about all the things she'd told her about Audrey and Adam Star. She shook her head, globs of shampoo flying all over the shower stall.

As Sophie worked the lather in her hair, she thought about Audrey Star and the day she had finally realized why Audrey was so mean and spiteful. It was because she knew she was different from everyone else, mentally challenged. She couldn't think ahead, couldn't remember most of what was behind her, and could only deal with the moment. Sophie had tried once to broach the subject with Audrey's doctor, but he'd held up his hand and told her point-blank that none of it was her concern and not to bring it up ever again. At the time, she had considered that part of patient-doctor confidentiality. And she had never mentioned it again, not even to Kala during the trial. She wondered now whether, if she had mentioned it to Kala, it would have made a difference at the outcome. Probably not, since she was the one on trial, not Audrey Star. Well, that was in the past, and she certainly couldn't change it now.

Downstairs on the lanai, the cell phone rang and rang as hot water sluiced through Sophie's hair and all over her body. When she was sure all the sand from the ocean was flowing down the drain, Sophie got out of the shower and dressed. She smelled so good she could hardly stand herself. She giggled as she dried off and powdered up, dressing in a light summery green sundress that showed off her glorious tan. She rooted around in the bottom of the closet till she found a pair of thong sandals that matched her dress. She looked in the mirror and decided she looked pretty darn good, probably the best she'd ever looked in her whole life. She wished Nick and Patty could see her.

Still giggling, Sophie tripped down the stairs. She whistled for Sula, who came on the run. "We're going to town, girl!" Sophie reached up to a hook by the front door and removed Sula's leash. The dog knew what that meant. She whimpered happily. New places, new scents, and a nice long walk with some treats thrown in for good measure. No sooner were they out of earshot of the lanai than the cell phone on the table in the lanai chirped to life.

On the walk into town, Sophie hummed to herself, "Today is Tuesday, today is Tuesday, today is Tuesday."

Sophie walked along at a leisurely pace, Sula at her side. People smiled, the universal language of hello, and some stopped to pet Sula. The big dog basked in the attention. An open-air market that sold souvenirs, cosmetics, and perfume drew Sophie like a magnet. She wandered the aisles and finally settled on two tubes of lipstick.

"What do you think, Sula? The Cherry Berry or the Pink Flamingo?" She waved her hand about with the two strips of lipstick as though the dog was going to make the decision for her. In the end, Sula did. She barked twice, so Sophie bought both tubes. She also bought some whimsical postcards with fat little cherubs dressed in grass skirts and leis in outrigger canoes. She had no idea who she was going to send them to, probably no one. It was mind boggling that she had just spent $47 for tubes of lipstick.

Outside again in the warm sunshine, Sophie continued to drink in the sights and sounds of the busy street. She sniffed the flower-scented air. It was potent enough to make her light-headed. She was loving every minute of this excursion.

Sophie continued to meander down the street, looking in shop windows, fingering the merchandise that was outside. She bought two T-shirts, one for Patty, a pretty pink shirt with the word *Hawaii* on the pocket, and one for Nick, a navy blue muscle shirt with a golfer on the pocket.

Sophie came to a stall where a grandmother and granddaughter were selling leis. She bought two for herself and waited while the granddaughter made a small one for Sula. Everyone smiled as she paid for them and walked on, finally stopping at an outdoor café of sorts. She ordered a pineapple ice and a bowl of water for Sula.

Sophie did then what she called people watching. It seemed like everyone who passed her table took the time to comment on Sula and pat her head. Sophie smiled in return, and said, "My dog," over and over. "My dog." Beautiful words, and Sula was officially hers. The first dog she'd ever owned.

"Time to go, Sula," Sophie said, tossing her paper cup into a trash container. She picked up the water bowl, set it on the table, a five-dollar bill tucked underneath. Ohhh, life was soooo good. She thought about everything and nothing as she crossed the street and walked back the way she'd come earlier. She checked the souvenirs, which were basically the same in every store. She was tempted to buy a bottle of sand, but the thought was so ludicrous that she passed on it. Three doors down, she stopped and bought a bottle, giggling the whole time. Her own personal souvenir.

Ninety minutes later, Sophie's solo trip into town was at an end. She removed her sandals, walked between several buildings down to the beach, and headed for home. No doubt about it, she was a happy camper.

Back at the house, Sophie set out fresh water for Sula, then went upstairs to change into shorts and a tank top. She was back on the lanai within minutes. It was time for her last chore from her list.

She called Information for the number of the airline and did her best to make a reservation for her and Sula for the following day. She was told Sula would have to fly in the cargo hold. That was unacceptable. She then tried buying the dog a first-class ticket, to no avail. She offered to buy out the entire first-class section and was told that wasn't going to happen.

Then she realized if she was going to spend that amount of money, she could just charter a flight. She made more calls, one after the other, until she was finally connected to a private charter company. She gulped at the cost but told herself it was for Sula and not herself. She rattled off her credit card number and was told someone would call her back by the close of business.

When the call finally came in, Sophie again gasped at the terms and conditions. First, the professional voice asked if she would be on the pilot's return flight. That gave Sophie pause for thought. If she was going to stay in Georgia any length of time, she had to provide accommodations for the pilot and hostess. She was told if it was a one-day layover, she was also responsible for accommodations for the pilot and hostess. Rattled, Sophie said she would call back shortly after she checked her plans.

Sophie started to pace the lanai, uncertain what she should do. It wasn't the money; she could afford whatever decision she decided to make. How long did she want to stay in Georgia? Just long enough to meet with the Star lawyers. Just long enough to see Nick and Patty. Just long enough to meet up with Jay, Linda, and Kala and thank them in person, pay off her bills, settle her finances, get some idea of where she stood in this new life of hers.

Five days, she finally decided. Five days, then Sula and she would head back to Hawaii. Her plan on her return would be to find a house of her own, buy it, and settle in. That was when she remembered reading that there was a house on the island that had belonged to the Stars. On some hilltop. The list of holdings said it was an estate. She needed to look into that before she left.

Sophie called the charter company back, relayed her plans

and was told the pilot was clear in two days. He was booked for tomorrow and the next day. Sophie agreed, and was told her charge would be put through on her credit card. She clapped her hands in glee, then called Kiki, asking him if he knew about the hilltop estate and if he could find someone to take her there. He said he would take her up the mountain the following morning at ten o'clock.

Happier than a pig in a mud slide, Sophie checked the messages on the cell phone. She had thirty-seven messages. Her eyes popped wide as she listened to them, her face wreathed in smiles. Thirty-one of them were from Nick, and six were from Patty. And the cell phone was blinking red—the battery was dead.

Quicker than lightning, she plugged in the charger and sat back to daydream until she had enough minutes charged to call Nick. While she waited she ran out to the mailbox. And there it was, a large padded envelope from Linda with her belongings. She was ripping at the envelope as she made her way back to the house. There were her pearls, her bracelet, her Timex watch, which was actually ticking and had the correct time on it, and, of course, the locket Nick had given her. Her hands shook as she clasped it around her neck. She slipped on the bracelet and decided the fake pearls weren't needed but she knew she'd never get rid of them. They were hers, bought and paid for herself with her savings. She knew then she could buy a dozen strands of real pearls if she wanted to. She could buy diamonds by the bushel if she wanted to. She never would, she knew. She had more than enough with what was right in front of her. Money could not buy happiness. It could buy security and contentment but not happiness.

"And how profound is that, Sophie Lee?"

Chapter 25

PATTY MOLNAR WAS SO EXCITED SHE HAD TO TAKE DEEP CALMING breaths. Sophie's plane was due to land in three hours. Patty had personally arranged the welcoming committee. She thought about Nick then, and the look on his face when he told her about his hour-long conversation with Sophie. He had been so happy until he got to the part where Sophie was only staying five days. She herself had been devastated at the short length of time Sophie planned to stay. Lord, how she missed her. How would they ever cram everything in to five short days with all the legal stuff Sophie had to attend to?

There had been so many questions about Jon that she and Nick had to deal with. They had agreed beforehand not to tell Sophie until they could do it in person. Since it was Patty's week to have Jon's urn, she had him in the car to hand over to Sophie. She hoped Sophie wouldn't fall apart. From the conversation they'd had, she knew Sophie wasn't the same person she was ten years ago. Sophie was tough, or at least Sophie said she was. Patty wondered if it was true. The conversation had been sisterly, full of a lot of *do you remembers?* and all of Sophie's plans for the future. The main plan was relocating and putting down roots someplace where she would be at peace.

Hawaii was that place, Sophie said. But it was so far away.

An ocean away, thousands of miles away. There was no way she'd be able to call Sophie and meet for some girl talk. Of course, she could use the Webcam, e-mail, and phone, but it wouldn't be the same. They would still be thousands of miles and an ocean away from each other. A tear formed in the corner of Patty's eye, then rolled down her cheek. She brushed at it. No time for tears. Today was a happy day. And it was Tuesday!

The last time she'd spoken to Sophie she'd said the charter flight she engaged had to be canceled because of a family crisis of some sort with the pilot's son. Sophie said she thought the boy had to have an emergency appendectomy, and she was okay with the delay because the earliest the pilot could commit to was Tuesday, today. Everything happens for a reason, Sophie had said happily. "Remember, I'm Tuesday's Child." Like she or any of the others could ever forget that fact.

Patty looked down at her watch. Time for what she hoped was the last meeting of her six-man investigative group. She'd file her last report with Kala and move on. With Sophie's return, Kala said they would be able to wrap it all up.

Already, the *Sophie Lee v. Ryan Spenser* articles were relegated to the back pages in the papers. There were too many disasters in the world to keep Spenser in the foreground.

Patty sighed as she picked up a pile of folders and headed to the conference room, which could accommodate twelve people easily at the one-of-a-kind teak table Kala had had specially made in Hawaii and shipped to Atlanta.

Patty poured a cup of coffee from the sideboard and settled herself to wait for the others as she was eight minutes early. In less than three hours, she was going to see Sophie, her best friend in the whole world.

Her thoughts were all over the map. She'd been offered a job with Fox News, and she was a hair away from signing on. Her old boss had sent one of his underlings to her house two days ago, asking her what she wanted, to avoid the lawsuit Jay had filed against the paper. She'd gotten such perverse pleasure flipping him the bird and reminding him that anything he or his boss had to say to her had to be transmitted through her lawyer, and she would certainly tell her lawyer about this improper communication.

What will be will be, she thought. The suit, a judge had ruled, had merit. Discrimination of any kind had to be taken seriously. In the past three days, she'd received numerous phone calls from other fired female employees asking to join her suit. She'd turned them all over to Jay, who was working diligently on the case. She knew that sooner or later, it would all be settled out of court; those things always were. She was okay with that because, for her, it wasn't about the money, it was about accountability. She, along with all the kids at St. Gabe's, had been taught that you own what you do, take responsibility. She lived by that rule.

The door opened, and Team Patty, as the group referred to themselves, trooped into the room, plopped down, and gave a collective sigh. All six of them looked weary, their eyes bloodshot, their hair mussed, their clothes wrinkled.

"We've been working around the clock to meet your deadline, Patty," Rob said. "If you hold on a minute, I'll give you everything we have. Bill, give me a hand, will you?"

Patty watched in awe as the two young men wheeled in two dollies with boxes lined to the top, ten in all.

"These are all the old cases that Ryan Spenser either prosecuted himself or oversaw for his ADAs. In the top box on the second dolly are the affidavits of the different defense lawyers who are out there spinning their wheels hoping to get some of their convictions overturned. It's not going to happen. There are no irregularities, and we had six pairs of eyes going over these cases with a fine-tooth comb. Sorry for the cliché, but Spenser is as pure as the driven snow. We told you the same thing about the Sophie Lee trial, but you didn't want to believe us," Rob Pope said.

"Can we go now? We haven't had a wink of sleep in three days, and no showers either, and we're a bit gamey," Bonnie said.

"You can turn all this over to your *licensed* investigators to handle now. We made it easy for them by writing a detailed summary of every single case," Rob said.

Chairs were pushed back, and the six law students prepared to leave the room. "You just ruined a guy who gave his all to the system, you know that, right?" Beth snarled. "You and the goddamn media. You all think you're God! Tell us all, because we want to know, how does Ryan Spenser get his life back? He did his job, and did it better than any prosecutor we came across, and he's been vilified. This whole thing damn well stinks!"

The door closed with a bang behind the students. Patty sat for a long time, just staring at the stacked boxes. She felt sick to her stomach. She wondered what Kala was going to say. What could she say, when it came right down to it? She tried to drown out her thoughts by thinking of Sophie's arrival, but Sophie was suddenly taking second place in her mind.

Patty reached for her cell phone and called Kala, who had elected to stay home to make Jay happy. She answered on the fifth ring. "You are interrupting my bubble bath, Patty," Kala said before Patty could even identify herself. Caller ID, in her opinion, was a curse. She liked the element of surprise as to who was on the other end of the phone.

"No one I know takes a bubble bath at two o'clock in the afternoon. Please don't tell me you have scented candles burning and are drinking wine," Patty retorted.

"Well, since you guessed what I'm doing, then I don't have to confirm or deny it, and I know at least one other person who takes bubble baths at this hour. Why are you calling me anyway?"

Patty told her why. Kala was silent for so long, Patty had to prod her to see if she was still on the line. "I heard you. I'm thinking. Do me a favor. Call Spenser's house and ask him if I can stop by. Tell him I need to discuss something important. Forty-five minutes. He doesn't live far from me. And no, he is not hiding out, although I wouldn't blame him if he was. Don't worry, I'll be at the airport in plenty of time to meet Sophie with you all."

"Kala, did you finish going through the journals?"

"I did last night. Why do you think I'm taking a bubble bath at two in the afternoon? I didn't even go to sleep last night. There's nothing there. We need the last and final journal, and it's nowhere to be found."

"Maybe we'll never find it, Kala," Patty said, sadness ringing in her voice. "Who is the other person who takes a bubble bath at two in the afternoon?"

"Jay, and he likes blue cypress and lavender bath salts because they calm the nerves," Kala said as she broke the connection.

"Oh," was all Patty could think of to say, but she made a mental note to buy some blue cypress and lavender bath salts.

Patty eyed the boxes in front of her before she swiveled her chair around to peck at the phone console. She pressed Jay's extension and waited. "All the files are in the conference room. Your *licensed* investigators can have them all now. But be warned, there is nothing in them. Spenser did absolutely nothing wrong. I called Kala and told her. She asked me to call Spenser to tell him she's on her way to his house, and I'll do it as soon as I hang up. Then I'm going home to shower and change. I'll see you all at the airport."

Ryan Spenser opened the door and stared at Kala, who was wearing a red hibiscus over her left ear and a white one over her right ear. "Covering your bases, eh?" he said, grinning.

"Sort of, kind of. Damn, it's hot out there. You got anything cold to drink, Spenser?"

"I do. Name your poison." He grinned again.

"How come you're so chipper?"

Spenser shrugged. "The weight of the world is off my shoulders. I'm a free agent for the first time in my life. I like the feeling."

Kala eyed the man who had been her adversary for so many years. It still stunned her that she actually liked him. She smiled at his attire: cargo shorts that were frayed at the hem, a stretched-out T-shirt that said he was a member of some fraternity whose letters were all but washed out. He was barefoot and hadn't shaved. She liked this new Spenser. Even though he was smiling, his teeth didn't look so polished. They just looked like he had a good dentist.

"Sun tea. I make it myself." Spenser reached into the freezer for two glasses that had frost all over them. Kala thought they looked like beer mugs.

"This is good!" Kala said, drinking deeply.

"I know. Take a load off," he said, pointing to one of the wooden stools in the kitchen. "What brings you here at this time of day?"

"You sound just like Patty Molnar. Why does everything have to work around a certain time of day? Why can't I take a bubble bath at two o'clock in the afternoon? Why can't I come here to your home at three o'clock in the afternoon? Is there some book out there that says we have to conform to a time schedule?"

Kala didn't realize how shrill her voice was until Spenser held up his hand and went, "Whoa there, Nellie!"

"Sit down, Spenser. I want you sitting when I tell you this, so when I offer my apology, you won't fall over." To make her point, Kala plucked the two flowers from her hair and placed them in the middle of the table. "Every one of your old cases came up whistle clean. . . . Why are you looking at me like that, Spenser?"

"Because I told you I did nothing wrong. And this all surprised you. That's why you're surrendering with the flowers?"

"Well, yes, I guess so. How could you be so damn perfect? Everyone screws up at some point. You never did. How is that possible?"

"All those *other people* you're referring to don't have a father like mine. I don't want to go there right now, Kala. I appreciate your coming here to tell me, though."

"I want to hold a press conference and tell the world, you standing right there alongside of me, with Sophie Lee in the middle. Tomorrow I'll arrange it. Sophie's plane lands in a few hours. I called her on the way over, and she's all for it. Believe it or not, Spenser, she holds no ill feelings toward you. She knows and understands you were just doing your job. That's not to say that during her ten-year incarceration, she didn't plot your death every night of her life when she was falling asleep."

"So what you're saying is, when I apologize in person, she isn't going to kick me in the nuts."

Kala smiled. "No, Sophie is not going to do that. That's not who she is. All along I've tried to tell you what a remarkable young woman she is. If I had a daughter, I'd want her to be just like Sophie Lee. I haven't mentioned it to her yet, but I'm going to suggest she forfeit the second ten million."

Spenser was off his chair in a flash. "Oh, no! No, no! That young woman deserves every penny you can milk out of this state. If it was up to me, I'd vote for fifty million. You could have gotten it, too, Kala, if you'd played ball a little harder. That's what they were prepared to pay out. Over time, of course."

"Now you tell me!" Kala drained the last of her sun tea.

Spenser laughed so hard his shoulders shook. "I did tell you, you just didn't pick up on it. I told you *not* to go for fifty million. That was supposed to be your clue, but you let it fly right over your head."

"Imagine that," Kala drawled, as she mentally calculated what a third of $50 million would come to for Aulani coffers. She shrugged. Win some, lose some.

"Yeah, imagine that."

"There was nothing in the journals. I brought one to show you. Audrey Star could barely write. I made myself crazy trying to decipher her daily recordings. It was all just your basic girly stuff, gushing and prattling on about nothing. We found where Adam hid all the jewelry that wasn't kept in the safe-deposit box. Right there on the same bookshelf as the diaries. Take a look at this," Kala said, reaching down into her briefcase to pull out one of the leather-bound journals.

Spenser leafed through the elegantly bound book and let loose with a soft whistle. "I had no idea. I had no clue the woman was mentally challenged. There was not even a hint from Adam Star. Not that it would have mattered in the end. It might have created more of a circus atmosphere, which would have really played hell with your client at trial. I'm glad we didn't know it because I would have exploited it to the nth degree. It would have been my job to do that."

"I know, and I'm also glad none of us knew it. Let that poor woman rest in peace. I wish I knew, though, why Adam married Audrey. For some reason I don't think it was the money. He said it wasn't. But then look what he did."

"Yes, look what he did. I know he confessed to killing his wife, but there's something about it that just doesn't ring true to me. I'm very glad for Sophie Lee's sake, but for some reason it just isn't adding up for me. For the life of me I cannot figure out what it is. Do you have any ideas about it?"

Kala shrugged as she got to her feet. "I'll have the office call you later today after they arrange for the press conference. I promise to be humble tomorrow."

Spenser laughed. "Enjoy your meeting with Sophie."

"I will. Thanks for the tea. You can keep that diary. We have a ton of them. All but the last one. Give it some thought, Spenser. You were there that day. Try to remember if you saw it, didn't think it was important, whatever."

"Kala, I can't afford to lose any more sleep over this. When I can't figure something out, I can't sleep. I was hoping tonight for a good night's sleep."

"If I can't sleep, why should you?" Kala quipped.

Chapter 26

THEY WERE EXCITED, BABBLING TO EACH OTHER, AS THEY watched the sleek charter plane's wheels hit the runway. The late-afternoon sun coated the plane and the surrounding air in a golden sheen that looked like a glistening nimbus. That did not go unnoticed by any of the six people waiting expectantly for Sophie Lee's arrival.

The plan was for all of them to return to the Aulani offices, where two bottles of Dom Pérignon were chilling for a small celebration. And then, Kala had said, "us old people will go about our business and let the young people get reacquainted." Meaning, of course, Sophie, Patty, and Nick. Patty had argued with Nick for hours, saying Sophie needed to stay with her. Nick could see the logic of it, and, of course, he was invited along, but still he didn't like it. He wanted Sophie to himself. He wanted so much, but he knew that Sophie couldn't be overwhelmed right then.

"Slow and steady" had been Ben's fatherly advice, and he knew it was good advice. Following it would be the hard part. His good hip ached. He ignored the ache and concentrated on the plane, which had just come to a standstill. Even though he wore sunglasses, the glare of the sun was blinding. Would he even be able to see Sophie clearly when she first appeared in the cabin doorway? He could hardly wait to drink in the sight of her.

Jay sidled up to Kala, his cell in hand. He read from a short text he'd just received. "Press conference is scheduled for ten o'clock at the courthouse. Spenser confirmed. We're good to go, Kala."

Kala nodded. Her big problem was what color flower to wear in her hair. Red or white? A wicked thought raced through her mind. She wondered if she could convince Spenser to wear a white hibiscus in his lapel, and she'd wear one in her hair. A united front. The bullshit is over. We're a team who in the end just wants justice to be served. No one's ego had to be stroked. Done. Over. Her heart kicked up an extra beat.

"The door is opening," Patty squealed.

"You look too serious, sweetheart," Ben whispered in Kala's ear. "Lighten up. By the way, when we go home, we are going to go through those mail sacks. An old friend of mine called me this morning to tell me he sent me something he wanted an opinion on and wanted to know why I hadn't responded. I explained about the mail, being away, then coming back to this circus. I promised to read through it this evening and get back to him ASAP."

"Works for me. I don't have anything planned for this evening. And you're right, I can't back out my convertible because Patty dumped the sacks behind it. That means we have a plan. Are you going to grill some tuna for us? I'll make the salad, and I'll even clean the grill."

"Now that's an offer I can't refuse. There's our girl, Kala!"

And there she was. Sophie wore a white waffle-weave sundress that showed off her glorious tan. Kala blinked at her fashionable haircut, the highlights in it, but she was stunned to see a cluster of white hibiscus tucked behind her right ear. She frowned and didn't know why. Around her neck, Sophie wore a scarlet lei that looked professionally made. The frown stayed on Kala's face. Even from where she was standing she could make out the gold locket around Sophie's neck. She wondered why the young woman wasn't moving. It looked to her like Sophie was posing, so that the moment was frozen in time. And then she saw the big dog heading down the steps. Sula! She'd forgotten about Sula.

Kala looked down at the shopping bag at Patty's feet. Jon's ashes.

The sun dimmed as a puffy white cloud sailed underneath. All of them sucked in their breath as Sophie picked up her feet and ran toward them, Sula sprinting ahead.

Sophie stopped short at the gate, Sula at her side. She looked at everyone and started to cry before she walked through to her loved ones.

Nick wanted to hold out his arms and wished with all his might that Sophie would rush into them. She did, but not right away.

Patty, tears rolling down her face, could only say, "God, I missed you, Sophie."

Jay and Linda smiled as they, too, wondered about the white flowers tucked into Sophie's hair.

Sophie stepped to the side of the little group and homed in on Kala. Her smile rivaled the sun that was shining again. Kala watched as Sophie advanced and withdrew the scarlet lei and draped it around her neck. "I made it myself on the way here. I picked the flowers fresh and kept them cooled in the refrigerator on the plane. I made it just before we landed." She hugged Kala so tight, Kala thought her ribs were cracked.

"Welcome home, Sophie," Kala whispered.

Sophie went down the line, kissing, hugging, and crying until she came to Nick. She stepped into his outstretched arms and kissed him on the cheek. "There are no words to tell you how much I missed you, Nick," she murmured against his cheek.

The three young people moved forward, leaving Jay, Linda, Kala, and Ben. A string of marshmallow clouds slid past the sun, allowing Kala to see the strange expression on Jay's face.

"Time to celebrate, people! Our girl is home, and this whole sorry mess is finally over. Why are you all looking like that?" Ben asked.

"Like what?" Kala asked testily.

"Like you suddenly lost your best friend. You all just got your best friend back. We should be happy, and there should be a spring in your steps. You're lagging," Ben responded.

"Yeah, why is that?" Linda asked.

"I think it's your imagination, Ben," Kala said. "Sophie looks beautiful, doesn't she, Linda?"

"She sure does. On my best day, I could never look that good," Linda said, but there was no envy in her voice.

"Honey, you are every bit as beautiful as Sophie every day of your life."

"That was certainly the right answer. Even if it isn't true." Linda giggled.

"That girl has come into her own. She's set for life. She doesn't have a worry in the world right now. What's that old ditty, Kala?" Not waiting for a response, Ben came up with the answer. "Ah, yes, the world is her oyster. Meaning, of course, there is a priceless pearl in said oyster. Did I get that right, Kala?"

Kala smiled. "Close enough, dear. Look at them! Have you ever seen a happier trio in your life? Such a remarkable friendship. Such deep loyalty. And they're orphans," Kala said. She didn't expect a comment, and there was none forthcoming.

The driving arrangements completed, everyone got in their cars to head to the Aulani offices for the celebration of Sophie's return.

An hour later, the first champagne cork flew across the room. They all toasted Sophie's return. They drained their glasses as Linda popped the second bottle. "This one is to sip before we call it a day," she said happily.

Conversation was light and merry, the mood exuberant. Smiling faces abounded.

Ben Jefferson made the first move by nudging Kala. It was time to leave. Another round of hugs followed.

Kala and Ben were the first out the door, followed minutes later by Sophie, Patty, and Nick. Linda and Jay stayed behind to tidy up and close the office.

"Okay, Jay, spit it out. What's bothering you?" Linda said as she swept the plastic champagne glasses into the trash basket. The empty champagne bottles followed. "And don't tell me nothing is bothering you. I know you too well."

"I just had a . . . kind of eerie feeling out there at the airport. I think Kala did, too. I think . . . I know this is going to sound silly, and maybe it's a girl thing, but I think it had something to do with the flowers."

Linda laughed until the tears rolled down her cheeks. "The flowers! The lei? Or the white flowers in Sophie's hair? You're right, that is silly. Sophie learned how to make the lei. She made it fresh just for Kala. And the white flowers in her hair the way Kala wears hers . . . that was just to show Kala she appreciated all that she's done for her."

Jay listened to his wife because he always listened to her. She had more street smarts and common sense than anyone he knew, and that included himself. "Okay, then maybe it was the color. Red is when Kala goes to war. White is for winning and victory. So why was the lei red? I think Kala was wondering the same thing. So there, Miss Smarty Pants. Explain it to me."

Linda laughed again. "Is it even remotely possible that when it was time to pick the flowers, the red ones were the prettiest? Maybe you didn't notice it because you're a guy, but there were tiny white flowers in among the red ones. Did you miss that, my genius husband?"

"Yeah, I guess I did. This is one of those whatever kind of things, I'm thinking. Do you want to go out to eat or cook at home?" Jay asked, a clear indication that any further discussion about red or white flowers was over and done with.

"Home. I have this crazy urge to cook for you, darling. I want to wait on you hand and foot."

"I do not want Lipton noodle soup and grilled cheese. I want real *food*. I want mashed potatoes, gravy, and a big slab of meat. You can have my salad. Oh, and I want a giant slice of blackberry pie with two scoops of vanilla ice cream."

Linda sighed. Happily. "Okay, it's Mulligans. It's early enough that we won't need a reservation. Carry on, fearless leader, and I'll be right behind you." Linda felt pleased with herself. Jay fell for it every time. She didn't have to cook, and that was her intention all along. "But, if you keep that puss on, I'm going home. Show me some teeth now in a big smile."

Jay grimaced, but Linda settled for what she called a half-assed smile.

Nine miles away Sophie, Patty, and Nick sat at Patty's kitchen table with large glasses of sweet tea in front of them. Sula slept under the window.

"This is really a cute little house, Patty. It's you. When are you guys going to tell me what's in the shopping bag you've been carrying around?"

Seeing the uncomfortable look on Patty's face, Nick jumped into the conversation. "So tell us what your plans are, Sophie."

"Like I said in the car on the way here, I'm staying five days. I want to go to St. Gabriel's to make a donation to Sister Julie and, of course, see all the nuns. That's a whole day right there. I want to hang with you guys as much as I can, but I have meetings with the lawyers at Star. I have to make decisions. At least that's what Kala told me. There is the news conference tomorrow. On the flight here, I was thinking I might like to go to the Star mansion and walk through it. I know how morbid that sounds, but for some strange reason I think I need to do that. Do you guys want to go with me?"

"Sure," Nick said. He would have said yes to anything Sophie suggested. "We were just there a week ago. In all the excitement at the airport and the office, I guess we forgot to tell you. We found Audrey Star's old journals. And the jewelry she kept at the mansion. You should see it, Sophie. Tons of diamonds and all kinds of fancy gold jewelry."

"There wasn't tons but there was a lot. Probably as much as the Queen of England has. What are you going to do with it all?" Patty asked curiously.

Sophie fingered the locket at her neck, then the bracelet on her wrist. "I don't have a clue. I have to speak to some investment people. I'm sure they'll have ideas. Was there anything there you two would like? If there is, help yourself."

"Are you serious?" Patty asked, her jaw dropping.

"I think I'll pass," Nick said.

Sophie looked at Patty. "Of course I'm serious. Take it all if you want."

"I couldn't do that, Sophie. And anyway, I'm no lawyer, but I think it belongs to the estate and has to go through probate. There was a pair of earrings I liked, though."

"Then when it's all said and done, they're yours," Sophie said happily. "What's in the bag, Sophie? And, I hate to bring this up, but what's for dinner? Do you think we could order a loaded pizza? I have been dying for pizza. And an ice-cold root beer. Did you guys go and buy me a present? Is that the surprise that's in the shopping bag?"

Nick had his cell phone in hand to call to order the pizza. He looked at Patty, and Patty looked at him. They both shrugged at the same time.

"It . . . it's not a gift but it . . . it's going to be a surprise," Patty said in a choked voice.

Sophie grew so still, Sula got up and walked over to her, sensing something the others couldn't define. "Why don't you just tell me what's in the bag? Is it Audrey's last journal, the one you all couldn't find?"

Nick looked so stricken, Patty had a hard time coming up with the words she was looking for. She finally blurted out, "Why would you think that?"

Sophie threw her hands up in the air. "I don't know. You said a surprise. That's the only surprise I can think of. You all said you couldn't find it. The last piece of the puzzle, so to speak. If that isn't it, then what is it? Don't tell me it's Sister Julie's famous seven-layer chocolate cake. That's it, right? Listen, I'm sensing something here, and I don't know what it is. It feels to me like we're all trying too hard to . . . to regain what we once had. We're different people today. Ten years is a long time. I guess you two think I'm different, or now that I'm suddenly rich, I'm going to turn into someone else. That's what I'm seeing here. Am I wrong? So, will one of you tell me what's in the damn bag already so we can get past this . . . awkward moment."

"It's Jon's ashes. Jon died several years after you went to prison. He got some kind of jungle bug, and with his weak immune system, he couldn't fight it off. We had him cremated. Patty and I take turns keeping his ashes. It was Patty's turn this week. She brought the urn to show you."

Sophie's face went totally blank. "Why didn't you tell me?"

"Because," Patty said, bitterness ringing in her voice, "you cut off all visitation and the mail that we sent you was returned. We did try, Sophie." Patty swiped at the tears rolling down her cheeks. Nick looked away before he knuckled his own eyes.

"I wonder why I didn't sense something. We were all so close. I am so sorry. When I first got off the plane and saw the only person missing was Jon, I was going to ask you both if you thought he would be able to come back if I sent him a ticket. I thought . . . I thought . . . I could fly you all to Hawaii, and we could have an island reunion. But in the excitement, I forgot, and that's not a good thing. I can't believe . . . Let me see the urn, Patty."

Patty bent over and removed the urn from the shopping bag. She held it close to her heart for a moment before she set it on the table. Sophie didn't touch it, but she stared at it for a long time. "Was there a service?"

"Of course there was a service. Why would you even ask that question, Sophie?" Patty snapped.

"We took the urn to St. Gabe's and had a service in the chapel. Father Latham officiated. It was sad but beautiful. Everyone cried. Why aren't you crying, Sophie?" Nick asked coolly.

"I guess I'm in shock and still trying to absorb that Jon is gone. In prison you learn not to show emotion. If you do, you're considered weak, and you become a target."

Neither Nick nor Patty asked Sophie what she meant by that.

"Listen, would you guys mind if I turn in? I didn't sleep at all last night because I was so excited about coming back. I'm really tired, and I can't remember ever drinking two full glasses of champagne in my life. If it's okay with you guys, we can do the pizza tomorrow. Plus, I just had the shock of my life."

"No problem, Sophie. Go on upstairs. Your room is the first door on the left. It has its own bathroom," Patty said.

There were no hugs, no kisses as Sophie left the kitchen. It was silent as she walked out to the living room, then to the foyer and up the staircase to the second floor. No one even said good night.

"Who was that person?" Nick asked in a strangled voice.

Patty flopped down on the kitchen chair. "I don't know, Nick. Certainly not the Sophie I knew and loved. What happened here?" The tears started to flow again.

Nick lowered himself to the chair and reached for Patty's hands. He squeezed them. "Prison does strange things to people. It changes them. You read about it all the time, and it's always on the news."

"But Sophie—I didn't think anything could change her. She was happy to see us, yes, but . . . I don't know how to put it, Nick. It's like she was going through the motions. She didn't shed a tear over Jon."

"She said you could have all the jewelry. That's Sophie, generous as always. And she was wearing the locket." Nick realized how lame his defense was when Patty made a very unladylike snort of sound.

"All of a sudden she has to go to all these meetings. She has to take care of that empire she inherited. She's rich now. She was going to fly us all to Hawaii for this grand reunion. The old Sophie would never have said things like that."

"I thought that was generous of her. How else could she have said it, Patty?"

"I don't know, Nick. All I'm saying is, this is not the old Sophie I knew and loved like a sister. If you think so, then you are just fooling yourself."

"I will admit I was disappointed. But like I said, we all changed. Why should we think Sophie wouldn't change? To her, we're probably different, too. Maybe she was disappointed in us and kept it to herself. Ten years is a long time. . . . I'm going home. Do you want to keep Jon or should I take him?"

"Go ahead, take him. I'll pick him up next week after Sophie leaves. I'm sorry, Nick. I know you were expecting things to be different. I wish . . . dammit, I just wish things were different."

"Good night, Patty. I'll talk to you tomorrow. Call me after the press conference, okay?"

"Sure." She walked Nick to the door, let him kiss her cheek, and accepted the brief hug they always shared. Nick was real. Sophie didn't feel real.

Chapter 27

KALA SLID HER EMPTY DINNER PLATE TO THE CENTER OF THE table. "The tuna was excellent, Ben. As always."

Ben knew it was worth his life if he didn't respond in kind. "And your salad was delicious even if you did just dump it out of a bag and smear some dressing all over it."

"Everyone is a critic," Kala laughed. "This is my favorite time of day. The sun is on the way down, the oppressive humidity doesn't seem as bad, and before you know it, the stars will be out, and we can make our first wish of the night. I think it's a full moon tonight, too. You know what they say about a full moon, don't you, Ben?"

Ben laughed. "That all the lunatics in the world come out from hiding, and the emergency rooms at the hospitals are so full the hospitals add extra staff when there's a full moon."

Kala nodded. Her fingers drummed on the glass-top table.

"You're not yourself tonight, Kala. You should be happy. Do you want to talk about whatever it is that's bothering you?"

"Well, for one thing, those stupid petunias in the pots are almost dead. I hate looking at dead flowers."

Ben blinked when he saw Kala reach up and rip the lei from her neck and toss it toward one of the petunia pots. "There, now there's some color!"

Ben chewed down on his lower lip as he got up to clear the

table. He was done in five seconds. Hard plastic plates, plastic glasses. Silverware went into the dishwasher. Done. He turned the grill on high to burn off the residue. When it cooled down, three good strokes with the wire brush, and the grill would be good to go the next time Kala wanted grilled something or other.

"Time to get to the mail bags. I've got to leave as soon as I find the package my buddy sent me. What are you going to do this evening?"

Kala shrugged. "Maybe I'll soak in the hot tub with a couple of glasses of wine while I shop on the shopping channel, then I'll go to bed."

"Sounds deadly to me," Ben said.

"To me, too, so I'll probably watch a rerun of something on TV. Let's get to those damn mail bags and get it over with."

Ben beat Kala to the garage in seconds. He unfolded two aluminum lawn chairs, which he placed half in the garage and half in the driveway. Then he rolled one of the huge trash cans and placed it between the two chairs. "All we have to do is go through it and toss what we don't want into the can. I'll wheel it back to the gate, and we're done. We should have done this days ago. Mail is sacred," he huffed.

"If you say so," Kala said through clenched teeth.

It took both of them to upend Kala's canvas bag of mail. She shuddered at the array of catalogs and flyers. She went to work separating the first-class mail into a pile; the junk mail was tossed into the trash can with barely a glance.

"You know, Kala, you have got to be on someone's mailing list. If you'd stop shopping from catalogs, you wouldn't be getting all this junk mail. Ah, here's what I'm looking for." Ben tossed what looked like a heavy manila envelope to the side and finished up with the rest of his junk mail.

"Fold up the bags and take them out to the mailbox. Patty said the mailman will pick them up. They have to be returned to the post office, and I don't want to make a trip there. And the reason I shop from catalogs is I hate driving through parking lots looking for a parking space, then standing in line to check out."

"Point taken, dear."

"Will you get that garden basket over there so I can put all this other stuff I have to go through into it? I see there are overdue notices for the house insurance and every other insurance I have. Not to mention the utility bills. How could I have forgotten all that stuff? That's not like me."

Ben tried to make his voice as soothing as possible. "In all fairness, Kala, you did have a lot on your mind—the trip, Sophie, the office, the whole ball of wax. You can pay online in ten minutes. If you're good to go here, I'm going to leave. I have to help my friend; he's counting on me."

"Go ahead. I'll see you in the morning. Are you going to be at the courthouse?" Kala asked as she folded the lawn chairs and stacked them up against the wall.

"If you want me there, I'll be there. I can even pick you up."

"Okay, that works. Nine-thirty should do it. Night, sweetie, and thanks for cooking dinner."

Kala waved to Ben as she pressed the remote that would close the garage door.

Inside the kitchen, she kicked off her shoes, opened her laptop, booted up, then poured a tall glass of wine for herself. She ripped at envelopes, typed in amounts, and sent off her payments, all within minutes. All the first-class mail and congratulatory cards taken care of, Kala looked at the two padded envelopes that were the last things she had to go through. One had a local address she didn't recognize, and the other was something she'd ordered from the shopper's channel. She ripped at the envelope. A purple pepper mill. Her favorite color. The other envelope was in a post office priority padded envelope. She ripped at it.

Kala's eyes rolled back in her head. She gripped the edge of the kitchen table with both hands because she thought she was going to black out. The minute she was able to focus, she reached for the tall wineglass and drained it. Her eyes watered, her throat burned, and she could barely catch her breath. She dropped her head between her knees and struggled to take great gulping breaths. She reached for her cat, Shaky, and brought him up to her lap. He purred and licked at her. She started to babble to the cat, not understanding a thing she was saying. Obviously, Shaky didn't understand it either. He stopped purring and hissed his displeasure before he hopped to the floor with a loud plop. His luxurious plumed tail swished angrily as he waddled from the room. In the doorway he turned, hissed again, then disappeared to his bed, wherever he had dragged it to earlier in the day.

A good ten minutes went by, the slowest ten minutes of Kala's life, as she struggled to get herself under control. The moment she felt like she was firing on all cylinders, Kala reached for the wine bottle and poured. So what if she got drunk? So what?

Kala looked down at the kitchen table. Audrey Star's last journal stared at her like some benevolent eye. In this case, a yellow spiral notebook kind of eye. She didn't touch it. Instead, she looked at the address on the priority envelope and the date. The mailing date was the very day Adam Star Clements had expired. The address looked familiar: 5665 Peachtree Dunwoody Road in northeast Atlanta. Of course! St. Joseph's Hospital!

Adam had had the journal all along. And as he had appointed her as the personal representative for his estate, it was only natural that he would send this last—what was it, a piece of evidence?—to her? Why?

Kala gulped at the wine, but she didn't drain her glass. Her hands were shaking so badly she could barely hold it. She wished then that Ben had stayed with her. A second later, she was glad he hadn't stayed with her.

Kala sat on her hands to stop them from trembling until she realized she wouldn't be able to open the diary or turn the pages. She got up and started to pace around her kitchen table, her arms and hands flapping like some silly marionette. She drank more wine straight from the bottle.

Finally, finally, Kala sat down at the table and opened Audrey Star's last and final journal. The time was ten-thirty by the digital clock on the range. At two-thirty, the wine bottle was empty, replenished with a second bottle, which was half-empty when Kala closed the journal. She knew she was drunk as a skunk when she got up and took precise little steps over to the kitchen counter, where she had her cell phone charging. She tried to focus on the numbers she was pressing, but it took her several tries before the phone was picked up on the other end. The voice demanded to know if the caller knew what time it was.

"It's late, Spenser, and I'm drunk. I don't have a clue as to what time it is. You need to come to my house right now. Right now, do you hear me? I just got finished reading Audrey Star's last journal. Are you coming or not?"

"Of course I'm coming. Where did you find it?"

"The post office sent it to me. It's been sitting in my damn garage for over a week now. They held my mail, and Patty just picked it up the other day. When are you coming? Do you know where I live?"

"I do know where you live, and I'm going out my door right now. Stay on the phone with me, do you hear me, Kala?"

"Spenser, this is not . . . Why aren't you here yet? I'll put the light on for you as soon as I can find it. I don't want you tripping over my cat when you get here."

Ryan Spenser broke every speed law in the town of Dunwoody, Georgia, that night. He arrived at Kala's house in eleven minutes. He laughed out loud when he saw the great Kala Aulani standing, more like leaning, in the open doorway, chugging from a bottle of wine.

"What took you so long?" Kala sniffed, as Spenser led her back to the kitchen.

"I think you've had enough of this," he said, pouring the

rest of the wine in the bottle down the drain. "Where do you keep your coffee?"

Kala waved her arm about. Spenser finally found it as Kala staggered to the downstairs bathroom. He shuddered at the horrible sounds finding their way to the kitchen. "You're sounding good in there!" he bellowed. "Keep it up, get it all out!" he bellowed again. He couldn't be sure, but he thought Kala shouted something that sounded like, "Shut the hell up, Spenser."

A long time later, when Kala found her way to the kitchen, Spenser looked up at his colleague. Her face was red and splotchy, her hair looked like a wild bush, but her eyes were focused. "You look like shit, Spenser," she said as she headed to the coffeepot.

"You don't exactly look like a Hawaiian beauty queen yourself." He grinned as he tried to smooth down his spiky hair. "You want to tell me what's in here, or do you want me to actually read it?"

Kala poured two cups of coffee. She handed one to Spenser. "You need to read it for yourself, okay? We can talk about it when you finish it. Whatever you don't understand about Audrey's chicken scratching, I can explain later. But you have to go through it. Where it ends is where Adam started writing. I'm going to go upstairs and take a shower."

"Are you okay, Kala?"

"Hell no, I'm not okay. Why would you ask me such a stupid question, Spenser?"

"Because I want to know," he said patiently. "I'm not going to like this, am I?" Spenser said, pointing to the yellow spiral notebook.

"No, Spenser, you are not going to like it any more than I did when I read it."

"Okay. By the way, how was the homecoming reunion?"

"Very pleasant. We toasted with two bottles of champagne. Then us old people left, and the young ones went to Patty's house. Sophie is staying with Patty. She's only going to be here five days, then she's going back to Hawaii. She said she loves it there. What's not to love? Hawaii is the land of sunshine and all that good stuff. I can't wait to get back there myself. Did you decide what you're going to do with the rest of your life?"

"My plans are a work in progress. But, I'm making inroads. Much to my father's dismay, I might add. Not that it matters to me what he thinks. The funny thing is, Kala, it matters to me what *you* think. Whoever thought I'd be saying something like that? Go figure."

Kala set her coffee cup down and placed her hands on Spenser's shoulders from behind. "The only thing that matters, Spenser, is that you be true to yourself." She gave his shoulders an extrafriendly squeeze before she headed upstairs to shower.

A long time later, smelling like her fragrant lanai in Hawaii, Kala joined Spenser in her kitchen. Her hair was wet and piled on top of her head. She was wearing the ancient comfortable bathrobe that was her best friend. There was fresh coffee. She poured herself a cup and sat down at the table. Spenser looked up once, his face expressionless before he lowered his eyes to keep reading. Kala could see he had just a few more pages to go.

Kala sipped at her coffee and waited patiently.

Chapter 28

PATTY BUSTLED AROUND IN THE KITCHEN AS SHE PREPARED breakfast. She glanced at the clock; Nick was running late. He should have been there by then. She listened to Sophie's footsteps overhead as she prepared for the press conference that was to take place at ten o'clock.

She herself had gotten up well over an hour ago. She liked to take an early-morning hour out on her little patio with a cup of coffee as she thought about her day. She'd been surprised the previous evening to get a call from Fox News asking her to represent the network. It was all politics, she knew that. The people at Fox knew she had the inside track with Kala and Sophie, so why not use her. It would be her first job for the network. She knew for a fact because Kala had told her that after the conference, neither she nor Ryan Spenser would be taking questions. That's where her inside track came in.

Patty turned the bacon in the fry pan. The waffle mix was ready to be poured, and the scrambled eggs were a huge wet lemon color in the bowl just waiting to be poured on the grill. Waffles, bacon, and scrambled eggs had always been the favorite meal of Nick, Sophie, and herself.

She looked up to see Nick standing in the doorway. How handsome he looked. He'd really dressed for the occasion in a summer suit, power tie, and sparkling white shirt. His unruly dark hair was slicked back. He looked like the professional he was. She herself was wearing a robe, but she'd applied her makeup earlier after her shower. All she had to do was scoot into the downstairs bathroom and slip into the dress she was wearing to the press conference.

"Hey there! Just in time. I'm making our favorite breakfast. I hope you brought your appetite. You look . . . wary. What's wrong?"

Nick sat down gingerly. He shrugged. "You know what they say about expectations? Guess mine weren't met. Sophie's different. She was wearing the locket, though."

"You noticed, huh." It wasn't so much a question as a comment. "I think she was just overwhelmed. We didn't talk or anything after you left. She never came down again, and I just sat down here and watched TV. It wasn't exactly the reunion I expected, but it's understandable. Hey, Fox called last night. My first assignment is to cover the press conference. Yeah, I know, it's all politics, but what the heck. Do you think Sophie will give me an exclusive interview?" She laughed. "Kala and Spenser okayed the exclusive. I heard on the early-morning news that Spenser's father, Speaker of the House Spenser, is going to be at the conference. Do I hear the words *photo op* anywhere?" She laughed again.

"We better get moving here. There's going to be all kinds of traffic this morning." Patty deftly finished cooking the breakfast and handed a plate to Nick. She looked at her own plate and wondered if she would be able to eat all the food piled on it. Sophie's plate would stay warm in the oven.

Normally a robust eater, Nick picked at his food while Patty pushed hers around, breaking off little pieces of her waffle, then mashing them into the scrambled eggs until she had a mess on her plate. There was no way she was going to eat any of it. Why, she wondered, had she even bothered to go to all the trouble?

I'm trying to hold on to something that is slipping from my grasp, she thought. She couldn't be sure, but she thought Nick was thinking the same thing. She knew him so well.

Sophie stood in the kitchen doorway, Sula at her side. Patty was stunned at how beautiful her friend looked. "Good morning, my two favorite people in the whole world," she gushed as she walked over to the door to let Sula out. "Ah, our favorite breakfast from the *old days.* I hate to tell you this, Patty, but I don't eat like that anymore. I think prison ruined my stomach. Then when I was in Hawaii, I had to learn to eat healthy, but I appreciate the thought and effort.

"Nick, how handsome you look," Sophie said as she kissed him lightly on the cheek. She walked around the table and did the same thing to Patty.

"How—how did you sleep, Sophie?" Nick asked.

"So-so. I kept thinking about all the things I have to cram into five days. I slept soundly toward morning. I'll just have juice and coffee, Patty," Sophie said, sitting down at her place setting.

I'll just have juice and coffee. A devil perched itself on Patty's shoulder. She pointed to the coffeepot and the fridge. "Help yourself. I just have orange juice."

"Really! I'm now addicted to pineapple juice. That's okay. You couldn't know that, Patty. I'll just have coffee."

Well, you're going to die of thirst if you think I'm going to get up and pour it for you, Patty thought. She did get up and head toward the downstairs bathroom. "I'm going to get dressed and head out. Nick will drive you to the courthouse. Don't worry about cleaning up, my day lady comes in today."

"Ooooh, you have come up in the world, haven't you? A day lady!" Sophie trilled. She made it sound like a day lady was the next thing to the queen's cleaning Patty's little house.

Patty wished she could wipe the sappy look off Nick's face. She shut the bathroom door with a little more force than was necessary. She was seething and didn't know why.

In the kitchen, when Sophie realized no one was going to pour her a cup of coffee, she got up and did it herself. She touched Nick's shoulder, and said, "So, Nick, how are things going? I know we spoke on the phone that day, but we were all so wired up all we did was reminisce. Tell me about yourself, because there's nothing I can tell you about me. I'm like some kind of open freaky book."

"A rich one," Nick said.

"That, too. That just boggles my mind. They said on the news that you were going to have your other hip done. Is that true?"

Nick thought she sounded like she cared. "It's true, but I still have a lot of therapy to go on the one that's been replaced. My golfing career is over, that's for sure. Some of my endorsements are sticking with me. Then there's product out there with my name on it. That stays in place.

"I see you're still wearing that locket I gave you."

"It's my most treasured possession. Linda mailed my meager belongings to me. I put it on right away. It almost makes me feel whole again. Do you have any idea what that means to me?"

Nick nodded. "About Jon," he said, changing the subject. "Are you okay with that?"

"Good Lord, no. I cried all night. That was one of the reasons I couldn't sleep. I really don't want to talk about Jon now. I'll grieve when I have more time."

I'll grieve when I have more time. Nick's eyes burned the way they always burned when he thought of his lifelong friend. "We probably should be going now," he said. "If you're ready," he said coolly. He was surprised at how calm and collected his voice was. "You can't bring the dog. You know that, right?"

"No, I didn't know that, but it's okay. Sula won't destroy Patty's little house. You know, Nick, I used to be in love with you. I dreamed about you all the time. When I was in prison, when all hope was gone of ever seeing you again, the dreams became so intense they actually allowed me to talk to a shrink. It helped a little. Unrequited love is a terrible thing, you know."

Nick felt his insides start to crumble. He hoped his voice was as light as he wanted, but he knew he failed miserably. "Does that mean you no longer love me?"

"Oh, you silly, you! Of course I love you. Like my brother, like Patty as my sister."

Thank God she hadn't asked him what his feelings were. Instead of responding to Sophie's explanation, Nick walked over to the bathroom door, and said, "We're leaving now, Patty."

The door opened, and Patty stepped out. "Whoa!" Nick whistled. "You look . . . spectacular! First day on the job for Fox, and you are going to be the star."

Patty laughed as she smoothed down her dress. She did look good in a wholesome next-door kind of way. "Bet you say that to all the girls! Jed loves this dress. He said it's me. Today, Kala and Spenser are the stars. No pun intended. I'm just going to do the reporting. You guys go ahead. I'm meeting Kala and Spenser before the press conference. Good luck, Sophie!"

"Thanks, Patty. Nick's right, you look gorgeous! By the way, are we still going to go to the Star mansion today?"

"If you want to." Patty's phone took that moment to ring. She reached for it on the counter, clicked on, and said, "Hi." She listened, her eyebrows almost shooting up to her hairline. "No kidding! And it was there all this time!" She continued to listen, then she frowned. "Gotcha! I'm leaving the house now. So are Nick and Sophie. See ya."

"What happened?" Nick asked.

"Kala found Audrey Star's last journal. It was in the mail sack I picked up over a week ago, along with Ben's mail. She didn't go through it till last night. She said she called Spenser, and he came over, and they went through it word for word, page by page. Where Audrey Star stopped writing, Adam started to write. I guess he wrote right up until he died. Kala said they were up all night. Listen, I gotta run. I'll see you at the courthouse. Drive carefully, Nick."

"Yes, Mother," Nick drawled.

Patty laughed as she raced out the door.

Nick held the door open for Sophie. "Do you want me to put the top up?"

"That would be nice," Sophie said, settling herself in the passenger side of the car. "What does all that mean, Nick?"

"You mean about finding the journal?"

"Yes."

"I don't know. Patty didn't say. She was excited, though. It takes a lot to get Patty excited. You must remember that about her. I assume it's all good."

"I wonder why Kala didn't call last night to tell *me.* This is all about me, and I have to find out this way, fourth-hand almost. Don't you agree, Nick?"

"I don't know. It can't be bad, so it has to be good. For you. I'm assuming all the unanswered questions are going to be answered."

There was an anxiousness in Sophie's voice Nick hadn't heard before. "Are you worried?"

"Wouldn't you be?" Sophie said coolly.

"Actually, no." Nick took his eyes off the busy highway just long enough to stare at Sophie. She looked . . . angry? Scared? "By the way, you look really pretty, Sophie. I meant to tell you that back at Patty's, but then she got that call."

"I haven't changed, Nick. I just got a haircut and a suntan. Oh, and a dog." She laughed, but the laughter sounded forced to Nick. "How long do you think the press conference will be?"

"Those things are usually no more than fifteen minutes, if that. I'm sure Spenser and Kala will be reading from a statement. They aren't going to take any questions. I guess you're just going to stand there so all of Atlanta can see you. I really don't know too much about how these legal things work. I'm speaking from an entertainment/sports perspective. I know that I personally hate them."

"I thought I was going to be interviewed."

"You are. Patty has the exclusive. You're part of the package."

"Part of the package? Is that what you said?" Sophie hissed.

"Maybe that was a poor choice of words. I wouldn't worry, Kala has done well by you up until now, and there's no reason to think she won't continue to do so."

"Don't forget how well paid she is, or the firm," Sophie hissed again.

"Since when did you become so money driven?"

"That's not it, Nick, and you know it. I just think I should have been consulted, and I shouldn't have had to hear all this from you. Not even Patty, who didn't really say anything except that Kala found Mrs. Star's journal. Something's not right," Sophie sniffed.

Now that what he thought of as his love life was in shambles, Nick was never so glad to park his car and get out. It took him several minutes to work the stiffness out of his hip and legs. Minutes too long for Sophie, who got out of the car and walked around to where Nick was wincing with pain. "Work through it, Nick. Don't let the pain win. I learned that in prison. It actually works. You have to shift to a neutral zone and work from there."

"This is physical pain, Sophie, not mental pain. There's a difference."

"No, there isn't. Pain is pain. Mental pain can be ten times worse than physical pain. I'm the living proof."

Satisfied that he'd worked out the kinks, Nick led the way to the elevator. He pressed the button, then stepped aside for Sophie to enter. She offered up what he thought of as a million-dollar smile. He stretched his own facial muscles into something that resembled a smile. They rode up the elevator in silence.

Standing in the hallway when they exited the elevator were the members of Camp Aulani and Ryan Spenser.

Nick hung back until Patty walked over to him. Inched her way was more like it, he thought. "What the hell is going on here?" he whispered. "I was expecting . . . not exactly a party atmosphere but something close to it. Why is everyone looking so damn serious? What was in that journal, Patty? By the way, Sophie doesn't love me."

"I'm glad to hear that," Patty said.

Nick stiffened. "What exactly does that mean, Patty?"

"It means Sophie has kicked us to the curb. We aren't kids or young adults anymore. Well, you and I are, but Sophie has not joined our two-man admiration club. She's moved on. Don't you get it? We're the past, we're bad memories now, and Jon is gone. Sophie has a new life now. You tell me where you think either one of us fits in to that new life of hers."

"She said she'll grieve for Jon when she has more time," Nick said in a choked voice.

Patty threw her arms around Nick and whispered in his ear, "Don't take it so hard. You still have me, Nick, and we both have Jon and all our memories—the good ones and now some that aren't so good."

Patty gave Nick an extrahard squeeze until he said "Uncle." "I have to go now," she said. "I belong out there with the press. Catch you later."

"This feels like a funeral procession," Nick said to no one in particular.

"You can say that again," Jay said. Linda nodded in agreement.

Then they were all outside in the bright sunshine. Spenser, seeing how large the crowd of media was, knew that there was no room inside that could hold everyone. It had been his decision to move it all outside, and they were running twenty minutes late, not that anyone was complaining, as a small podium had to be erected along with several miles of cable.

Spenser took the lead at Kala's insistence. Even though the sun was blinding, he removed his sunglasses, as did Kala. Everyone else kept theirs on.

"Ladies and gentlemen, thank you all for coming. Miss Aulani and I have a joint statement to make. We will not be taking any questions, but in several hours we'll have a press release for you at the Aulani law firm. Or we can fax it to you, it's your choice. Right now, we'd both like to introduce you to Sophie Lee." Sophie stepped forward, smiled a little-girl smile, then stepped back to take her place between Spenser and Kala.

"Last night, Mr. Spenser and I found Audrey Star's last journal," Kala began. "We spent the entire night going through it. But before I get into that, I want to assure all of you, and all the lawyers out there who tried cases against Mr. Spenser, and still might think there were irregularities in some of those cases. You are wrong. We hired investigators who dissected each and every case. There was no wrongdoing on Mr. Spenser's part whatsoever. All of you out there vilified this man to sell papers, to get headlines. You ruined his life. A life he dedicated to this city. I say shame on all of you.

"What we learned from Audrey Star's last journal is this. Audrey and her husband had a suicide pact, but Mr. Star, or Mr. Clements, whatever you prefer to call him, changed his mind. Audrey Star committed suicide. You will all be given copies of the journal once we finish with it."

It was Spenser's turn again. "Mr. Star's confession to killing his wife to free Sophie Lee was something none of us contemplated. He wanted to die without the world knowing his wife committed suicide because she was mentally challenged. In the end, whether Audrey Star committed suicide or her husband killed her, Sophie Lee was wrongly imprisoned. All we hope for now is that Sophie Lee can get on with her life with the assistance the state of Georgia will give her for wrongly imprisoning her. That's it, ladies and gentlemen."

Spenser turned aside to let Kala and Sophie go ahead of him. They all ignored the shouted questions from the media.

Inside, they all fled to a room Spenser had had the good sense to prepare before the conference. There was a huge urn of coffee and a plate of pastries sitting in the middle of the table. No one said a word.

"You did well out there, honey," Ben whispered in her ear. He turned to shake Spenser's hand. "You were just as good, son."

"Can I see the journal?" Sophie asked.

"Afraid not, Sophie. It's evidence," Kala said.

"Are you certain it's Mrs. Star's journal?" she asked.

"We're positive. We compared the handwriting to all the other journals. There is not one scintilla of doubt."

"I would have thought you'd want me to authenticate it since I saw it," Sophie said.

"It wasn't necessary, Sophie. You are free now to do whatever you want. You don't have to stay hidden. In a few days, people won't remember who you are or what happened. Your life will be whatever you want it to be. You just have to do the interview with Patty, and you can be on your way. We'll say good-bye now. I wish you well. When you finally locate somewhere permanent, advise me, so I can forward all the estate papers you'll need to sign and go through. We're making great headway, and should wrap it all up in a few weeks."

Tears rolled down Sophie's cheeks. "I don't know how to thank you, Kala. The words don't seem to be enough. I wish there was something I could do for you. If there is, just tell me."

Kala smiled. "I just did my job the way Ryan did his job. It's over now. I don't like to dwell in the past. Have a good life, Sophie."

Everyone hugged, shook hands, or kissed each other. Finally, the only two people left in the room were Patty and Sophie.

"Let's get to it, Sophie," Patty said, switching on her recorder.

Back outside in the hallway Kala spotted the Speaker of the House at the same time Spenser did.

"Oh, shit!" Spenser said. "He never misses a photo op. Wait for me, Kala."

Kala and Ben watched as Spenser walked over to his father. They shook hands. They said a few words, and Spenser was back at their side, a stricken expression on his face.

Suddenly, red-hot rage coursed through Kala. She excused herself and told Spenser and Ben to wait outside for her. She literally ran down the hall, calling out, "Mr. Speaker, Mr. Speaker, can I talk to you for a minute in private?"

"Certainly, Ms. Aulani. Do you have something to say to me?"

"Damn straight I do, Mr. Speaker, and I sure hope to hell you're man enough to hear me out."

The Speaker heard her out, his face draining of all color when Kala said, "You don't deserve a son like Ryan. Didn't you ever wonder, even once, why he never called you 'Dad'? Because you don't deserve that title, that's why. You have to earn it. I personally don't give two hoots in hell what you do in Washington, DC. But I do care about what you do here in my home state with my friend Ryan. You are a loser in every sense of the word. That's all I have to say. Enjoy your trip back to Washington, and I hope this little photo op was all you wanted it to be."

Kala turned around and hurried to the exit where Ben and Spenser were waiting for her. "What did you want to talk to my father about?" Spenser asked.

"I wanted to tell him he isn't as photogenic as he thinks he is."

Spenser laughed as they made their way down the courthouse steps. "Where are we going?" he finally asked.

"Back to my office. There's one more bottle of champagne we need to drink, then Ben and I are going home. We have a wedding to get ready for."

"I hope I'm invited," Spenser said.

"Now that you bring that up, Spenser, I was waiting for just the right moment to ask you if you'd be my best man. Kala and I would like that very much."

Spenser's smile rivaled the sun. "I don't know what to say. Yes, of course. I'm honored, I'm flattered. I can't wait."

"I want you to give me away, Spenser. I need to tell you, though, you are my second choice. I asked Jay, and he adamantly refused. He said he wasn't giving me away to anyone."

Spenser swallowed hard. "I can do that, too, Kala. I really can. I don't mind being second choice."

"Okay, then, let's go celebrate."

Two hours later, the minicelebration was over. Spenser was gone, and Ben went to get the car. Kala's things were packed up once more. This was her final exit from the Aulani law firm.

"So, you're finally getting out of our hair, eh?" Jay said.

"You finally got something right. And I'm not coming back. You need me, call me at home. Home as in Hawaii. Ben and I are outta here first thing in the morning. Get that damned will probated so I can cut all my ties with the Star estate. And do not, I repeat, do not call me for anything frivolous, like you miss me."

"It won't happen. Have a safe trip. See ya at your wedding unless you chicken out."

"No chance."

"Well then, this is good-bye." They hugged, but this time there were no tears. Sadness, yes.

The console on Kala's desk buzzed. She pressed the button as she waved to Jay.

"Sophie Lee is here, Kala," Linda said.

"Tell her to come on back."

"Damn," was all Kala could mutter under her breath.

"Can't get enough of this place, is that it?" Kala said by way of a greeting. She watched as Sophie closed the door behind her. "Is something wrong, Sophie?"

"No. I did the interview. Patty said it went well. I left my itinerary here last night. In all the excitement, I guess I just forgot it. The receptionist gave it to me. I guess I wanted to say good-bye one last time."

"I hope it is the last time, Sophie."

"That's not a very nice thing to say, Kala."

"You killed Audrey Star, didn't you?"

"Yes, Kala, I killed Audrey Star. When Adam wouldn't go through with their suicide pact, she begged me to do it. I couldn't say no. I didn't tell you because it was only a few years after Dr. Kevorkian had been sentenced to a long prison term for second-degree murder, and I didn't think Spenser really had enough evidence to convince a jury I was guilty of anything. Turns out I was wrong about his persuasive powers. Or maybe it was just luck.

"Either way, I broke the law to do what I thought was right and what Mrs. Star wanted done. And the law took its pound of flesh, ten years of my life. If what I did makes me a bad person in your eyes, then I'm sorry about that."

Sophie tucked her itinerary into her purse. "But there's one thing I'm not sorry about—attorney-client privilege."

"Sophie?"

"Yes!"

"Have you forgotten something?"

"What's that, Kala?"

"TODAY IS NOT TUESDAY!

"Okay, people, showtime!" Kala said in a neutral-sounding voice.

Epilogue

December, five months later
Hawaii

THE ISLAND WAS AWASH IN FEVERISH ACTIVITY. THE SNOWBIRDS, a.k.a. tourists, had arrived in force; the approaching Christmas season and Kala Aulani's nuptials only added to the intense excitement. An island wedding was a serious thing, and everyone felt duty-bound to pitch in to make it a perfect day for the new bride.

The sun wasn't up, but Kala hadn't slept more than a few hours in the last hectic days. Guests from the mainland had arrived in slow dribbles, so it was one trip after the other to the airport. Thanks to her large family, accommodations for all worked out just fine. Food was constantly being cooked and served. Kala herself rushed from one thing to another as an island wedding required a lot of preparation, and since she was a perfectionist in all things, she had offered input out the wazoo as her relatives grumbled. She was leaving nothing to chance.

That night was the wedding rehearsal, followed by a luau. She sent out no invitations—that was not how it was done. The whole island was invited to Kala Aulani's wedding. That was standard operating procedure, and there was no getting around it. Not that Kala would even try. Tradition was tradition.

It was still dark out, as dark as Kala's thoughts, and that shouldn't be. No matter how hard she'd tried during these last five months, she couldn't get Sophie Lee out of her mind. She'd told no one about her deep dark secret. She pinched herself, hoping the dark, ugly thoughts would disappear. She needed to concentrate on her wedding and how happy she was supposed to be. She looked down at her wrist. In twenty minutes, she had to leave for the airport to pick up Ryan Spenser. She had deliberately withheld Spenser's arrival time because she didn't want the shuttle brigade to pick him up. She wanted to be the one to do it. She hadn't even told Ben.

She had plenty of time, she was dressed. All she had to do was walk out to her car, climb in, and make the thirty-minute drive to the airport.

Kala thought about her life these last five months. She'd thought on her return that she would find peace and harmony. She had found those things, but she just hadn't been able to leave her baggage behind. It was with her every day. And she couldn't tell anyone about it. Sophie was right about attorney-client privilege. And with the original conviction overturned and a directed verdict of not guilty entered, she couldn't be tried again because of the prohibition against double jeopardy.

Perhaps Kala could have put it behind her, shelved it, so to speak, but Sophie had returned to the island and lived up on the North Shore in the state-of-the-art Star mansion. Kala had read in one of the newspapers that it was the estate that had been used when Hollywood filmed *Magnum, P. I.* At first she didn't believe it, and she still wasn't sure she believed it. The article said Sophie Lee spent the winter months on the island and the summer months in New York, to be close to the corporate headquarters of Star Enterprises. If true, that meant Sophie Lee was presently on the island. And if she knew as much as she said she knew about Hawaiian customs, she could, if she wanted, show up at Kala's wedding. That was why Kala couldn't put it behind her.

What surprised Kala more than anything was the way Nick and Patty had accepted Sophie's departure. As far as she knew, there had been no further communication with Sophie once she'd left Atlanta.

Patty was happy with her new job at Fox, which really wasn't so new anymore. She was planning her own wedding for the spring, and Kala and Ben would have to return to Atlanta for that. Nick had had his second surgery, was doing well, so well that he had recently become engaged to his physical therapist and had even brought her with him for the wedding. He was writing a book and had opened his own golf shop and was giving golfing lessons to underprivileged children.

Linda was pregnant and deliriously happy. Jay walked around in a daze, worrying about what kind of father he would be. A wonderful father, Kala had told him.

Ben said he'd found his niche and loved teaching a law class two nights a week. Kala's plan to open a storefront law office was still on the drawing board. She wasn't sure if it would ever materialize. The law these days held no appeal for her. She hoped that would change in time. If it didn't, oh, well.

Her little family was all present and accounted for. And, finally, it was time to head to the airport.

Kala was in the car, the engine running, when she remembered the leis she'd made the night before for Spenser. She ran back into the house and took them out of the fridge. How could she have forgotten something so important? Overload, that was how.

Forty minutes later, Kala saw Spenser waiting at the curb, his luggage stacked up next to him. She hopped out, hugged her new best friend, then draped the leis around his neck. "Welcome to Hawaii, Spenser!" Kala said. "You're lookin' good, pal."

"I wish I could say the same for you, Kala. You've lost

weight. And what are you doing with dark circles under your eyes? Too much excitement. I hope you aren't having second thoughts. Ben is one in a million," Spenser said, sliding into the car. "By the way, I'm in love, in case you're interested. I hired this young doctor for our summer camp and one thing led to another and I'm going to ask her to marry me over Christmas. I would have brought her with me, but she's just getting over a really bad flu, and the doctor said she couldn't fly. And before you can ask, my father has been acting like a father of late. It's a chore for him, but he is trying. I'm trying, too. One of these days, if it's meant to be, we'll be a real father and son. I'm happy, that's the main thing."

"See, things really do work out if you're patient enough to wait for them," Kala said lightly.

The sun was up already, and it was sufficiently light out for Spenser to marvel about the exotic island.

Kala moved to the right and pulled into an all-night café on the beach. "I need to talk to you, Spenser," she said as she brought her car to a full stop and turned off the engine. She turned to face her friend. "Look, I'm going to do and say something I never ever thought I would do. But, right now, I don't care. I need you to listen to me, Spenser."

Spenser held up his hand. "Let's get out of the car, Kala, and sit over there at that picnic table. Looks like the place is open, and we can get some coffee. If there's one thing I cannot stand, it's airline coffee. This is my chance to taste that coffee you brag about all the time."

They ordered from a sleepy-looking waitress who was just minutes away from the end of her shift. When the coffee came, Spenser held up his hand again, and said, "Before you say what I think you're going to say, and ruin your life, let me say it first.

"I know that Sophie Lee killed Audrey Star. I figured it out when I went through the journal. You would have, too, if you weren't . . . ah . . . under the weather that night. I was going to come by the day after the conference, but you had already left for Hawaii. Everything happens for a reason, Kala. Ours not to reason why. There's nothing either of us could do even now. Every new law student knows about double jeopardy. She can't be tried again. What I don't know is if you figured it out on your own, or if Sophie confessed to you. I don't want to know either. Now, do you feel better?"

Kala blinked. Well, damn, she did feel better. She felt like a ton of bricks had been lifted from her shoulders. "You know what, Spenser? I do. God, I am so glad we had this talk. There is one more thing, though, that I want you to know. That last day, the day of the conference, that wasn't a Tuesday!"

Spenser laughed and couldn't stop. "Did you tell her that?"

Kala grinned. "I did! I wish you could have seen her face. Right then and there, I knew I had ruined her brand-spanking-new life. God works in mysterious ways. We both know that."

"That we do, that we do! So tell me about the wedding preparations. I hear it's going to be one hell of a wingding."

"This might be a good time to tell you that you, as best man, have to get up with Ben and . . ."

Spenser laughed. "I already know all about the loincloth. Hey, I had so much time on my hands these last five months, I joined a gym. I am ripped. I look forward to showing off. I even went to a tanning bed, so I wouldn't embarrass you with my fish-belly white body."

Kala chuckled.

"Look at me, Kala. Life is good. Let's both agree not to dwell on the past. Sophie Lee is the past. We both acted honorably. And to tell you the truth, Kala, I'm not sure the outcome is all that terrible. We follow the rules of the legal profession and uphold the laws as they are. Sophie Lee broke those laws. But was what she actually did, apart from the fact that it was against the law, really so bad? Does what she did make her a bad person?

"I wish I knew the answer to that question. Yes, I'm offended by lawbreaking. But are there times when, as Dickens so aptly put it, 'the law is a ass'? Again, I wish I knew.

"So, as far as I'm concerned, what happened is just life. Like it or not, we have to accept it."

Kala smiled, a genuine smile, and looked deep into Ryan's eyes. "I knew I liked you for a reason, Spenser. You're my kind of people even if we have a secret we can't share with anyone."

Kala Aulani's wedding to Ben Jefferson was everything she had hoped and dreamed it would be. Everyone near and dear attended the nuptials and the luau. It was said later that Ben Jefferson and Ryan Spenser stole the show with their authentic dance at the luau. The once-a-week island paper carried a beautiful color picture of the bride and groom on the front page.

Days later, after the happy couple had left on their world cruise, their guests were waiting at the airport to board their flights back to the mainland. They were each handed a copy of the island paper to read on the plane, along with leis. It was Spenser who picked out Sophie Lee in the paper, standing at the back of the crowd of hundreds at the luau. She was alone, the huge dog at her side, a big smile on her face, and her fist in the air.

It wasn't a Tuesday either.